# A HEROINE OF FRANCE

Evelyn Everett-Green

1st WORLD
LIBRARY
Literary Society

# A Heroine of France

## Evelyn Everett-Green

© 1st World Library – Literary Society, 2005
PO Box 2211
Fairfield, IA 52556
www.1stworldlibrary.org
First Edition

LCCN: 2004195615

Softcover ISBN: 1-4218-0436-0
Hardcover ISBN: 1-4218-0336-4
eBook ISBN: 1-4218-0536-7

Purchase *"A Heroine of France"*
as a traditional bound book at:
www.1stWorldLibrary.org/purchase.asp?ISBN=1-4218-0436-0

1st World Library Literary Society is a nonprofit
organization dedicated to promoting literacy by:

- Creating a free internet library accessible from any
  computer worldwide.
- Hosting writing competitions and offering book
  publishing scholarships.

***A Heroine of France***
*contributed by Tim, Ed & Rodney*
*in support of*
*1st World Library Literary Society*

# CONTENTS

# I.

## HOW I FIRST HEARD OF THE MAID.

"The age of Chivalry - alas! - is dead. The days of miracles are past and gone! What future is there for hapless France? She lies in the dust. How can she hope to rise?"

Sir Guy de Laval looked full in our faces as he spoke these words, and what could one reply? Ah me! - those were sad and sorrowful days for France - and for those who thought upon the bygone glories of the past, when she was mistress of herself, held high her head, and was a power with hostile nations. What would the great Charlemagne say, could he see us now? What would even St. Louis of blessed memory feel, could he witness the changes wrought by only a century and a half? Surely it were enough to cause them to turn in their graves! The north lying supine at the feet of the English conqueror; licking his hand, as a dog licks that of his master, lost to all sense of shame that an English infant in his cradle (so to speak) should rule through a regent the fair realm of France, whilst its own lawful King, banished from his capital and from half his kingdom, should keep his Court at Bourges or Chinon, passing his days in idle revelry, heedless of the eclipse of former greatness, careless of the further aggressions threatened by the ever-encroaching foe.

Was Orleans to fall next into the greedy maw of the English adventurers? Was it not already threatened? And how could it be saved if nothing could rouse the King from his slothful indifference? O for the days of Chivalry! - the days so long gone by!

Whilst I, Jean de Novelpont, was musing thus, a curious look overshadowed the face of Bertrand de Poulengy, our comrade and friend, with whom, when we had said adieu to Sir Guy a few miles farther on, I was to return to Vaucouleurs, to pay a long-promised visit there. I had been journeying awhile with Sir Guy in Germany, and he was on his way to the Court at Chinon; for we were all of the Armagnac party, loyal to our rightful monarch, whether King or only Dauphin still, since he had not been crowned, and had adopted no truly regal state or authority; and we were earnestly desirous of seeing him awaken from his lethargy and put himself at the head of an army, resolved to drive out the invaders from the land, and be King of France in truth as well as in name. But so far it seemed as though nothing short of a miracle would effect this, and the days of miracles, as Sir Guy had said, were now past and gone.

Then came the voice of Bertrand, speaking in low tones, as a man speaks who communes with himself; but we heard him, for we were riding over the thick moss of the forest glade, and the horses' feet sank deep and noiseless in the sod, and our fellows had fallen far behind, so that their laughter and talk no longer broke upon our ears. The dreamy stillness of the autumn woodlands was about us, when the songs of the birds are hushed, and the light falls golden through the yellowing leaves, and a glory more solemn than that of springtide lies upon the land.

Evelyn Everett-Green

Methinks there is something in the gradual death of the year which attunes our hearts to a certain gentle melancholy; and perchance this was why Sir Guy's words had lacked the ring of hopeful bravery that was natural to one of his temperament, and why Bertrand's eyes were so grave and dreamy, and his voice seemed to come from far away.

"And yet I do bethink me that six months agone I did behold a scene which seems to me to hold within its scope something of miracle and of mystery. I have thought of it by day, and dreamed of it by night, and the memory of it will not leave me, I trow, so long as breath and being remain!"

We turned and looked at him - the pair of us - with eyes which questioned better than our tongues. Bertrand and I had been comrades and friends in boyhood; but of late years we had been much sundered. I had not seen him for above a year, till he joined us the previous Wednesday at Nancy, having received a letter I did send to him from thence. He came to beg of me to visit him at his kinsman's house, the Seigneur Robert de Baudricourt of Vaucouleurs; and since my thirst for travel was assuaged, and my purse something over light to go to Court, I was glad to end my wanderings for the nonce, in the company of one whom I still loved as a brother.

From the first I had noted that Bertrand was something graver and more thoughtful than had been his wont. Now I did look at him with wonder in my eyes. What could he be speaking of?

He answered as though the question had passed my lips.

"It was May of this present year of grace," he said, "I mind it the better that it was the Feast of the Ascension, and I had kept fast and vigil, had made my confession and received the Holy Sacrament early in the day. I was in my lodging overlooking the market place, and hard by the Castle which as you know hangs, as it were, over the town, guarding or threatening it, as the case may be, when a messenger arrived from my kinsman, De Baudricourt, bidding me to a council which he was holding at noon that day. I went to him without delay; and he did tell me a strange tale.

"Not long since, so he said, an honest prud'homme of the neighbouring village of Burey le Petit, Durand Laxart by name, had asked speech with him, and had then told him that a young niece of his, dwelling in the village of Domremy, had come to him a few days since, saying it had been revealed to her how that she was to be used by the God of Heaven as an instrument in His hands for the redemption of France; and she had been told in a vision to go first to the Seigneur de Baudricourt, who would then find means whereby she should be sent to the Dauphin (as she called him), whom she was to cause to be made King of France."

"Mort de Dieu!" cried Sir Guy, as he gazed at Bertrand with a look betwixt laughter and amaze, "and what said your worshipful uncle to that same message?"

"At the first, he told me, he broke into a great laugh, and bid the honest fellow box the girl's ears well, and send her back to her mother. But he added that the man had been to him once again, and had pleaded that at least he would see his niece before sending her away; and since by this time he was himself somewhat

Evelyn Everett-Green

curious to see and to question this village maiden, who came with so strange a tale, he had told Laxart to bring her at noon that very day, and he desired that I and certain others should be there in the hall with him, to hear her story, and perhaps suggest some shrewd question which might help to test her good faith."

"A good thought," spoke Sir Guy, "for it is hard to believe in these dreamers of dreams. I have met such myself - they talk great swelling words, but the world wags on its way in spite of them. They are no prophets, they are bags of wind. They make a stir and a commotion for a brief while, and then they vanish to be heard of no more."

"It may be so," answered Bertrand, whose face was grave, and whose steadfast dark-blue eyes had taken a strange shining, "I can only speak of that which I did see and hear. What the future may hold none can say. God alone doth know that."

"Then you saw this maid - and heard her speech. What looked she like? - and what said she?"

"I will tell you all the tale. We were gathered there in the great hall. There were perhaps a score of us; the Seigneur at the head of the council table, the Abbe Perigord on his right, and the Count of La Roche on his left. There were two priests also present, and the chiefest knights and gentlemen of the town. We had all been laughing gaily at the thought of what a village maid of but seventeen summers - or thereabouts - would feel on being introduced into the presence of such a company. We surmised that she would shrink into the very ground for shame. One gentleman declared that it was cruel to ask her to face so many strangers of condition so much more exalted than her own; but De Baudricourt cried out, 'Why man, the wench is clamouring to be taken to the King at his Court! If she cannot face a score of simple country nobles here, how can she present herself at Chinon? Let her learn her place by a sharp lesson here; so may she understand that she had best return to her distaff and spindle and leave the crowning of Kings to other hands!' And it was in the midst of the roar of laughter which greeted this speech that the door opened slowly - and we saw the maid of whom we had been talking."

"And she doubtless heard your mirth," spoke I, and he bent his head in assent.

"I trow she did," he answered, "but think you that the ribald jests of mortal men can touch one of the angels of God? She stood for a moment framed in the doorway, and I tell you I lie not when I declare that it seemed to all present as though a halo of pure white light encircled her. Where the light came from I know not; but many there were, like myself, who noted it. The far end of the hall was dim and dark; but yet we saw her clear as she moved forward. Upon her face was a shining such as I have seen upon none other. She wore the simple peasant dress of her class, with the coif upon her head; yet it seemed to me - ay, and to others too - as though she was habited in rich apparel. Perchance it was that when one had seen her face, one could no longer think upon her raiment. If a queen - if an angel - if a saint from heaven stood in stately calm and dignity before one's eyes, how could we think of the raiment worn? We should see nothing but the grandeur and beauty of the face and form!"

"Mort de Dieu!" cried Sir Guy with his favourite oath, "but you look, good Bertrand, as though you had gazed upon some vision from the unseen world!"

"Nay," he answered gravely, "but I have looked upon the face of one whom God has visited through His saints. I have seen the reflection of His glory in human eyes; and so I can never say with others that the days of miracles are past."

Bertrand spoke with a solemnity and earnestness which could not but impress us deeply. Our eyes begged him to continue, and he told the rest of his tale very simply.

"She came forward with this strange shining in her eyes. She bent before us with simple reverence; but then lifted herself up to her full height and looked straight at De Baudricourt without boldness and without fear, as though she saw in him a tool in the hand of God, and had no other thought for him besides.

"'Seigneur,' she said, 'my Lord has bidden me come to you, that you may send me to the Dauphin; for He has given me a message to him which none else may bear; and He has told me that you will do it, therefore I know that you will not fail Him, and your laughter troubles me not.'

"'Who is your Lord, my child?' asked De Baudricourt, not laughing now, but pulling at his beard and frowning in perplexity.

"'Even the Lord of Heaven, Sire,' she answered, and her hands clasped themselves loosely together whilst her eyes looked upward with a smile such as I have seen on none other face before. 'He that is my Lord and your Lord and the Lord of this realm of France. But it is His holy will that the Dauphin shall be its King, and that he shall drive back the English, and that the crown shall be set upon his head. And this, with other matters which are for his ear alone I am sent to tell him; and you, good my lord, are he who shall send me to my King.'

"Thus she spoke, and looked at us all with those shining eyes of hers; yet it seemed to me she scarce saw us. Her glance did go beyond, as though she were gazing in vision upon the things which were to be."

"She was beautiful, you say?" asked Sir Guy, whose interest was keenly aroused; but who, I saw, was doubtful whether Bertrand had not been deceived by some witchery of fair face and graceful form; for Bertrand, albeit a man of thews and sinews and bold as a lion in fight, was something of the dreamer too, as warriors in all ages have sometimes been.

"Yes - as an angel of God is beautiful," he answered, "ask me not of that; for I can tell you nothing. I know not the hue of her hair or of her eyes, nor what her face was like, nor her form, save that she was tall and very slender; but beautiful - ah yes! - with the beauty which this world cannot give; a beauty which silenced every flippant jest, shamed every scoffing thought, turned ridicule into wonder, contempt into reverence. Whether this wonderful maiden came in truth as a messenger of God or no, at least not one present but saw well that she herself believed heart and soul in her divine commission."

"And what answer did the Seigneur de Baudricourt make to her?"

Evelyn Everett-Green

"He gazed upon her full for awhile, and then he suddenly asked of her, 'And when shall all these wonders come to pass?'

"She, with her gaze fixed still a little upwards, answered, 'Before mid-Lent next year shall succour reach him; then will the city of Orleans be in sore straight; but help shall come, and the English shall fly before the sword of the Lord. Afterwards shall the Dauphin receive consecration at Rheims, and the crown of France shall be set upon his head, in token that he is the anointed of the Lord.'

"'And who has told you all this, my child?' asked De Baudricourt then, answering gently, as one speaks within a church.

"'Mes voix,' she answered, speaking as one who dreams, and in dreaming listens.

"'What voices?' asked De Baudricourt, 'and have you naught but voices to instruct you in such great matters?'

"'Yes, Sire,' she answered softly, 'I have seen the great Archangel Michael, his sword drawn in his hand; and I know that he has drawn it for the deliverance of France, and that though he has chosen so humble an instrument as myself, yet that to him and to the Lord of Heaven will he the victory and the glory.'

"When she had thus spoken there was a great silence in the hall, in which might have been heard the fall of a pin, and I vow that whether it were trick of summer sunshine or no, the light about the maiden seemed to grow brighter and brighter. Her face was just slightly uplifted as one who listens, and upon her lips there was a smile.

"'And I know that you will send me to the Dauphin, Robert de Baudricourt,' she suddenly said, 'because my voices tell me so.'

"We all looked at De Baudricourt, who sat chin on hand, gazing at the maiden as though he would read her very soul. We waited, wondering, for him to speak At last he did.

"'Well, my girl, I will think of all this. We have till next year, by your own showing, ere these great things shall come to pass. So get you home, and see what your father and mother say to all this, and whether the Archangel Michael comes again or no. Go home - be a good girl, and we will see what we will see.'"

"Was that all he promised?" spoke Sir Guy with a short laugh. "I trow the maiden dreamer would not thank him for that word! A deliverer of princes to be bidden to go home and be a good girl! What said she to that counsel?"

"Ay, well you may ask," spoke Bertrand with subdued emotion. "Just such a question sprang to my lips as I heard my kinsman's answer. I looked to see her face fall, to see sparks of anger flash from her eyes, or a great disappointment cloud the serene beauty of her countenance. But instead of this a wonderful smile lighted it, and her sweet and resonant voice sounded clear through the hall.

"'Ah, now Seigneur, I know you for a good and true man! You speak as did my voices when first I heard

Evelyn Everett-Green

them. "Jeanne, sois bonne et sage enfant; va souvent a l'eglise"; that was their first message to me, when I was but a child; and now you say the same to me - be a good girl. Thus I know that your heart is right, and that when my Lord's time is come you will send me with His message to the Dauphin.'

"And so saying she bent again in a modest reverence before us. Yet let me tell you that as she did so, every man of us sprang to his feet by an impulse which each one felt, yet none could explain. As one man we rose, and bowed before her, as she retired from the hail with the simple, stately grace of a young queen. Not till the door had closed behind her did we bethink us that it was to a humble peasant girl we had paid unconscious homage. We who had thought she would well-nigh sink to the dust at sight of us, had been made to feel that we were in the presence of royalty!"

"Tu Dieu! but that is a strange story!" quoth Sir Guy with knitted brows. "For many a long day I have heard nought so strange! What think you of it yourself, good Bertrand? For by my troth you speak like a man convinced that a miracle may even yet be wrought for France at the hand of this maid."

"And if I do, is that so strange? Cannot it be that the good God may still speak through His saints to the sons of men, and may raise up a deliverer for us, even as He did in the days of old for His chosen people? Is His arm shortened at all? And is it meet that we Christian knights should trust Him less than did the Jews of old?"

Sir Guy made no reply, but fell into thought, and then asked a sudden question:

"Who is this peasant maid of whom you speak? And where is she now? Is she still abiding content at home, awaiting the time appointed by her visions?"

"I trow that she is," answered Bertrand. "I did hear that she went home without delay, as quietly as she had come. Her name is Jeanne d'Arc. She dwells in the village of Domremy over yonder. Her father is an honest prud'homme of the place. She has brothers and a sister. She is known in the village as a pious and gentle maid, ever ready to tend the sick, hold vigil for the dead, take charge of an ailing child, or do any such simple service for the neighbours. She is beloved of all, full of piety and good works, constant in attendance at church, regular in her confession and at mass. So much have I heard from her kinsman Laxart, though for mine own part I have not seen her again."

"And what thinks De Baudricourt of her mission? Does he ever speak of it?"

"Not often; and yet I know that he has not forgotten it. For ofttimes he does sink into a deep reverie; and disjointed words break from him, which tell me whither his thoughts have flown.

"At the first he did say to me, 'Let the girl go home; let us see if we hear more of her. If this be but a phantasy on her part; if she has been fasting and praying and dreaming, till she knows not what is true and what is her own imagining, why, time will cure her of her fancies and follies. If otherwise - well, we will see when the time comes. To act in haste were to act with folly.'

"And so he dismissed the matter, though, as I say, he

Evelyn Everett-Green

doth not forget it, and I think never a day comes but he thinks on it."

"And while the Lord waits, the English are active!" cried Sir Guy with a note of impatience in his voice. "They are already threatening Orleans. Soon they will march in strength upon it. And if that city once fall, why what hope is there even for such remnants of his kingdom as still remain faithful south of the Loire? The English will have them all. Already they call our King in mockery 'the King of Bourges;' soon even that small domain will be reft away, and then what will remain for him or for us? If the visions of the maiden had been true, why doth not the Lord strike now, before Salisbury of England can invest the city? If Orleans fall, all is lost.'"

"But Jeanne says that Orleans shall be saved," spoke Bertrand in a low voice, "and if she speaks sooth, must not she and we alike leave the times and seasons in the hand of the Lord?"

Sir Guy shrugged his shoulders, and gave me a shrewd glance, the meaning of which I was at no loss to understand. He thought that Bertrand's head had been something turned, and that he had become a visionary, looking rather for a miracle from heaven than for deliverance from the foe through hard fighting by loyal men marching under the banner of their King. Truth we all knew well that little short of a miracle would arouse the indolent and discouraged Charles, cowed by the English foe, doubtful of his own right to call himself Dauphin, distrustful of his friends, despairing of winning the love or trust of his subjects. But could it indeed be possible that such a miracle could be wrought, and by an instrument so humble as a village maid - this Jeanne d'Arc?

But the time had come when we must say adieu to our comrade, and turn ourselves back to Vaucouleurs, if we were not to be benighted in the forest ere we could reach that place. We halted for our serving men to come up; and as we did so Bertrand said in a low voice to Sir Guy:

"I pray you, Seigneur de Laval, speak no word to His Majesty of this maid and her mission, until such time as news may reach him of her from other sources."

"I will say no word," answered the other, smiling, and so with many friendly words we parted, and Bertrand and I, with one servant behind us, turned our horses' heads back along the road by which we had come.

"Bertrand," I said, as the shadows lengthened, the soft dusk fell in the forest, and the witchery of the evening hour fell upon my heart, "I would that I could see this maiden of whom you speak, this Jeanne d'Arc of the village of Domremy."

He turned and looked me full in the face; I saw his eyes glow and the colour deepen in his cheeks.

"You would not go to mock, friend Jean de Metz?" he said, for so I am generally named amongst my friends.

"Nay," I answered truthfully, "there is no thought of mockery in my heart; yet I fain would see the Maid."

He paused awhile in thought and then made answer:

Evelyn Everett-Green

"At least we may ride together one day to Domremy; but whether or no we see the Maid will be according to the will of Heaven."

## II.

## HOW I FIRST SAW THE MAID.

I did not forget my desire to see this maiden of Domremy, nor did Bertrand, I trow, forget the promise, albeit some days passed by ere we put our plan into action.

Bad news kept coming in to the little loyal township of Vaucouleurs. There was no manner of doubt but that the English Regent, Bedford, was resolved to lose no more time, but seek to put beneath his iron heel the whole of the realm of France. Gascony had been English so long that the people could remember nothing different than the rule of the Roy Outremer - as of old they called him. Now all France north of the Loire owned the same sway, and as all men know, the Duke of Burgundy was ally to the English, and hated the Dauphin with a deadly hatred, for the murder of his father - for which no man can justly blame him. True, his love for the English had cooled manifestly since that affair of Duke Humphrey of Gloucester and Jacquelaine of Brabant, in which as was natural, he took the part of his brother; but although the Duke of Bedford was highly indignant with Duke Humphrey, and gave him no manner of support in his rash expedition, yet the Duke of Burgundy resented upon the English what had been done, and although it did

Evelyn Everett-Green

not drive him into the arms of the Dauphin, whom he hated worse, it loosened the bond between him and our foes, and we had hoped it might bring about a better state of things for our party. Yet alas! - this seemed as far as ever from being so; and the Burgundian soldiers still ravaged along our borders, and it seemed ofttimes as though we little loyal community of the Duchy of Bar would be swallowed up altogether betwixt the two encroaching foes. So our hearts were often heavy and our faces grave with fear.

I noted in the manner of the Governor, whose guest I had now become, a great gravity, which in old days had not been there; for Robert de Baudricourt, as I remembered him, had ever been a man of merry mood, with a great laugh, a ready jest, and that sort of rough, bluff courage that makes light of trouble and peril.

Now, however, we often saw him sunk in some deep reverie, his chin upon his hand, his eyes gazing full into the blaze of the leaping fire of logs, which always flamed upon the hearth in the great hall, where the most part of his time was spent. He would go hunting or hawking by day, or ride hither and thither through the town, looking into matters there, or sit to listen to the affairs of the citizens or soldiers as they were brought before him; and at such times his manner would be much as it had ever been of yore - quick, almost rough, yet not unkindly - whilst the shrewd justice he always meted out won the respect of the people, and made him a favourite in the town.

But when the evening fell, and the day's work was done, and after supper we sat in the hall, with the dogs slumbering around us, talking of any news which might have come in, either of raids by the roving

Burgundians, or the advance of the English towards Orleans, then these darker moods would fall upon him; and once when he had sat for well-nigh an hour without moving, his brow drawn and furrowed, and his eyes seemingly sunk deeper in his head, Bertrand leaned towards me and whispered in mine ear:

"He is thinking of the Maid of Domremy!"

De Baudricourt could not have heard the words, yet when he spoke a brief while later, it almost seemed as though he might have done so.

"Nephew," he said, lifting his head abruptly and gazing across at us, "tell me again the words of that prophecy of Merlin's, spoken long, long ago, of which men whisper in these days, and of which you did speak to me awhile back."

"Marry, good mine uncle, the prophecy runs thus," answered Bertrand, rising and crossing over towards the great fire before which his kinsman sat, "'That France should be destroyed by the wiles of a woman, and saved and redeemed by a maiden.'"

The bushy brows met in a fierce scowl over the burning eyes; his words came in a great burst of indignation and scorn.

"Ay, truly - he spake truly - the wise man - the wizard! A woman to be the ruin of the kingdom! Ay, verily, and has it not been so? Who but that wicked Queen Isabeau is at the bottom of the disgraceful Treaty of Troyes, wherein France sold herself into the hands of the English? Did she not repudiate her own son? Did not her hatred burn so fiercely against him that she was ready to tarnish her own good fame and declare him illegitimate, rather than that he should succeed his father as King of France? Did she not give her daughter to the English King in wedlock, that their child might reign over this fair realm? Truly has the kingdom been destroyed by the wiles of a woman! But I vow it will take more than the strength of any maiden to save and redeem it from the woes beneath which it lies crushed."

"In sooth it doth seem so," answered Bertrand with grave and earnest countenance, "but yet with the good God nothing is impossible. Hath He not said before this that He doth take of the mean and humble to confound the great of the earth? Did not the three hundred with Gideon overcome the hosts of the Moabites? Did not the cake of barley bread overturn the tent and the camp of the foe?"

"Ay, if the good God will arise to work miracles again, such things might be; but how can we look for Him to do so? What manner of man is the Dauphin of France that he should look for divine deliverance? 'God helps those who help themselves,' so says the proverb; but what of those who lie sunk in lethargy or despair, and seek to drown thought or care in folly and riotous living - heedless of the ruin of the realm?"

"There is another proverb, good mine uncle, that tells how man's extremity is God's opportunity," quoth Bertrand thoughtfully; "if we did judge of God's mercy by man's worthiness to receive the same, we might well sink in despair. But His power and His goodness are not limited by our infirmities, and therein alone lies our hope."

De Baudricourt uttered a sound between a snort and a grunt. I knew not what he thought of Bertrand's answer; but that brief dialogue aroused within me afresh the desire I had before expressed to see the maid, Jeanne of Domremy; and as the sun upon the morrow shone out bright and clear, after a week of heavy rain storms, we agreed that no better opportunity could we hope for to ride across to the little village, and try whether it were possible to obtain speech with the young girl about whom such interest had been aroused in some breasts.

We spoke no word to De Baudricourt of our intention. Bertrand knew from his manner that he was thinking more and more earnestly of that declaration on the part of the village maiden that her Lord - the King of Heaven - had revealed to her that she must be sent to the Dauphin, to help him to drive out the English from his country, and to place the crown of France upon his head, and that he, Robert de Baudricourt, was the instrument who would be used to speed her on her way. Bertrand knew that this thought was weighing upon the mind of his kinsman, and the more so as the time for the fulfilment of the prophecy drew nearer.

Autumn had come. Winter was hard at hand; and before Mid-Lent the promised succour to France was to arrive through the means of this maiden - this Jeanne d'Arc.

"He is waiting and watching," spoke Bertrand, as we rode through the forest, the thinning leaves of which allowed the sunlight to play merrily upon our path. "He says in his heart that if this thing be of God, the Maid will come again when the time draws near; but that if it is phantasy, or if she be deluded of the Devil,

Evelyn Everett-Green

perchance his backwardness will put a check upon her ardour, and we shall hear no more of it. The Abbe Perigord, his Confessor, has bidden him beware lest it be a snare of the Evil One" - and as he spoke these words Bertrand crossed himself, and I did the like, for the forest is an ill place in which to talk of the Devil, as all men know.

"But for my part, when I think upon her words, and see again the look of her young face, I cannot believe that she has been thus deceived; albeit we are told that the Devil can make himself appear as an angel of light."

This was the puzzle, of course. But surely the Church had power to discern betwixt the wiles of the Evil One and the finger of God. There were words and signs which any possessed of the Devil must needs fly before. I could not think that the Church need fear deception, even though a village maid might be deceived.

The forest was very beautiful that day, albeit travelling was something slow, owing to the softness of the ground, and the swollen condition of the brooks, which often forced us to go round by the bridges instead of taking the fords; so that we halted a few miles from Domremy to bait our horses and to appease our own hunger, for by that time our appetite was sharp set.

It was there, as we sat at table, and talked with mine host, that we heard somewhat more of this Maid, whom we had started forth in hopes to see.

Bertrand was known for the kinsman of De Baudricourt and all the countryside knew well the tale, how that Jeanne d'Arc had gone to him in the springtide of the year, demanding an escort to the Dauphin King of France, for whom she had a message from the King of Heaven, and whom she was to set upon his throne.

"When she came home again, having accomplished nothing," spoke the innkeeper, leaning his hands upon the table and greatly enjoying the sound of his own voice, "all the village made great mock of her! They called her the King's Marshal, the Little Queen, Jeanne the Prophetess, and I know not what beside. Her father was right wroth with her. Long ago he had a dream about her, which troubled him somewhat, as he seemed to see his daughter in the midst of fighting men, leading them on to battle."

"Did he dream that? Surely that is something strange for the vision of a village prud'homme anent his little daughter."

"Ay truly, though at the time he thought little of it, but when all this came to pass he recalled it again; and he smote Jeanne upon the ear with his open hand, and bid her return to her needle and her household tasks, and think no more of matters too great for her. Moreover, he declared that if ever she were to disgrace herself by mingling with men-at-arms, he would call upon her brothers to drown her, and if they disobeyed him, he would take and do it with his own hands!"

"A Spartan father, truly!" murmured Bertrand.

"O ay - but he is a very honest man, is Jacques d'Arc; and he was very wroth at all the talk about his daughter, and he vowed she should wed an honest man, as she is now of age to do, and so forget her dreams and her visions, and take care of her house and her husband and the children the good God should send them - like other wedded wives."

"Then has she indeed wedded?" asked Bertrand earnestly.

"Ah, that is another story!" answered our host, wagging his head and spreading out his hands. "It would take too long were I to tell you all, messires; but so much will I tell. They did find a man who had long desired the pretty Jeanne for his wife, and he did forswear himself and vow that he had been betrothed to Jeanne with her own free will and consent, and that now he claimed her as his wife. Jeanne, whose courage is high, though she be so quiet and modest in her daily life, did vehemently deny the charge, whereupon the angry father and his friend, the claimant of her hand, did bring it into the court, and the Maid had to defend herself there from the accusation of broken faith. But by St. Michael and all his angels! - how she did confound them all! She asked no help from lawyers, though one did offer himself to her. She called no witnesses herself; but she questioned the witnesses brought against her, and also the man who would fain have become her lord, and out of their own mouths did she convict them of lying and hypocrisy and conspiracy, so that she was triumphantly acquitted, and her judges called her a most wonderful child, and told her mother to be proud of such a daughter!"

I saw a flush rise to Bertrand's cheek, a flush as of pride and joy. And indeed, I myself rejoiced to hear the end of the tale; for it did seem as though this maiden had been persecuted with rancour and injustice, and that is a thing which no man can quietly endure to hear or see.

"And how have they of Domremy behaved themselves to her since?" I asked; and Bertrand listened eagerly for the answer.

"Oh, they have taken her to favour once more; her father has been kind again; her mother ever loved Jeanne much, for her gentleness and beauty and helpfulness at home. All the people love her, when not stirred to mockery by such fine pretensions. If she will remain quietly at home like a wise and discreet maiden, no one will long remember against her her foolish words and dreams."

As we rode through the fields and woodlands towards Domremy, the light began to take the golden hue which it does upon the autumn afternoon, and upon that day it shone with a wonderful radiance such as is not uncommon after rain. We were later than we had meant, but there would be a moon to light us when the sun sank, and both we and our horses knew the roads well; or we could even sleep, if we were so minded, at the auberge where we had dined. So we were in no haste or hurry. We picked our way leisurely towards the village, and Bertrand told me of the Fairy Well and the Fairy Tree in the forest hard by, so beloved of the children of Domremy, and of which so much has been heard of late, though at that time I knew nothing of any such things.

But fairy lore has ever a charm for me, and I bid him show me these same things. So we turned a little aside into the forest, and found ourselves in a lovely glade, where the light shone so soft and golden, and where the songs of the birds sounded so sweet and melodious, that I felt as though we were stepping through an enchanted world, and well could I believe that the

Evelyn Everett-Green

fairies danced around the well, sunk deep in its mossy dell, and fringed about with ferns and flowers and the shade of drooping trees.

But fairies there were none visible to our eyes, and we moved softly onwards towards the spreading tree hard by. But ere we reached it, we both drew rein as by a common impulse, for we had seen a sight which arrested and held us spellbound, ay, and more than that, for the wonder and amaze of it fell also upon the horses we bestrode. For scarcely had we drawn rein, before they both began to tremble and to sweat, and stood with their forefeet planted, their necks outstretched, their nostrils distended; uttering short, gasping, snorting sounds, as a horse will do when overcome by some terror. But for all this they were as rigid as if they had been carved in stone.

And now, what did we see? Let me try and tell, so far as my poor words may avail. Beneath a spreading tree just a stone's throw to the right of where we stood, and with nothing between to hinder our view of her, a peasant maiden, dressed in the white coif, red skirt, and jacket and kerchief of her class, had been bending over some fine embroidery which she held in her hands. We just caught a glimpse of her thus before the strange thing happened which caused us to stop short, as though some power from without restrained us.

Hard by, as I know now, stood the village, shut out from view by the trees, with its little church, and the homestead of Jacques d'Arc nestling almost within its shadow. At the moment of which I speak the bell rang forth for the Angelus, with a full, sweet tone of silvery melody; and at the very same instant the work dropped from the girl's hands, and she sank upon her knees. At the first moment, although instinctively, we reined back our horses and uncovered our heads, I had no thought but that she was a devout maiden following the office of the Church out here in the wood. But as she turned her upraised face a little towards us, I saw upon it such a look as I have never seen on human countenance before, nor have ever seen (save upon hers) since. A light seemed to shine either from it or upon it - how can I tell which? - a light so pure and heavenly that no words can fully describe it, but which seemed like the radiance of heaven itself. Her eyes were raised towards the sky, her lips parted, and through the breathless hush of silence which had fallen upon the wood, we heard the soft, sweet tones of her voice.

"Speak, my Lord - Thy servant heareth!"

It was then that our horses showed the signs of terror of which I have before spoken. For myself, I saw nothing save the shining face of the Maid - I knew who it was - there was no need for Bertrand's breathless whisper - "It is she - herself!" - I knew it in my heart before.

She knelt there amid the fallen leaves, her face raised, her lips parted, her eyes shining as surely never human eyes have shone before. A deep strange hush had fallen over all nature, broken only by the gentle music of the bell. The ruddy gold light of approaching sunset bathed all the wood in glory, and the rays fell upon the kneeling figure, forming a halo of glory round it. But she did not heed, she did not see. She was as one in a trance, insensible to outward vision. Once and again her lips moved, but we heard no word proceed from them, only the rapt look upon her face increased in intensity, and once I thought (for I could not turn my gaze away) that I saw the gleam of tears in her eyes.

The bell ceased as we stood thus motionless, and as the last note vibrated through the still air, a change came over the Maid. Her head drooped, she hid her face in her hands, and thus she knelt as one absorbed in an intensity of prayer. Even as this happened, the peculiar glory of the sunlight seemed to change. It shone still, but without such wonderful glow, and our horses at the same time ceased their trembling and their rigid stillness of pose. They shook their heads and jingled their bits, as though striving to throw off some terrifying impression.

"Let us withdraw from her sight," whispered Bertrand touching my arm, and very willingly I acceded to this suggestion, and we silently pressed into the shadow of some great oaks, which stood hard by, the trunks of which hid us well from view. It seemed almost like a species of sacrilege to stand there watching the Maid at her prayers, and yet I vow, that until the bell ceased we had no more power to move than our horses. Why we were holden by this strange spell I know not. I can only speak the truth. We saw nothing and we heard nothing of any miraculous kind, and yet we were like men in a dream, bound hand and foot by invisible bonds, a witness of something unseen to ourselves, which we saw was visible to another.

Beneath the deep shadow of the oaks we looked back. The Maid had risen to her feet by this, and was stooping to pick up her fallen work. That done, she stood awhile in deep thought, her face turned towards the little church, whence the bell had only just ceased to sound.

I saw her clearly then - a maiden slim and tall, so slender that the rather clumsy peasant dress she wore could not give breadth or awkwardness to her lithe figure. The coif had slipped a little out of place, and some tresses of waving hair had escaped from beneath it, tresses that looked dark till the sun touched them, and then glowed like burnished gold. Her face was pale, with features in no way marked, but so sweet and serene was the expression of the face, so wonderful was the depth of the great dark eyes, that one was lost in admiration of her beauty, albeit unable to define wherein that beauty lay.

When we started forth, I had meant to try and seek speech with this Jeanne - this Maid of Domremy - and to ask her of her mission, and whether she were still believing that she would have power to carry it out; but this purpose now died within me.

How could I dare question such a being as to her visions? Had I not seen how she was visited by sound or sight not sensible to those around her? Had I not in some sort been witness to a miracle? Was it for us to approach and ask of her what had been thus revealed? No! - a thousand times no! If the good God had given her a message, she would know when and where to deliver it. She had spoken before of her voices. Let them instruct her. Let not men seek to interfere. And so we remained where we were, hidden in the deep shadows, whilst Jeanne, with bent head and lingering, graceful steps, utterly unconscious of the eyes that watched her, went slowly out of sight along the glade leading towards the village and her home.

Only when she had disappeared did we venture to move on in her wake, and so passed by the low-browed house, set in its well-tended little garden, where the d'Arc family lived. It lay close to the church, and bore a look of pleasant homelike comfort. We saw Jeanne bending tenderly over a chair, in which reclined the bent form of a little crippled sister. We even heard the soft, sweet voice of the Maid, as she answered some question asked her from within the open door. Then she lifted the bent form in her arms, and I did note how strong that slim frame must be, for the burden seemed as nothing to her as she bore it within the house; and then she disappeared from view, and we rode onwards together.

"There, my friend," spoke Bertrand at last, "I have kept my promise, you have seen the Maid."

"Yes," I answered gravely, "I have seen the Maid," and after that we spoke no word for many a mile.

# III.

## HOW THE MAID CAME TO VAUCOULEURS.

It may yet be remembered by some how early the snow came that year, to the eastern portion of France at least. I think scarce a week had passed since our journey to Domremy, before a wild gale from the northeast brought heavy snow, which lay white upon the ground for many long weeks, and grew deeper and deeper as more fell, till the wolves ravaged right up to the very walls of Vaucouleurs, and some of the country villages were quite cut off from intercourse with the world.

Thus it came about that I was shut up in Vaucouleurs with my good comrade and friend Bertrand, in the Castle of which Robert de Baudricourt was governor, and for awhile little news reached us from the outside world, though such news as did penetrate to our solitude was all of disaster for the arms of France.

We never spoke to De Baudricourt of our expedition to Domremy, nor told him that we had seen the Maid again. Yet methinks not a day passed without our thinking of her, recalling something of that wonderful look we had seen upon her face, and asking in our hearts whether indeed she were truly visited by heavenly visions sent by God, and whether she indeed heard voices which could reach no ears but hers.

Evelyn Everett-Green

I observed that Bertrand was more regular in attendance at the services of the Church, and especially at Mass, than was usual with young knights in those days, and for my part, I felt a stronger desire after such spiritual aids than I ever remember to have done in my life before. It became a regular thing with us to attend the early Mass in the little chapel of the Castle; and, instead of growing lax (as I had done before many times in my roving life), as to attending confession and receiving the Holy Sacrament, I now began to feel the need for both, as though I were preparing me for some great and solemn undertaking. I cannot well express in words the feeling which possessed me - ay, and Bertrand toc - for we began to speak of the matter one with another - but it seemed to us both as though a high and holy task lay before us, for which we must needs prepare ourselves with fasting and prayer; I wondered if, perhaps, it was thus that knights and men in days of old felt when they had taken the Red Cross, and had pledged themselves to some Crusade in the East.

Well, thus matters went on, quietly enough outwardly, till the Feast of the Nativity had come and gone, and with that feast came a wonderful change in the weather. The frost yielded, the south wind blew soft, the snow melted away one scarce knew how, and a breath of spring seemed already in the air, though we did not dare to hope that winter was gone for good and all.

It was just when the year had turned that we heard a rumour in the town, and it was in this wise that it reached our ears. De Baudricourt had been out with his dogs, chasing away the wolves back into their forest lairs. He had left us some business to attend to for him within the Castle, else should we doubtless have been of the party. But he was the most sagacious huntsman of the district, and a rare day's sport they did have, killing more than a score of wolves, to the great joy of the townsfolk and of the country people without the walls. It was dark ere he got home, and he came in covered with mud from head to foot; the dogs, too, were so plastered over, that they had to be given to the servants to clean ere they could take their wonted places beside the fire; and some of the poor beasts had ugly wounds which needed to be washed and dressed.

But what struck us most was that De Baudricourt, albeit so successful in his hunt, seemed little pleased with his day's work. His face was dark, as though a thunder cloud lay athwart it, and he gave but curt answers to our questions, as he stood steaming before the fire and quaffing a great tankard of spiced wine which was brought to him. Then he betook himself to his own chamber to get him dry garments, and when he came down supper was already served. He sat him down at the head of the table, still silent and morose; and though he fell with right good will upon the viands, he scarce opened his lips the while, and we in our turn grew silent, for we feared that he had heard the news of some disaster to the French arms, which he was brooding over in silent gloom.

But when the retainers and men-at-arms had disappeared, and we had gathered round the fire at the far end of the hall, as was our wont, then he suddenly began to speak.

"Went ye into the town today?" he suddenly asked of us.

Evelyn Everett-Green

We answered him, Nay, that we had been occupied all day within the Castle over the services there he had left us to perform.

"And have you heard nought of the commotion going on there?"

"We have heard nought. Pray what hath befallen, good sir? Is it some disaster? Hath Orleans fallen into the hands of the English?"

For that was the great fear possessing all loyal minds at this period.

"Nay, it is nought so bad as that," answered De Baudricourt, "and yet it is bad enough, I trow. That mad girl from Domremy is now in the town, telling all men that Robert de Baudricourt hath been appointed of God to send her to the Dauphin at Chinon, and that she must needs start thither soon, to do the work appointed her of heaven.

"Dents de Dieu! - the folly of it is enough to raise the hair on one's head! Send a little paysanne to the King with a wild story like hers! 'Tis enough to make the name of De Baudricourt the laughingstock of the whole country!"

I felt a great throb at heart when I heard these words. Then the Maid had not forgot! This time of waiting had not bred either indifference or doubt. The time appointed was drawing near, and she had come to Vaucouleurs once more, to do that which was required of her!

O, was it not wonderful? Must not it be of heaven, this

thing? And should we seek to put the message aside as a thing of nought?

Bertrand was already speaking eagerly with his kinsman; but it seemed as though his words did only serve to irritate the Governor the more. In my heart I was sure that had he been certain the Maid was an impostor, he would have been in no wise troubled or disturbed, but would have contented himself by sharply ordering her to leave the town and return home and trouble him no more. It was because he was torn by doubts as to her mission that he was thus perturbed in spirit. He dared not treat her in this summary fashion, lest haply he should be found to be fighting against God; and yet he found it hard to believe that any deliverance for hapless France could come through the hands of a simple, unlettered peasant girl; and he shrank with a strong man's dislike from making himself in any sort an object of ridicule, or of seeming to give credence to a wild tale of visions and voices, such as the world would laugh to scorn. So he was filled with doubt and perplexity, and this betrayed itself in gloomy looks and in harsh speech.

"Tush, boy! You are but an idle dreamer. I saw before that you were fooled by a pretty face and a silvery voice. Go to! - your words are but phantasy! Who believes in miracles now?"

"If we believe in the power of the good God, shall we not also believe that He can work even miracles at His holy will?"

"Poof - miracles! - the dreams of a vain and silly girl!" scoffed De Baudricourt, "I am sick of her name already!"

Evelyn Everett-Green

Then he suddenly turned upon me and spoke.

"Jean de Metz, you are a knight of parts. You have sense and discretion above your years, and are no featherhead like Bertrand here. Will you undertake a mission from me to this maiden? Ask of her the story of her pretended mission. Seek to discover from her whether she be speaking truth, or whether she be seeking to deceive. Catch her in her speech if it may be. See whether the tale she tells hang together, and then come and report to me. If she be a mad woman, why should I be troubled with her? She cannot go to the Dauphin yet, come what may. The melting snows have laid the valleys under water, the roads are impassable; horses would stick fast in the mire, and we are not at the end of winter yet. She must needs wait awhile, whatever her message may be, but I would have you get speech of her, and straightly question her from me. Then if it seem well, I can see her again; but if you be willing, you shall do so first."

I was more than willing. I was rejoiced to have this occasion for getting speech with the Maid. I spoke no word of having had sight of her already, but fell in with De Baudricourt's wish that I should go to her as if a mere passing stranger, and only afterwards reveal myself as his emissary. I slept but little all that night, making plans as to all that I should speak when I saw her on the morrow, and, rising early, I betook myself to Mass, not to the private chapel of the Castle, but to one of the churches in the town, though I could not have said why it was that I was moved to do this.

Yet as I knelt in my place I knew, for there amongst the worshippers, her face upraised and full of holy joy, her eyes alight with the depth of her devotion, her hands clasped in an ecstasy of prayer, was the Maid herself; and I found it hard to turn my eyes from her wonderful face, to think upon the office as it was recited by the priest.

I did not seek speech of her then, for she tarried long in the church over her prayers. I felt at last like one espying on another, and so I came away. But after breakfast, as the sun shone forth and began to light up the narrow streets of the little town, I sallied forth again alone, and asked of the first citizen I met where could be found the dwelling place of one Jeanne d'Arc, from Domremy, who was paying a visit to the town.

I had scarce need to say so much as this. It seemed that all the people in the town had heard of the arrival of the Maid. I know not whether they believed in her mission, or whether they scoffed at it; but at least it was the talk of the place how she had come before, and fearlessly faced the Governor and his council, and had made her great demand from him, and how she had come once again, now that the year was born and Lent approaching, in the which she had said she must seek and find the Dauphin. Thus the man was able at once to give me the information I asked, and told me that the girl was lodging with Henri Leroyer the saddler, and Catherine his wife, naming the street where they dwelt, but adding that I should have no trouble in finding the house, for the people flocked to it to get a sight of the Maid, and to ask her questions concerning her mission hither, and what she thought she was about to accomplish.

And truly I did find that this honest citizen had spoken the truth, for as I turned into the narrow street where Leroyer lived, I saw quite a concourse of people

Evelyn Everett-Green

gathered about the house, and though they made way for me to approach, knowing that I was from the Castle, I saw that they were very eager to get sight or speech of the Maid, who was standing at the open door of the shop, and speaking in an earnest fashion to those nearest her.

I made as though I were a passing stranger, who had just heard somewhat of her matter from the bystanders, and I addressed her in friendly fashion, rather as one who laughs.

"What are you doing here, ma mie? And what is this I hear? Is it not written in the book of fate that the King or Dauphin of France must be overcome of England's King, and that we must all become English, or else be driven into the sea, or banished from the realm?"

Then for the first time her wonderful eyes fastened themselves on my face, and I felt as though my very soul were being read.

"Nay, sire," she answered, and there was something so flute-like and penetrating in her tones that they seemed to sink into my very soul, "but the Lord of Heaven Himself is about to fight for France, and He has sent me to the Governor here, who will direct me to the Dauphin, who knows nothing of me as yet. But I am to bring him help, and that by Mid-Lent. So I pray you, gentle knight, go tell Robert de Baudricourt that he must needs bestir himself in this business, for my voices tell me that the hour is at hand when, come what may, I must to Chinon, even though I wear my legs to the knees in going thither."

"Why should I tell this to the Seigneur de

Baudricourt?" I asked, marvelling at her words and the fashion of her speech.

"Because he has sent you to me," she answered, her eyes still on my face, "and I thank him for having chosen so gracious a messenger; for you have a good heart, and you are no mocker of the things my Lord has revealed to me; and you will be one of those to do His will, and to bring me safely to the Dauphin."

Half confounded by her words I asked:

"Who is your Lord?"

"It is God," she answered, and bent her head in lowly reverence.

And then I did a strange thing; but it seemed to be forced upon me from above by a power which I could not withstand. I fell suddenly to my knees before her, and put up my clasped hands, as we do when we pay homage for our lands and honours to our liege lord. And, I speak truth, and nought else, the Maid put her hands over mine just as our lord or sovereign should do, and though I dare swear she had never heard my name before, she said:

"Jean de Novelpont de Metz, my Lord receives you as His faithful knight and servant. He will be with us now and to the end."

And the people all uncovered and stood bareheaded round us, whilst I felt as though I had received a mandate from Heaven.

Then I went into the house with Jeanne, and asked her

of herself, and of her visions and voices. She told me of them with the gentle frankness of a child, but with a reverence and humility that was beautiful to see, and which was in strange contrast to some of the things she spoke, wherein she told how that she herself was to be used of Heaven for the salvation of France.

I cannot give her words as she spoke them, sitting there in the window, the light upon her face, her eyes fixed more often upon the sunny sky than upon her interlocutor, though now and again she swept me with one of her wonderful glances. She told me how from a child she had heard voices, which she knew to be from above, speaking to her, bidding her to be good, to go to the church, to attend to her simple duties at home. But as she grew older there came a change. She remembered the day when first she saw a wonderful white light hovering above her; and this light came again, and yet again; and the third time she saw in it the figure of an angel - more than that - of the Archangel Michael himself - the warrior of Heaven; and from him she first received the message that she was to be used for the deliverance of her people.

She was long in understanding what this meant. St. Michael told her she should receive other angelic visitors, and often after this St. Catherine and St. Margaret appeared to her, and told her what was required of her, and what she must do. At first she was greatly affrighted, and wept, and besought them to find some other for the task, since she was but a humble country maid, and knew nothing of the art of warfare, and shuddered at the sight of blood. But they told her to be brave, to trust in the Lord, to think only of Him and of His holy will towards her. And so, by degrees, she lost all her fears, knowing that it was not of herself she would do this thing, and that her angels would be with her, her saints would watch over her, and her voices direct her in all that she should speak or do.

"And now," she added, clasping her hands, and looking full into my face, "now do they tell me that the time is at hand. Since last Ascensiontide they have bid me wait in quietness for the appointed hour; but of late my voices have spoken words which may not be set aside. I must be sent to the Dauphin. Orleans must be saved from the hosts of the English which encompass it. I am appointed for this task, and I shall accomplish it by the grace of my Lord and His holy saints. Then the crown must be set upon the head of the Dauphin, and he must be anointed as the king. After that my task will be done; but not till then. And now I must needs set forth upon the appointed way. To the Dauphin I must go, to speak to him of things I may tell to none other; and the Sieur Robert de Baudricourt is appointed of Heaven to send me to Chinon. Wherefore, I pray you, gentle knight, bid him no longer delay; for I am straitened in spirit till I may be about my Lord's business, and He would not have me tarry longer."

I talked with her long and earnestly. Not that I doubted her. I could not do so. Although no voices came to me, yet my heart was penetrated by a conviction so deep and poignant that to doubt would have been impossible. France had been sold and betrayed by one bad woman; but here was the Maid who should arise to save! I knew it in my heart; yet I still spoke on and asked questions, for I must needs satisfy De Baudricourt, I must needs be able to answer all that he would certainly ask.

"How old are you, fair maiden?" I asked, as at length I

rose to depart, and she stood, tall and slim, before me, straight as a young poplar, graceful, despite her coarse raiment, her feet and hands well fashioned, her limbs shapely and supple.

"I was seventeen last week," she answered simply, "the fifth of January is my jour de fete."

"And your parents, what think they of this? What said they when you bid them farewell for such an errand?"

The tears gathered slowly in her beautiful eyes; but they did not fall. She answered in a low voice:

"In sooth they know not for what I did leave them. They believed I went but to visit a sick friend. I did not dare to tell them all, lest my father should hold me back: He is very slow to believe my mission; he chides me bitterly if ever word be spoken anent it. Is it not always so when the Lord uses one of His children? Even our Lord's brethren and sisters believed not on Him. How can the servant be greater than his Lord?"

"You fear not, then, to disobey your parents?"

I had need to put this question; for it was one that De Baudricourt had insisted upon; for he knew something of Jacques d'Arc's opposition to his daughter's proposed campaign.

"I must obey my Lord even above my earthly parents," was her steadfast reply; "His word must stand the first. He knows all, and He will pardon. He knows that I love my father and my mother, and that if I only pleased myself I should never leave their side."

Then suddenly as she spoke a strange look of awe fell upon her; I think she had forgotten my presence, for when she spoke, her words were so low that I could scarce hear them.

"I go to my death!" she whispered, the colour ebbing from her face, "but I am in the hands of my Lord; His will alone can be done."

I went out from her presence with bent head. What did those last words signify - when hitherto all she had spoken was of deliverance, of victory? She spoke them without knowing it. Of that I was assured; and therefore I vowed to keep them locked in my heart. But I knew that I should never forget them.

I found Robert de Baudricourt awaiting my coming in the great hall, pacing restlessly to and fro. Bertrand was with him, and I saw by the tense expression upon his face that he was eager for my report. I gave him one quick glance upon entering, which I trow he read and understood; but to De Baudricourt I spoke with caution and with measured words, for he was a man whose scorn and ridicule were easily aroused, and I knew that Bertrand had fallen into a kind of contempt with him, in that he had so quickly believed in the mission of the Maid.

"Well, and what make you of the girl? Is she witch, or mad, or possessed by some spirit of vainglory and ambition? What has she said to you, and what think you of her?"

"In all truth, my lord, I believe her to be honest; and more than this, I believe her to be directed of God. Strange as it may seem, yet such things have been before, and who are we to say that God's arm is shortened, or that He is not the same as in the days of old? I have closely questioned the Maid as to her visions and voices, and I cannot believe them delusions of the senses. You may ask, are they of the Devil? Then would I say, if there be doubt, let the Abbe Perigord approach her with holy water, with exorcisms, or with such sacred words and signs as devils must needs flee before. Then if it be established that the thing is not of the Evil One, we may the better regard it as from the Lord of whom she speaks. At least, if she can stand this test, I would do this much for her - give her a small escort to Chinon, with a letter to the Dauphin. After that your responsibility will cease. The matter will be in the hands of the King and his advisers."

"Ay, after I have made myself the laughingstock of the realm!" burst out De Baudricourt grimly; yet after he had questioned me again, and yet again, and had even held one interview himself with the Maid, who came of her own accord to the Castle to ask for him one day, he seemed to come to some decision, after much thought and wavering.

Bringing out one of his rattling oaths, he cried:

"Then if she can bear the touch of holy water, and the sign of book and taper and bell - and I know not what beside - then shall she be sent to the King at Chinon, and I, Robert de Baudricourt, will send her - come what may of the mission!"

# IV.

## HOW THE MAID WAS TRIED AND TESTED.

I had myself proposed the test, and yet when the moment came I was ashamed of myself. The Abbe had put on his robes and his stole; a vessel containing holy water stood before him on the table; the book of the Blessed Gospels was in his hands, a boy with a taper stood at his side. The place was the hall of the Castle, and the Governor with a few of those most in his confidence stood by to see what would follow. I was at his right hand.

Bertrand brought in the Maid. I know not what he had said to her, or whether he had prepared her for what was about to take place; but however that may have been, her face wore that calm and lofty serenity of expression which seemed to belong to her. As she approached she made a lowly reverence to the priest, and stood before him where Bertrand placed her, looking at him with earnest, shining eyes.

"My daughter," spoke the Abbe gravely, "have you security in your heart that the visions and voices sent to you come of good and not of evil? Many men and women have, ere this, been deceived - yea, even the holy Saints themselves have been tempted of the devil, that old serpent, who is the great deceiver of the hearts

Evelyn Everett-Green

and spirits of men. Are you well assured in your heart that you are not thus deceived and led away by whispers and suggestions from the father of lies?"

There was no anger in her face, but a beautiful look of reverent, yet joyful, confidence and peace.

"I am well assured, my father, that it is my Lord who speaks to me through His most holy and blessed Saints, and through the ever-glorious Archangel Michael."

"And yet, my daughter, you know that it is written in the Holy Scriptures that the devil can transform himself into an angel of light."

"Truly that is so, my father; but is it not also written that those who put their trust in the Lord shall never be confounded?"

"Yes, my daughter; and I pray God you may not be confounded. But it is my duty to try and test the spirits, so as to be a rock of defence to those beneath my care. Yet if things be with you as you say, you will have no fear."

"I have no fear, my father," she answered, and stood with folded hands and serene and smiling face whilst he went through those forms of exorcism and adjuration which, it is said, no evil spirit can endure without crying aloud, or causing that the person possessed should roll and grovel in agony upon the ground, or rush frantically forth out of sight and hearing.

But the Maid never moved, save to bend her head in

reverence as the Thrice Holy Name was proclaimed, and as the drops of holy water fell upon her brow. To me it seemed almost like sacrilege, in face of that pure and holy calm, to entertain for one moment a doubt of the origin of her mission. Yet it may be that the test was a wise one; for De Baudricourt and those about him watched it with close and breathless wonder, and one and another whispered behind his hand:

"Of a surety she is no witch. She could never stand thus if there was aught of evil in her. Truly she is a marvellous Maid. If this thing be of the Lord, let us not fight against Him."

The trial was over. The Maid received the blessing of the Abbe, who, if not convinced of the sacredness of her mission, was yet impotent to prove aught against her. It is strange to me, looking back at those days, how far less ready of heart the ecclesiastics were to receive her testimony and recognise in her the messenger of the Most High than were the soldiers, whether the generals whom she afterwards came to know, or the men who crowded to fight beneath her banner. One would have thought that to priests and clergy a greater grace and power of understanding would have been vouchsafed; but so far from this, they always held her in doubt and suspicion, and were her secret foes from first to last.

I made it my task to see her safely home; and as we went, I asked:

"Was it an offence to you, fair Maid, that he should thus seek to test and try you?"

"Not an offence to me, Seigneur," she answered gently,

"but he should not have had need to do it. For he did hear my confession on Friday. Therefore he should have known better. It is no offence to me, save inasmuch as it doth seem a slighting of my Lord."

The people flocked around her as she passed through the streets. It was wonderful how the common townsfolk believed in her. Already she was spoken of as a deliverer and a saviour of her country. Nay, more, her gentleness and sweetness so won upon the hearts of those who came in contact with her, that mothers prayed of her to come and visit their sick children, or to speak words of comfort to those in pain and suffering; and such was the comfort and strength she brought with her, that there were whispers of miraculous cures being performed by her. In truth, I have no knowledge myself of any miracle performed by her, and the Maid denied that she possessed such gifts of healing. But that she brought comfort and joy and peace with her I can well believe, and she had some skill with the sick whom she tended in her own village, so that it is likely that some may have begun to mend from the time she began to visit them.

As for De Baudricourt, his mind was made up. There was something about this girl which was past his understanding. Just at present it was not possible to send her to the King, for the rains, sometimes mingled with blinding snow storms, were almost incessant, the country lay partially under water, and though such a journey might be possible to a seasoned soldier, he declared it would be rank murder to send a young girl, who, perchance, had never mounted a horse before, all that great distance. She must needs wait till the waters had somewhat subsided, and till the cold had abated, and the days were somewhat longer.

The Maid heard these words with grave regret, and even disapproval.

"My Lord would take care of me. I have no fear," she said; but De Baudricourt, although he now faithfully promised to send her to Chinon, would not be moved from his resolution to wait.

For my part, I have always suspected that he sent a private messenger to Chinon to ask advice what he should do, and desired to await his return ere acting. But of that I cannot speak certainly, since he never admitted it himself.

If the delay fretted the Maid's spirit, she never spoke with anger or impatience; much of her time was spent in a little chapel in the crypt of the church at Vaucouleurs, where stood an image of Our Lady, before which she would kneel sometimes for hours together in rapt devotion. I myself went thither sometimes to pray; and often have I seen her there, so absorbed in her devotions that she knew nothing of who came or went.

By this time Bertrand and I had steadfastly resolved to accompany the Maid not only to Chinon, but upon whatsoever campaign her voices should afterwards send her. Although we were knights, we neither of us possessed great wealth; indeed, we had only small estates, and these were much diminished in value from the wasting war and misfortunes of the country. Still we resolved to muster each a few men-at-arms, and form for her a small train; for De Baudricourt, albeit willing to send her with a small escort to Chinon, had neither the wish nor the power to equip any sort of force to accompany her, though there would be no

Evelyn Everett-Green

small danger on the journey, both from the proximity of the English in some parts, and the greater danger from roving bands of Burgundians, whose sole object was spoil and plunder, and their pastime the slaughter of all who opposed them.

And now we began to ask one another in what guise the Maid should travel; for it was obvious that her cumbrous peasant garb was little suited for the work she had in hand, and we made many fanciful plans of robing her after the fashion of some old-time queen, such as Boadicea or Semiramis, and wondered whether we could afford to purchase some rich clothing and a noble charger, and so convey her to the King in something of regal state and pomp.

But when, one day, we spoke something of this to the Maid herself, she shook her head with a smile, and said:

"Gentle knights, I give you humble and hearty thanks; but such rich robes and gay trappings are not for me. My voices have bidden me what to do. I am to assume the dress of a boy, since I must needs live for a while amongst soldiers and men. I am sent to do a man's work, therefore in the garb of a man must I set forth Our good citizens of Vaucouleurs are already busy with the dress I must shortly assume. There is none other in which my work can be so well accomplished."

And in truth we saw at once the sense of her words. She had before her a toilsome journey in the companionship of men. She must needs ride, since there was no other way of travelling possible; and why should the frailest and tenderest of the party be burdened by a dress that would incommode her at every turn?

And when upon the very next day she appeared in the Castle yard in the hose and doublet and breeches of a boy, and asked of us to give her her first lesson in horsemanship, all our doubts and misgivings fled away. She wore her dress with such grace, such ease, such simplicity, that it seemed at once the right and fitting thing; and not one of the soldiers in the courtyard who watched her feats that day, passed so much as a rude jest upon her, far less offered her any insult. In truth, they were speedily falling beneath the spell which she was soon to exercise upon a whole army, and it is no marvel to me that this was so; for every day I felt the charm of her presence deepening its hold upon my heart.

Never have I witnessed such quickness of mastery as the Maid showed, both in her acquirement of horsemanship and in the use of arms, in both of which arts we instructed her day by day. I had noted her strength and suppleness of limb the very first day I had seen her; and she gave marvellous proof of it now. She possessed also that power over her horse which she exercised over men, and each charger that she rode in turn answered almost at once to her voice and hand, with a docility he never showed to other riders. Yet she never smote or spurred them; the sound of her voice, or the light pressure of knee or hand was enough. She had never any fear from the first, and was never unhorsed. Very soon she acquired such skill and ease that we had no fears for her with regard to the journey she soon must take.

Although filling the time up thus usefully, her heart was ever set upon her plan, and daily she would wistfully ask:

"May we not yet sally forth to the Dauphin?"

Still she bore the delay well, never losing opportunities for learning such things as might be useful to her; and towards the end of the month there came a peremptory summons to her from the Duke of Lorraine, who was lying very ill at Nancy.

"They tell me," he wrote to De Baudricourt, "that you have at Vaucouleurs a woman who may be in sooth that Maid of Lorraine who, it has been prophesied, is to arise and save France. I have a great curiosity to see her; wherefore, I pray you, send her to me without delay. It may be that she will recover me of my sickness. In any case, I would fain have speech of her; so do not fail to send her forthwith."

De Baudricourt had no desire to offend his powerful neighbour, and he forthwith went down to the house of Leroyer, taking Bertrand and me with him, to ask of the Maid whether she would go to see the Duke at his Court, since the journey thither was but short, and would be a fitting preparation for the longer one.

We found her sitting in the saddler's shop, with one of his children on her lap, watching whilst he fashioned for her a saddle, which the citizens of Vaucouleurs were to give her. Bertrand and I were to present the horse she was to ride, and I had also sent to my home for a certain holiday suit and light armour made for a brother of mine who had died young. I had noted that the Maid had just such a slim, tall figure as he, and was certain that this suit, laid away by our mother in a cedar chest, would fit her as though made for her. But it had not come yet, and she was habited in the tunic and hose she now wore at all times. Her beautiful hair still hung in heavy masses round her shoulders, giving to her something of the look of a saintly warrior on painted window.

Later on, when she had to wear a headpiece, she cut off her long curling locks, and then her hair just framed her face like a nimbus; but today it was still hanging loose upon her shoulders, and the laughing child had got his little hands well twisted in the waving mass, upon which the midday sun was shining clear and strong. She had risen, and was looking earnestly at De Baudricourt; yet all the while she seemed to be, as it were, listening for other sounds than those of his voice.

When he ceased she was silent for a brief while, and then spoke.

"I would fain it had been to the Dauphin you would send me, Seigneur; but since that may not be yet, I will gladly go to the Duke, if I may but turn aside to make my pilgrimage to the shrine of St Nicholas, where I would say some prayers, and ask help."

"Visit as many shrines as you like, so as you visit the Duke as well," answered De Baudricourt, who always spoke with a sort of rough bluffness to the Maid, not unkindly, though it lacked gentleness. But she never evinced fear of him, and for that he respected her. She showed plenty of good sense whilst the details of the journey were being arranged, and was in no wise abashed at the prospect of appearing at a Court. How should she be, indeed, who was looking forward with impatience to her appearance at the Court of an uncrowned King?

Bertrand and I, with some half-dozen men-at-arms,

were to form her escort, and upon the very next day, the sun shining bright, and the wind blowing fresh from the north over the wet lands, drying them somewhat after the long rains, we set forth.

The Maid rode the horse which afterwards was to carry her so many long, weary miles. He was a tall chestnut, deep in the chest, strong in the flank, with a proudly arching neck, a great mane of flowing hair, a haughty fashion of lifting his shapely feet, and an eye that could be either mild or fierce, according to the fashion in which he was treated. On his brow was a curious mark, something like a cross in shape, and the colour of it was something deeper than the chestnut of his coat. The Maid marked this sign at the first glance, and she called the horse her Crusader. Methinks she was cheered and pleased by the red cross she thus carried before her, and she and her good steed formed one of those friendships which are good to see betwixt man and beast.

Our journey was not adventurous; nor will I waste time in telling overmuch about it. We visited the shrine, where the Maid passed a night in fasting and vigil, and laid thereon a little simple offering, such as her humble state permitted. The next day she was presented to the Duke of Lorraine, as he lay wrapped in costly silken coverlets upon his great bed in one of the most sumptuous apartments of his Castle.

He gazed long and earnestly at the Maid, who stood beside him, flinching neither from his hollow gaze, nor from the more open curiosity or admiration bestowed upon her by the lords and ladies assembled out of desire to see her. I doubt me if she gave them a thought. She had come to see the sick Duke, and her thoughts were for him alone.

There was something very strange and beautiful in her aspect as she stood there. Her face was pale from her vigil and fast; her hair hung round it in a dark waving mass, that lighted up at the edges with gold where the light touched it. Her simple boy's dress was splashed and travel stained; but her wonderful serene composure was as marked here as it had been throughout. No fears or tremors shook her, nor did any sort of consciousness of self or of the strangeness of her position come to mar the gentle dignity of her mien or the calm loveliness of her face.

The Duke raised himself on his elbow the better to look at her.

"Is this true what I have heard of you, that you are the Maid of Lorraine, raised up, according to the word of the wizard Merlin, to save France in the hour of her extremity?"

"I am come to save France from the English," she answered at once; "to drive them from the city of Orleans, to bring the Dauphin to Rheims, and there see the crown set upon his head. This I know, for my Lord has said it. Who I am matters nothing, save only as I accomplish the purpose for which I am sent."

Her sweet ringing voice sounded like a silver trumpet through the room, and the lords and ladies pressed nearer to hear and see.

"In sooth, the Maid herself - the Maid who comes to save France!"

Such was the whisper which went round; and I marvelled not; for the look upon that face, the glorious shining in those eyes, was enough to convince the most sceptical that the beatific vision had indeed been vouchsafed to them.

The Duke fell back on his pillows, regarding her attentively.

"If then, Maiden, you can thus read the future, tell me, shall I recover me of this sickness?" he gasped.

"Of that, sire, I have no knowledge," she answered. "That lies with God alone; but if you would be His servant, flee from the wrath to come, which your sins have drawn upon you. Turn to the Lord in penitence. Do His will. Be reconciled to your wife; for such is the commandment of God. Perchance then you will find healing for body and soul. But seek not that which is hidden. Do only the will of the Lord, and trust all to Him."

She was hustled from the room by the frightened attendants, who feared for her very life at the hands of their irate lord. He had done many a man to death for less than such counsel. But the Maid felt not fear.

"He cannot touch me," she said, "I have my Lord's work yet to accomplish."

And in truth the Duke wished her no ill, though he asked not to see her more. Perhaps - who knows - these words may have aroused in him some gleams of penitence for his past life. I have heard he made a better end than was expected of him when his time came. And before the Maid left the Castle he sent her a present of money, and said he might even send his son to help the Dauphin, if once Orleans were relieved, and her words began to fulfil themselves.

So then we journeyed home again, and we reached Vaucouleurs on the afternoon of the twelfth day of February. The Maid had been smiling and happy up till that time, and, since the weather was improving, we had great hopes of soon starting forth upon the journey for Chinon. Nevertheless, the streams were still much swollen, and in some places the ground was so soft that it quaked beneath our horses' feet. We travelled without misadventure, however, and I wondered what it was that brought the cloud to the brow of the Maid as we drew nearer and nearer to Vaucouleurs.

But I was to know ere long; for as we rode into the courtyard of the Castle the Maid slipped from her horse ere any could help her, and went straight into the room where the Governor was sitting, with her fearless air of mastery.

"My lord of Baudricourt, you do great ill to your master the Dauphin in thus keeping me from him in the time of his great need. Today a battle has been fought hard by the city of Orleans, and the arms of the French have suffered disaster and disgrace. If this go on, the hearts of the soldiers will be as water, the purpose of the Lord will be hindered, and you, Seigneur, will be the cause, in that you have not hearkened unto me, nor believed that I am sent of Him."

"How know you the thing of which you speak, girl?" asked De Baudricourt, startled at the firmness of her speech.

Evelyn Everett-Green

"My voices have told me," she answered; "voices that cannot lie. The French have met with disaster. The English have triumphed, and I still waste my time in idleness here! How long is this to continue, Robert de Baudricourt?"

A new note had come into her voice - the note of the general who commands. We heard it often enough later; but this was the first time I had noted it. How would De Baudricourt take it?

"Girl," he said, "I will send forth a courier at once to ride with all speed to the westward. If this thing be so, he will quickly meet some messenger with the news. If it be as you have said, if this battle has been fought and lost, then will I send you forth without a day's delay to join the King at Chinon."

"So be it," answered the Maid; and turned herself to the chapel, where she spent the night in prayer.

It was Bertrand who rode forth in search of tidings, his heart burning within him. It was he who nine days later entered Vaucouleurs again, weary and jaded, but with a great triumph light in his eyes. He stood before De Baudricourt and spoke.

"It is even as the Maid hath said. Upon the very day when we returned to Vaucouleurs, the English - a small handful of men - overthrew at Rouvray a large squadron of the French, utterly routing and well-nigh destroying them. The English were but a small party, convoying herrings to the besiegers of Orleans. The ground was strewn with herrings after the fight, which men call the Battle of the Herrings. Consternation reigns in the hearts of the French - an army flies before a handful! The Maid spake truly; the need is desperate. If help reach not the Dauphin soon, all will be lost!"

"Then let the Maid go!" thundered the old man, roused at last like an angry lion; "and may the God she trusts in guard and keep her, and give to her the victory!"

Evelyn Everett-Green

## V.

## HOW THE MAID JOURNEYED TO CHINON.

So the thing had come to pass at last - as she had always said it must. Robert de Baudricourt was about to send her to the Court of the Dauphin at Chinon. The weary days of waiting were at an end. She was to start forthwith; she and her escort were alike ready, willing, and eager. Her strange mystic faith and lofty courage seemed to have spread through the ranks of the chosen few who were to attend her.

I trow, had she asked it, half the men of Vaucouleurs would have gladly followed in her train; for the whole town was moved to its core by the presence of the Maid in its midst. Almost were the townsfolk ready to worship her, only that there was something in her own simplicity and earnest piety which forbade such demonstration. All knew that the Maid herself would be first to rebuke any person offering to her homage other than true man can and ought to offer to true woman.

And now let me speak here, once and for all, of the love and reverence and devotion which the Maid had power to kindle in the hearts of those with whom she came in contact. I can indeed speak of this, for I am proud to this day to call myself her true knight. From the first I felt towards her as I have felt to none since - not even to the wife of my manhood's tried affections. It was such a love as may be inspired by some almost angelic, presence - there was no passion in it. I believe I speak truly when I say that not one of the Maid's true followers and knights and comrades-in-arms, ever thought of her as possible wife - ever even dreamed of her as lover. She moved amongst us as a being from another sphere. She inspired us with a courage, a power, and a confidence in her and in our cause, which nothing could shake or daunt. She was like a star, set in the firmament of heaven. Our eyes, our hearts turned towards her, but she was never as one of us.

Still less was she as other women are, fashioned for soft flatteries, ready to be wooed and won. Ah, no! With the Maid it was far otherwise. Truly do I think that of herself she had no thought, save as she was the instrument appointed of her Lord to do the appointed work. To that task her whole soul was bent. It filled her to the full with an ecstasy of devotion which required no words in which to express itself. And I can faithfully say that it was not the beauty of her face, the sweetness of her ringing voice, nor the grace and strength of her supple form which made of men her willing followers and servants.

No, it was a power stronger and more sacred than any such carnal admiration. It came from the conviction, which none could fail to reach, that this Maid was indeed chosen and set apart of Heaven for a great and mighty work, and that in obeying her, one was obeying the will of God, and working out some purpose determined in the counsels of the heavenlies.

With her man's garb and light armour, the Maid had

assumed an air of unconscious command which sat with curious graceful dignity upon the serene calm of her ordinary demeanour. Towards her followers of the humbler sort she ever showed herself full of consideration and kindliness. She felt for their fatigues or privations in marching, was tenderly solicitous later on for the wounded. Above all, she was insistent that the dying should receive the consolations of religion, and it was a terrible thought to her that either friend or foe should perish unshriven and unassoiled.

Her last act at Vaucouleurs, ere we started off in the early dawn of a late February day, was to attend Mass with all her following.

An hour later, after a hasty meal provided by De Baudricourt, we were all in the saddle, equipped and eager for the start. The Maid sat her chestnut charger as to the manner born. The pawings of the impatient animal caused her no anxiety. She was looking with a keen eye over her little band of followers, taking in, as a practised leader of men might do, their equipment and general readiness for the road. She pointed out to me several small defects which required adjusting and rectifying.

Already she seemed to have assumed without effort, and as a matter of course, the position of leader and general. There was no abatement of her gentle sweetness of voice or aspect, but the air of command combined with it as though it came direct and without effort as a gift from heaven. None resented it; all submitted to it, and submitted with a sense of lofty joy and satisfaction which I have never experienced since, and which is beyond my power to describe.

There was one change in the outward aspect of the Maid, for her beautiful hair had been cut off, and now her head was crowned only by its cluster of short curling locks, upon which today she wore a cloth cap, though soon she was to adopt the headpiece which belonged to the light armour provided. She had been pleased by the dress of white and blue cut-cloth which I had humbly offered her, and right well did it become her. The other suit provided by the townsfolk was carried by one of the squires, that she might have change of garment if (as was but too probable) we should encounter drenching rains or blustering snow storms.

So far she had no sword of her own, nor had she spoken of the need of such a weapon for herself. But as we assembled in the courtyard of the Castle, getting ourselves into the order of the march, De Baudricourt himself appeared upon the steps leading into the building, bearing in his hands a sword in a velvet scabbard, which he gravely presented to the Maid.

"A soldier, lady, has need of a weapon," were his words, as he placed it in her hands; "take this sword, then. I trow it will do you faithful service; and may the Lord in whom you trust lead you to victory, and save this distracted realm of France from the perils which threaten to overwhelm her!"

"I thank you, Seigneur de Baudricourt," she answered, as she took the weapon, and permitted me to sling it for her in the belt for the purpose which she already wore, "I will keep your gift, and remember your good words, and how that you have been chosen of heaven to send me forth thus, and have done the bidding of the Lord, as I knew that so true a man must needs do at the

Evelyn Everett-Green

appointed time. For the rest, have no fear. The Lord will accomplish that which He has promised. Before the season now beginning so tardily has reached its height, the Dauphin will be the anointed King of France, the English will have suffered defeat and Orleans will be free!"

"Heaven send you speak sooth, fair Maid," answered the rugged old soldier, as he eyed the slim figure before him with something of mingled doubt, wonder, and reverence in his eyes.

Then as though some strange impulse possessed him, he took her hand and kissed it, and bending the knee before her, said:

"Give me, I pray you, a blessing, ere you depart!"

A wonderful light sprang into her eyes. She laid her hand upon the grizzled head, and lifted her own face, as was her wont, to the sunny sky.

"The blessing of the King of Heaven be upon you, Robert de Baudricourt, in that you have been an instrument chosen of Him. The grace and love of our Blessed Lady be yours, in that you have shown kindness and favour to a simple maid of the people, set apart by Heaven for a certain task. The favour and protection of the Saints be yours, in that you have believed the words of one who spake of them, and have been obedient to the command sent to you from them!"

She ceased speaking; but still continued to gaze upward with rapt and earnest eyes. Every head was bared, and we all gazed upon her, as upon one who looks through the open Gate of Heaven, and to whom is vouchsafed a glimpse of the Beatific Vision.

Then clear and sweet her voice rose once more. Her face was transfigured; a great light seemed to shine either upon or from it, no man could say which.

"O Lord God, Father of the Heavenlies, O sweet Jesu, Saviour of mankind, O Blessed Mother, Queen of Heaven, O Holy Michael, Archangel of the shining sword, O Blessed Saints - Catherine and Margaret, beloved of Heaven - give to these, Your children, Your blessing, Your help, Your protection, Your counsel! Be with us in our journeyings - in our uprising and down lying, in our going out and coming in - in all we put our hands unto! Be with us and uphold us, and bring us in safety to our journey's end; for we go forth in the strength which is from above, and which can never fail us till the work appointed be accomplished!"

Then we rode forth, out of the courtyard, and into the streets of the town, which were thronged and lined with townsfolk, and with people from the surrounding villages, who had crowded in to see the wonderful Maid, and witness the outgoing of the little band which was to accompany her to Chinon.

Two of the Maid's brothers had sought to be of her train, and one went with us upon that day. The second she sent back with a letter (written at her dictation by my fingers, for she herself knew not letters, though of so quick an understanding in other matters) to her parents, praying earnestly for their forgiveness for what must seem to them like disobedience, and imploring their blessing. And this letter she dispatched by Jean, permitting Pierre to accompany us on

Evelyn Everett-Green

the march.

Her mother and two younger brothers, at least, believed in her mission by this time; but her father was doubtful and displeased, fearful for her safety, and suspicious of her credentials; and the eldest son remained of necessity at home to help his father, and whether or no he believed in his sister's call, I have never truly heard. But I know it pleased her that Pierre should be in her escort, though she was careful not to show him any marked favour above others; and as in days to come she was more and more thrown with the great ones of the land, she of necessity was much parted from him, though the bond of sisterly love was never slackened; and both Pierre, and afterwards Jean, followed her through all the earlier parts of her victorious career.

Leaving Vaucouleurs, we had need to march with circumspection, for the country was in no settled state, and it was probable that rumours of our march might have got abroad, and that roving bands of English or Burgundian soldiers might be on the look out for us; for already it was being noised abroad that a miraculous Maid had appeared to the aid of France, and though, no doubt, men jeered, and professed incredulity, still it was likely that she would be regarded in the light of a valuable prize if she could be carried off, and taken either to Duke Philip or to the Regent Bedford in Paris.

We had with us a King's archer from Chinon, who had been sent with news of the disaster at Rouvray. He was to conduct us back to Chinon by the best and safest routes. But he told us that the country was beset by roving bands of hostile soldiers, that his comrades had been slain, and that he himself only escaped as by a miracle; and his advice was urgent that after the first day we should travel by night, and lie in hiding during the hours of daylight - a piece of advice which we were fain to follow, being no strong force, able to fight our way through a disturbed country, and being very solicitous for the safety of the precious Maid who was at once our chiefest hope and chiefest care.

This, then, we did, after that first day's travel in the bright springtide sunshine. We were attended for many a mile by a following of mounted men from the district round, and when, as the sun began to wester in the sky, they took their leave of us, the Maid thanked them with gracious words for their company and good wishes, though she would not suffer them to kiss her hand or pay her homage; and after that they had departed, we did halt for many hours, eating and resting ourselves; for we meant to march again when the moon was up, and not lose a single night, so eager was the Maid to press on towards Chinon.

Of our journey I will not speak too particularly. Ofttimes we were in peril from the close proximity of armed bands, as we lay in woods and thickets by day, avoiding towns and villages, lest we should draw too much notice upon ourselves. Ofttimes we suffered from cold, from hunger, from drenching rains and bitter winds. Once our way was barred by snow drifts, and often the swollen rivers and streams forced us to wander for miles seeking a ford that was practicable.

But whatever were the hardships encountered, no word of murmuring ever escaped the lips of the Maid; rather her courage and sweet serenity upheld us all, and her example of patience and unselfishness inspired even

Evelyn Everett-Green

the roughest of the men-at-arms with a desire to emulate it. Never, methinks, on such a toilsome march was so little grumbling, so little discouragement, and, above all, so little swearing. And this, in particular, was the doing of the Maid. For habit is strong with us all, and when things went amiss the oath would rise to the lips of the men about her, and be uttered without a thought.

But that was a thing she could not bear. Her sweet pained face would be turned upon the speaker. Her clear, ringing tones would ask the question:

"Shall we, who go forward in the name of the Lord, dare to take His holy name lightly upon our lips? What are His own words? Swear not at all. Shall we not seek to obey Him? Are we not vowed to His service? And must not the soldier be obedient above all others? Shall we mock Him by calling ourselves His followers, and yet doing that without a thought which He hath forbidden?"

Not once nor twice, but many times the Maid had to speak such words as these; but she never feared to speak them, and her courage and her purity of heart and life threw its spell over the rough men she had led, and they became docile in her hands like children, ready to worship the very ground she trod on.

Long afterwards it was told me by one of mine own men-at-arms that there had been a regular plot amongst the rougher of the soldiers at the outset to do her a mischief, and to sell her into the hands of the Burgundians or the English. But even before leaving Vaucouleurs the men had wavered, half ashamed of their own doubts and thoughts, and before we had proceeded two days' journey forward, all, to a man, would have laid down their lives in her service.

The only matter that troubled the Maid was that we were unable to hear Mass, as she longed to do daily. The risk of showing ourselves in town or village was too great. But there came a night, when, as we journeyed, we approached the town of Fierbois, a place very well known to me; and when we halted in a wood with the first light of day, and the wearied soldiers made themselves beds amid the dried fern and fallen leaves, I approached the Maid, who was gazing wistfully towards the tapering spire of a church, visible at some distance away, and I said to her:

"Gentle Maid, yonder is the church of Sainte Catherine at Fierbois, and there will be, without doubt, early Mass celebrated within its walls. If you will trust yourself with Bertrand and myself, I trow we could safely convey you thither, and bring you back again, ere the day be so far advanced that the world will be astir to wonder at us."

Her face brightened as though a sunbeam had touched it. She needed not to reply in words. A few minutes later, and we were walking together through the wood, and had quickly reached the church, where the chiming of the bell told us that we should not be disappointed of our hope.

We knelt at the back of the church, and there were few worshippers there that morning. I could not but watch the face of the Maid, and suddenly I felt a curious thrill run through me, as though I had been touched by an unseen hand. I looked at her, and upon her face had come a look which told me that she was listening to

Evelyn Everett-Green

some voice unheard by me. She clasped her hands, her eyes travelled toward the altar, and remained fixed upon it, as though she saw a vision. Her lips moved, and I thought I heard the murmured words:

"Blessed Sainte Catherine, I hear. I will remember. When the time comes I shall know what to do."

When the priest had finished his office we slipped out before any one else moved, and reached the shelter of the woods again without encountering any other person. I almost hoped that the Maid would speak to us of what had been revealed to her in that church, but she kept the matter in her own heart. Yet, methinks, she pondered it long and earnestly; for although she laid her down as if to sleep, her eyes were generally wide open, looking upwards through the leafless budding boughs of the trees as though they beheld things not of this earth.

It was upon this day that I wrote, at the Maid's request, a letter to the uncrowned King at Chinon, asking of him an audience on behalf of Jeanne d'Arc, the maiden from Domremy, of whom he had probably heard. This letter I dispatched to Sir Guy de Laval, asking him to deliver it to the King with his own hands, and to bring us an answer ere we reached Chinon, which we hoped now to do in a short while.

The missive was carried by the King's archer, who knew his road right well, and was acquainted with the person of Sir Guy. He was to ride forward in all haste, whilst we were to follow in slower and more cautious fashion.

I think it was about the fifth day of March when the

great towers of Chinon first broke upon our gaze. We had been travelling all the night, and it was just as the dawn was breaking that we espied the huge round turrets rising, as it were, from amid the mists which clung about the river and its banks. There we halted, for no message had yet come from the King; but upon the Maid's face was a look of awe and radiant joy as she stood a little apart, gazing upon the goal of her toilsome journey. No fear beset her as to her reception, just as no fears had troubled her with regard to perils by the way.

"God clears the road for me," she said, when news had been brought from time to time of bands of soldiers whom we had narrowly escaped; and now, as she looked upon the towers of Chinon, growing more and more distinct as the daylight strengthened, her face wore a smile of serene confidence in which natural fear and shrinking had no part.

"The Dauphin will receive me. Fear nothing. The work which is begun will go forward to its completion. God hath spoken in His power. He hath spoken, and His word cannot fail."

So after we had fed she lay down, wrapped in a cloak, and fell asleep like a child; whilst I rode forward a little way along the plain, for I had seen a handful of horsemen sallying forth, as it seemed from the Castle, and I hoped that it was Sir Guy bearing letter or message from the King.

Nor was I mistaken in this hope. Soon I was certain of my man, and Sir Guy in turn recognising me, spurred forward in advance of his followers, and we met alone in the plain, Bertrand, my companion, being with me.

Evelyn Everett-Green

"So there really is to be a miracle worked, and by a Maid!" cried Sir Guy, as we rode with him towards our camp; "Mort de Dieu - but it is passing strange! All the Court is in a fever of wonder about this Angelic Maid, as some call her; whilst others vow she is either impostor or witch. Is it the same, Bertrand, of whom you did speak upon the day we parted company?"

"The same; and yet in one way not the same, for since then she hath grown apace in power and wonder, so that all who see her marvel at her, and some be ready to worship her. But we will say no more. You shall see for yourself, and the King also shall see, if he refuse not to receive one who comes to him as the messenger of God."

"I am sent to conduct the Maid presently to the Castle," answered Sir Guy. 'There is now great desire to see her and hear her, and to try and test the truth of her mission. The Generals scoff aloud at the thought of going to battle with a maid for leader. The Churchmen look grave, and talk of witchcraft and delusion. The ladies of the Court are in a fever to see her. As for the King and his Ministers, they are divided in mind 'twixt hope and fear; but truly matters are come to such desperate pass with us that, if some help come not quickly, the King will flee him away from his distracted realm, and leave the English and Burgundians to ravage and subdue at will!"

"God forbid!" said I, and crossed myself.

Scarce had I spoken the words before I saw approaching us on her chestnut charger the Maid herself, who rode forward to meet us at a foot's pace, and reined back a few yards from us, her eyes fixed full upon the face of Sir Guy, who uncovered, I scarce know why, for how should he knew that this youthful soldier was indeed the Maid herself?

"You come from the Dauphin," she said; "go tell him that the darkest hour but heralds the dawn. He must not flee away. He must stay to face his foes. I will lead his armies to victory, and he shall yet be crowned King of France. Let him never speak more of deserting his realm. That shall not - that must not be!"

Sir Guy was off his horse by now; he bent his knee to the Maid.

"I will tell the King that the Deliverer hath truly come," he said; and taking her hand, ere she could prevent it, he reverently kissed it.

Evelyn Everett-Green

# VI.

## HOW THE MAID CAME TO THE KING.

So Guy de Laval had fallen beneath the spell of the Maid, even as we had done. He spoke of it to me afterwards. It was not because of her words, albeit she had plainly shown knowledge of that which he had been saying before her approach. It was not the beauty of her serene face, or the dignity of her mien. It was as though some power outside of himself urged him to some act of submission. An overshadowing presence seemed to rest upon him as with the touch of a hand, and he who had laughed at the idea of the restoration of miracles suddenly felt all his doubts and misgivings fall away.

We rode together back to our camp, and there we talked long and earnestly of many things. The Maid had much to ask of Sir Guy, but her questions were not such as one would have guessed. She never inquired how the Dauphin (as she always called him) had first heard of her, how he regarded her, what his Ministers and the Court thought of her mission, whether they would receive her in good part, what treatment she might expect when she should appear at Chinon.

No; such thoughts as these seemed never to enter her head. She was in no wise troubled as to the things which appertained to herself. Not once did a natural curiosity on this ground suggest such inquiries; and though we, her followers, would fain have asked many of these questions, something in her own absence of interest, her own earnestness as to other matters, restrained us from putting them.

It was of the city of Orleans she desired to know. What was the condition of the garrison? What were the armies of England doing? What was the disposition of the beleaguering force? Was any project of relief on foot amongst the Dauphin's soldiers? Did they understand how much depended upon the rescue of the devoted town?

Guy de Laval was able to answer these questions, for he had himself ridden from Chinon to Orleans with messages to the Generals in the beleaguered city. He reported that the blockade was not perfected; that provisions could still find their way - though with risk, and danger of loss - into the town, and that messengers with letters could pass to and fro by exercising great caution, and by the grace of Heaven. He told her of the great fortresses the English had built, where they dwelt in safety, and menaced the town and battered its walls with their engines of war.

The garrison and the city were yet holding bravely out, and the Generals Dunois and La Hire were men of courage and capacity. But when the Maid asked how it came about that the English - who could not be so numerous as the French forces in the town - had been suffered to make these great works unmolested, he could only reply with a shake of the head, and with words of evil omen.

Evelyn Everett-Green

"It is the terror of the English which has fallen upon them. Since the victory of Agincourt, none have ever been able to see English soldiers drawn up in battle array without feeling their blood turn to water, and their knees quake under them. I know not what the power is; but at Rouvray it was shown forth again. A small force of soldiers - but a convoy with provisions for the English lines - overcame and chased to destruction a French army ten times its own strength. It is as though the English had woven some spell about us. We cannot face them - to our shame be it spoken! The glorious days of old are past. If Heaven come not to our aid, the cause of France is lost!"

"Heaven has come to the aid of France," spoke the Maid, with that calm certainty which never deserted her; "have no fear, gentle knight. Let the Dauphin but send me to Orleans, and the English will speedily be chased away."

"It will need a great army to achieve that, fair Maid," spoke Sir Guy; "and alas, the King has but a small force at his disposal, and the men are faint hearted and fearful."

"It is no matter," answered the Maid, with shining eyes; "is it anything to my Lord whether He overcomes by many or by few? Is His arm shortened at all, that He should not fulfil that which He has promised? France shall see ere long that the Lord of Hosts fights for her. Will not that be enough?"

"I trow it will," answered De Laval, baring his head.

It was not until the evening was drawing on that we entered the fortress of Chinon, where the King held his

Court. A very splendid castle it was, and when, later in my life, I once visited the realm of England, and looked upon the Castle of Windsor there, it did bring back greatly to my mind that Castle of Chinon, with its towers and battlements overhanging, as it were, the river, and the town clustered at its foot.

We had delayed our approach that our wearied and way-worn men might rest and give a little care to their clothes and arms, so that we presented not too travel-stained and forlorn an appearance. We desired to do honour to the Maid we escorted, and to assume an air of martial pomp, so far as it was possible to us.

Sir Guy had ridden on in front to announce our coming. He told me that the King was full of curiosity about the Maid, and that the ladies of the Court were consumed with wonder and amaze; but that the Prime Minister, De la Tremouille, was strenuously set against having aught to do with that "dreamer of dreams," as he slightingly called her, whilst the King's confessor was much of the same mind, in spite of what was reported about her from the priests who had seen and examined her.

There was no mistaking the sensation which our approach occasioned when at last we reached the walls of the Castle. Soldiers and townspeople, gentlemen and servants, were assembled at every coign of vantage to watch us ride in; and every eye was fixed upon the Maid, who rode as one in a dream, her face slightly raised, her eyes shining with the great joy of an object at last achieved, and who seemed unconscious of the scrutiny to which she was subjected, and unaware of the excitement which her presence occasioned.

For the most part deep silence reigned as we passed by. No acclamation of welcome greeted us, nor did any murmurs of distrust smite upon our ears. There was whispering and a rustling of garments, and the clank of arms; but no articulate words, either friendly or hostile, till, as we passed the drawbridge, one of the sentries, a great, brawny fellow, half French half Scottish, uttered an insult to the Maid, accompanying his words by a horrible blasphemy.

My hand was upon my sword hilt. I could have slain the man where he stood; but I felt the Maid's touch on my shoulder, and my hand sank to my side. She paused before the sentry, gazing at him with earnest eyes, full of mournful reproach and sorrow.

"O Lord Jesu, forgive him!" she breathed softly, and as the fellow, half ashamed, but truculent still, and defiant, turned upon her as though he would have repeated either his insult or his blasphemy, she held up her hand and spoke aloud, so that all who stood by might hear her words:

"O, my friend, speak not so rashly, but seek to make your peace with God. Know you not how near you stand to death this night? May God pardon and receive your soul!"

The man shrank back as one affrighted. It was scarce two hours later that as he was crossing a narrow bridge-like parapet, leading from one part of the Castle to another, he fell into the swollen and rapid stream beneath, and was heard of no more. Some called it witchcraft, and said that the Maid had overlooked him; but the more part regarded it as a sign that she could read the future, and that things unknown to others were open to her eyes; and this, indeed, none could doubt who were with her at this time, as I shall presently show.

I had expected that Sir Guy would come to lead us into the chamber of audience, where we were told the King would receive us. But he did not come, and we were handed on from corridor to corridor, from room to room, first by one richly-apparelled servant of the Court, then by another.

Our men-at-arms, of course, had been detained in one of the courtyards, where their lodgings were provided. Only Bertrand and I were suffered, by virtue of our knighthood, to accompany the Maid into the presence of royalty; and neither of us had ever seen the King, or knew what his outward man was like.

But she asked no questions of us as to that, nor how she was to comport herself when she reached the audience chamber. Neither had she desired to change her travel-stained suit for any other, though, in truth, there was little to choose betwixt them now; only methinks most in her case would have provided some sort of gay raiment wherewith to appear before the King. But the Maid thought nought of herself, but all of her mission, and she held that this was a matter which could be touched by no outward adorning or bravery of apparel.

None who passed through the galleries and corridors of the Castle of Chinon in these days would have guessed to what a desperate pass the young King's affairs had come. Music and laughter resounded there. Courtiers fluttered about in gorgeous array, and fine ladies like painted butterflies bore them company. Feasting and

Evelyn Everett-Green

revelry swallowed up the days and nights. No clang of arms disturbed the gaieties of the careless young monarch.

If despair and desperation were in his heart, he pushed them back with a strong hand. He desired only to live in the present. He would not look beyond. So long as he could keep his Court about him, he would live after this fashion; and when the English had swept away the last barriers, and were at the very gates, then he would decide whether to surrender himself upon terms, or to fly to some foreign land. But to face the foe in gallant fight was an alternative which had never been entertained by him, until such time as he had received the message from the Maid; and then it was rather with wonder and curiosity than any belief in her mission that he had consented to receive her.

A pair of great double doors was flung open before us. We stood upon the threshold of a vast room, lighted by some fifty torches, and by the blaze of a gigantic fire which roared halfway up the vast chimney. This great audience chamber seemed full of dazzling jewels and gorgeous raiment. One could scarce see the faces and figures in the shifting throng for the wonder of this blaze of colour.

But there was no dais on which the King was seated in state, as I had expected. No figure stood out conspicuous in the throng as that of royalty. I gazed at one and another, as we stood in the doorway, our eyes still half dazzled by the glare of light and by the brilliance of the assembled company, but I could by no means distinguish the King from any of the rest. Many men, by their gorgeous raiment, might well be the greatest one present; but how to tell?

All were quiet now. They had fallen a little back, as though to gaze upon the newcomer. Smiling faces were turned upon us. Eager eyes were fastened upon the Maid's face. She stood there, with the glare of the torches shining over her, looking upon the scene with her calm, direct gaze, without tremor of fear or thought of shame.

One of the great Seigneurs - I know not which - came forward with a smile and a bow, and gave her his hand to lead her forward.

"I will present you to the King," he said; and made in a certain direction, as though he would lead her to a very kingly-looking personage in white and crimson velvet, blazing with diamonds; but ere he had taken many steps, the Maid drew her hand from his, and turning herself in a different direction, went forward without the least wavering, and knelt down before a young man in whose attire there was nothing in any way gorgeous or notable.

"Gentle Dauphin," she said, in that clear voice of hers which always made itself heard above other sounds, though at this moment a great hush prevailed throughout the audience chamber, and wondering eyes were fixed full upon the Maid, "God give you good life, and victory over your enemies!"

Astonishment was in the young man's face; but he took the Maid by the hand, and said:

"You mistake, fair damsel; it is not I that am the King. See, he is there; let me take you to him."

But she would not be raised; she knelt still at his feet,

Evelyn Everett-Green

and the hand which he had given her she held to her
lips.

"Gentle Dauphin, think not to deceive me. I know you,
who you are. You are he to whom I am sent, to win
you the victory first, and then to place the crown of
France upon your head. It is you, and none other, who
shall rule in France!"

The young man's face had changed greatly now. A
deep agitation replaced the former smile of mockery
and amusement. Several of the courtiers were exchan-
ging meaning glances; in the hush of the hall every
spoken word could be heard.

"Child, how dost thou know me?" asked the King, and
his voice shook with emotion.

Her answer was not strange to us, though it might have
been so to others.

"I am Jeanne the Maid," she replied, as if in so saying
she was saying enough to explain all; "I am sent to you
by the King of Heaven; and it is His Word that I have
spoken. You shall be crowned and consecrated at
Rheims, and shall be lieutenant of the King of Heaven,
Who is King of France, but Who wills that you shall
reign over that fair realm!"

"Have you a message from Him to me?" asked the
King, speaking like a man in a dream.

"Ay, verily I have," answered the Maid, "a message
which none but you must hear; for it is to you alone
that I may tell it."

Then the King took her by the hand, and raised her up, gazing at her with a great wonder and curiosity; and he led her behind a curtain into a deep recess of the window, where prying eyes could not see them, nor inquisitive ears overhear her words.

And so soon as they had disappeared there, a great hum and buzz of wonder ran throughout the hall, and we saw Sir Guy detach himself from a knot of gay courtiers, and come hastily towards us.

"Is it not wonderful!" he cried. "And I had feared that she would be deceived, and that the mockers would have the laugh against her in the first moment. Though how they looked for her to have knowledge of the King's person I know not. Surely none can doubt but that she is taught by the Spirit of God."

"It was done to prove her!"

"Ay, it was the thought of De la Tremouille, who has ridiculed her pretensions (the word is his) from first to last. But it was a thought welcomed by all, as a passing merry jest. Thus was it that I was not permitted to come and lead you in. They did fear lest I should tell what was intended, and describe to the Maid the person or the dress of the King. And now none can doubt; and, in sooth, it may be a wondrous thing for His Majesty himself, and take from him for ever that hateful fear which I always do declare has helped to paralyse him, and hold him back from action."

I lowered my voice to a whisper as I said:

"You mean the fear lest he was not the true son of the King?"

Evelyn Everett-Green

"Yes; his wicked mother hinted away her own honour in her desire to rob him of his crown. He has known her for an evil woman. Was it not likely he would fear she might speak truth? Those who know him best know that he has often doubted his right to style himself Dauphin or King; but methinks after today that doubt must needs be set at rest. If the Maid who comes from the King of Heaven puts that name upon him, need he fear to take it for his own?"

As we were thus speaking the Sieur de Boisi joined us. He was perchance more fully in the King's confidence than any other person at Court, and he was kinsman to De Laval, with whom he had plainly already had much talk upon this subject. He drew us aside, and whispered a story in our ears.

"His Majesty did tell it me himself," he said, "for there be nights when he cannot sleep, and he calls me from my couch at his bed's foot, and makes me lie beside him, that we may talk at ease; and he told me, not long since, how that this trouble and doubt were so growing upon him, that once he had fasted for a whole day, and had passed the night upon his knees in the oratory, praying for a sign whereby he might truly know whether he were the real heir, and the kingdom justly his. For that were it not so, he would sooner escape to Spain or Scotland to pass his days in peace; but that if the Lord would send him a sign, then he would seek to do his duty by the realm."

With awe we looked into each other's faces.

"The sign has come!" whispered Bertrand.

"Truly I do think it," answered De Boisi.

"Surely His Majesty will recognise it as such!" said Sir Guy.

"I see not how it can be otherwise; and it will be like a great load lifted from his heart."

"And he will surely hesitate no more," I said, "but will forthwith give her a band of armed men, that she may sally forth to the aid of the beleaguered Orleans!"

But De Boisi and De Laval looked doubtful.

"I know not how that will be. For there are many who will even now seek to dissuade the King, and will talk of witchcraft, and I know not what beside. The Abbes and the Bishops and the priests are alike distrustful and hostile. The Generals of the army openly scoff and jeer. Some say that if the Maid be sent to Orleans, both La Hire and Dunois will forthwith retire, and refuse all further office there. What can a peasant maid know of the art of war? They ask, and how can she command troops and lead them on to victory, where veterans have failed again and again? And then the King knows not what to reply - "

"But she hath given him wherewith to reply!" broke out Bertrand, with indignation in his tones. "She comes not in her own strength, but as the envoy of the King of Heaven. Is that not enough?"

"Enough for us who have seen and heard her," answered Sir Guy; "but will it prove enough for those who only hear of her from others, and who call her a witch, and say that she works by evil spells, and has been sent of the Devil for our deception and destruction and undoing?"

Evelyn Everett-Green

"Then let them send for one of the Generals from Orleans, and let him judge for himself!" cried Bertrand hotly; "you say the city is not so closely blockaded but that with care and caution men may get in or out? Then let some one send and fetch one of these commanders; and if he be not convinced when he sees her, then he will be of very different stuff from all else who have doubted, but whose doubts have been dispelled."

"In faith, that is no bad thought," spoke De Boisi thoughtfully, "and I trow it might be possible of accomplishment. I will certainly speak with the King of it. He is young; he is not firm of purpose; his own heart has never before been set upon his kingdom. One cannot expect a man's nature to change in a day, even though his eyes may have been opened, and his misgivings set at rest. If one of the Generals were won to her side, the troubles that beset us would be well-nigh overcome."

A great clamour of sound from the larger audience chamber, from which we had retired to talk at ease, warned us now that the King and the Maid had appeared from their private conference. His face was very grave, and there was more of earnestness and nobility in his expression than I had thought that countenance capable of expressing. The Maid was pale, as though with deep emotion; but a glorious light shone in her eyes, and when the Court ladies and gallants crowded round her, asking her questions, and gazing upon her as though she were a being from another sphere, she seemed lifted up above them into another region, and though she answered them without fear, she put aside, in some wonderful way, all those questions which were intrusions into holy things, speaking so fearlessly and so simply that all were amazed at her.

She came to us at last, weary, yet glad at heart; and her first question was for her followers, and whether they had been lodged and fed. We supped with her at her request, and in private, and her face was very calm and glad, though she spoke nothing of what had passed between her and the King.

Only when Bertrand said:

"You have done a great work today," did she look at him with a smile as she replied:

"My work hath but just begun, and may yet be hindered; but have no fear. The Lord has spoken, and He will bring it to pass. He will not fail us till all be accomplished."

## VII.

## HOW THE MAID WAS HINDERED;
## YET MADE PREPARATION.

I have no patience to write of the things which followed. I blush for the King, for his Council, yea, even for the Church itself! Here was a messenger sent from God, sent to France in the hour of her direst need. This messenger had been tried and tested by a score of different methods already, and had in every case come forth from the trial like gold submitted to the fire. Priests had examined and found nothing evil in her. Again and again had she spoken of that which must follow - and so it had been. If her voices were not from God, then must they be from the devil; yet it had been proved again, and yet again, that this was impossible, since she feared nought that was holy or good, but clave unto such, and was never so joyful and glad at heart as when she was able to receive the Holy Sacrament, or kneel before the Altar of God whilst Mass was being said.

She had proved her claim to be called God's messenger. She had justified herself as such in the eyes of the King and in the judgment of the two Queens and of half the Court. And yet, forsooth, he must waver and doubt, and let himself be led by the counsels of those who had ever set themselves against the Maid and her mission; and to the shame of the Church be it spoken, the Archbishop of Rheims was one of those who most zealously sought to persuade him of the folly of entrusting great matters to the hands of a simple peasant girl, and warned the whole Court of the perils of witchcraft and sorcery which were like to be the undoing of all who meddled therein.

I could have wrung the neck of the wily old fox, whom I did more blame than I did his friend and advocate, De la Tremouille; for the latter only professed carnal wisdom and prudence, but the Archbishop spoke as one who has a mandate from God, and he at least should have known better.

And so they must needs send her to Poictiers, to a gathering of ecclesiastics, assembled by her enemy, the Archbishop himself, to examine into her claims to be that which she professed, and also into her past life, and what it had been.

I scarce have patience to write of all the wearisome weeks which were wasted thus, whilst this assembly sat; and the Maid - all alone in her innocence, her purity, her sweetness, and gentle reverence - stood before them, day after day, to answer subtle questions, face a casuistry which sought to entrap her into contradiction or confusion, or to wring from her a confession that she was no heaven-sent messenger, but was led away by her own imaginations and ambitions.

It was an ordeal which made even her devoutest adherents tremble; for we knew the astuteness of the churchmen, and how that they would seek to win admissions which they would pervert to their own uses afterwards. Yet we need not have feared; for the

Evelyn Everett-Green

Maid's simplicity and perfectly fearless faith in her mission carried her triumphant through all; or perhaps, indeed, her voices whispered to her what answers she should make, for some of them were remembered long, and evoked great wonder in the hearts of those who heard them.

One Dominican monk sought to perplex her by asking why, since God had willed that France should be delivered through her she had need of armed men?

Full fearlessly and sweetly she looked at him as she made answer:

"It is my Lord's will that I ask for soldiers, and that the Dauphin shall give me them. The men shall fight; it is God who gives the victory."

Another rough questioner amongst her judges sought to confuse her by asking what language her voices spoke. They say that a flash flew from her eyes, though her sweet voice was as gentle as ever as she made answer:

"A better language than yours, my father."

And again, when the same man sought to know more of her faith and her love of God, having shown himself very sceptical of her voices and visions, she answered him, with grave dignity and an earnest, steadfast gaze:

"I trow I have a better faith than yours, my father."

And so, through all, her courage never failed, her faith never faltered, her hope shone undimmed.

"They must give me that which I ask; they cannot withstand God. They cannot hurt me. For this work was I born, and until it be accomplished I am safe. I have no fear."

Only once did she show anger, and then it was with a quiet dignity of displeasure, far removed from petulance or impatience. They asked of her a sign that she was what she professed to be.

"I have not come to Poictiers to give a sign," she answered, holding her head high, and looking fearlessly into the faces of those who sat to judge her. "Send me to Orleans, with as small a band as you will. But send me there, and you shall see signs and to spare that I come in the power of the King of Heaven."

And so in the end her faith and courage triumphed. The verdict ran somewhat thus:

"We have found in her nothing but what is good. To deny or hinder her intentions to serve the King would be to show ourselves unworthy of the assistance of God."

Yes, they had to come to it; and I trust that there were many sitting there whose hearts smote them for ever having doubted, or sought to baffle or entrap her. I cannot tell how far the judges were moved by the growing feeling in the town and throughout the district. But the people crowded to see the Maid pass by, and all were ready to fall at her feet and worship her. In the evenings they visited her at the house of Jean Ratabeau, the Advocate General, whose wife formed for her (as did every good and true woman with whom she came into contact during her life) an ardent admiration and affection.

And to their earnest questions she gave ready answer, sitting in the midst of an eager crowd, and telling them in her sweet and simple way the story of her life in Domremy, and how she had first heard these voices from Heaven, or seen wondrous visions of unspeakable glories; and how she had learnt, by slow degrees, that which her Lord had for her to do, and had lost, by little and little, the fear which first possessed her, till now she knew not of the name of the word. She had but to follow where her voices guided.

And the people believed in her, heart and soul. Her fame spread far and wide, and had she lifted but a finger, she might have been at the head of an armed band of citizens and soldiers, yea, and many gentlemen and knights as well, all vowed to live and die in her service. But this was not what was her destiny.

"I thank you, my friends," she would say, if such a step were proposed by any ardent soul, impatient of this long delay; "but thus it may not be. My Lord has decreed that the Dauphin shall send me forth at the head of his armies, and with a troop of his soldiers; and he will do this ere long. Be not afraid. We must needs have patience, as did our Lord Himself, and be obedient, as He was. For only as we look to Him for grace and guidance can we hope to do His perfect will."

Thus spoke the Maid, who, being without letters, and knowing, as she said, no prayers save the Pater Noster, Ave Maria, and Credo, yet could speak in such fashion to those who sought her. Was it wonder that the people believed in her? that they would have been ready to tear in pieces any who durst contemn her mission, or declare her possessed of evil spirits?

Yet I will not say that it was fear which possessed the hearts of her judges, and decided their ruling in this matter. I trow they could not look upon her, or hear her, without conviction of heart. Nevertheless it is possible that the respect for popular enthusiasm led them to speak in such high praise of the Maid, and to add that she was in the right in assuming the dress which she wore. For she had been sent to do man's work, and for this a man's garb was the only fitting one to wear. And this ruling was heard with great acclamation of satisfaction; for her dress had been almost more commented upon than any other matter by some, and that the Church had set its sanction upon that which common sense deemed most right and fitting, robbed the most doubtful of all scruple, and gave to the Maid herself no small pleasure.

"I do in this, as in all other things, that which I have been bidden," she said. "But I would not willingly act unseemly in the eyes of good men and virtuous women; wherefore I am glad that my judges have spoken thus, and I thank them from my heart for their gentle treatment of me."

It was ever thus with the Maid. No anger or impatience overset her sweet serenity and humility. She would not let herself take offence, or resent these ordeals to which, time after time, she was subjected. Nay, it was she who defended the proceedings when we attacked them, saying that it behoved men to act with care and caution in these great matters, and that her only trouble in the delay was the sufferings and sorrows of the poor beleaguered garrison and citizens in Orleans, to whose

Evelyn Everett-Green

help and relief she longed to fly.

So certain was she that before long she would be upon her way, that at Poictiers she composed that letter to the English King, his Regent, and his Generals which has been so much talked of since. It was a truly wonderful document to be penned by a village maiden; for in it she adjured them to cease from warring with the rightful King of France, whom God would have to rule the realm for Him, to go back to their own country, leaving peace behind them instead of war, and imploring them then to join with the King of France in a crusade against the Saracens. She speaks of herself as one who has power to drive them from the kingdom if they will not go in peace as adjured. Calling herself throughout "The Maid," she tells them plainly that they will not be able to stand against her; that she will come against them in the power of the King of Heaven, Who will give to her more strength than ever can be brought against her; and in particular she begs of them to retire from the city of Orleans; else, if they do not, they shall come to great misfortune there.

This letter took some time in the composition, and was written for her by Sir Guy de Laval, though we were all in her counsel as she dictated it.

By this I do not mean that we advised her. On the contrary, we gazed at her amazed, knowing how fruitless such an injunction must be to the haughty victorious nation, who had us, so to speak, in the dust at her feet. But the Maid saw with other eyes than ours.

"It may be that there will be some holy man of God in their camp to whom my Lord will reveal His will, as He hath done to me, and will show the things which must come to pass. I would so willingly spare all the bloodshed and misery which war will bring. It is so terrible a thing for Christian men to war one with another!"

So this letter, with its superscription "JHESUS MARIA," was written and dispatched to the English, and the Maid turned her attention to other matters near her heart, such as the design and execution of those banners which were to be carried before her armies in battle, and lead them on to victory. And these same words, "Jhesus Maria," she decreed should appear upon each of the three standards, in token that she went not forth in her own strength, nor even in that of the King of France; but in the power which was from above, and in the strength given by those who sent her.

Now there came to Poictiers to see the Maid at this time many persons from other places, and amongst these was a Scotchman called Hauves Polnoir, who brought with him his daughter, a fair girl, between whom and the Maid a great love speedily sprang up. These Polnoirs were the most skilful workers in embroideries and such like of all the country round, and to them was entrusted the making of the three banners, according to the instructions of the Maid.

There was first the great white silken standard, with the golden fleur-de-lys of France, and a representation on the reverse of the Almighty God between two adoring angels; then a smaller banner, with a device representing the Annunciation, which she always gave to one of her immediate attendants or squires to carry into battle; and for herself she had a little triangular banneret of white, with an image of the Crucified Christ upon it, and this she carried herself, and it was destined to be the rallying point of innumerable engagements, for the sight of that little fluttering pennon showed the soldiers where the Maid was leading them, and though this was in the thickest and sorest of the strife, they would press towards it with shouts of joy and triumph, knowing that, where the Maid led, there victory was won.

All these matters were arranged whilst we were kept in waiting at Poictiers; and the Polnoirs returned to Tours to execute the orders there in their own workshop. The Maid promised to visit them on her way from Chinon to Orleans, and so bid them a kindly farewell. Perhaps I may here add that when the Dauphin, upon his coronation, insisted upon presenting the Maid with a sum of money, the use she made of it, after offering at various shrines, was to provide a marriage dowry for Janet Polnoir. Never did she think of herself; never did she desire this world's goods.

This was shown very plainly upon her triumphant return to Chinon, with the blessing and sanction of the Church upon her mission, with the enthusiasm of the people growing and increasing every day, and her fame flying throughout the length and breadth of the realm. By this time the King and all his Court knew that a deliverer had been raised up in our midst, and instead of lowly lodgings being allotted to the Maid and her train, the whole Tower of Coudray was set apart for the use of herself and her suite. The custodian De Belier and his wife had charge of her, and to her were now appointed a staff, of which the brave Jean d'Aulon was the chief, and to which Bertrand and Sir Guy de Laval and myself belonged, together with many more knights and gentlemen, all anxious to do service under her banner. Also she had in her train some persons of lowlier degree, such as her brothers, for whom she always had tender care, and who believed devoutly in her mission, although they saw of necessity less and less of one another as the Maid's mission progressed, and took her into a different world.

But all this grandeur was no delight to her, save inasmuch as it showed that at last her mission was recognised and honoured. When asked what she would have for herself in the matter of dress and armour, her answer was that she had already all she required, although she only possessed at this time one suit more than she had started forth with from Vaucouleurs. Although she saw the courtiers fluttering about like butterflies, and noted how men, as well as women, decked themselves in choice stuffs and flashing jewels, she asked none of these things for herself; and when the Queen of Sicily, always her best and kindest friend, sent to her some clothing of her own designing - all white, and beautifully worked, some with silver, and some with gold thread and cord, and a mantle of white velvet, lined with cloth of silver - she looked at the beautiful garments with something between a smile and a sigh; then turning towards the great lady who stood by to watch her, she first kissed her hand, and then, with sudden impulse of affection, put her arms about her neck, and was drawn into a close embrace.

"Are you not pleased with them, my child?" spoke Queen Yolande gently; "they would have decked you in all the colours of the rainbow, and made you to blaze with jewels; but I would not have it The Virgin Maid, I told them, should be clad all in white, and my word prevailed, and thus you see your snowy raiment. I had thought you would be pleased with it, ma mie."

"Madame, it is beautiful; I have never dreamed of such. It is too fine, too costly for such as I. I am but a peasant maid - "

"You are the chosen of the King of Heaven, my child. You must think also of that. You are now the leader of the King's armies. You have to do honour alike to a Heavenly and an earthly Monarch; and shall we let our champion go forth without such raiment as is fitting to her mission?'

Then the Maid bent her head, and answered with sweet gladness:

"If it is thus that the world regards me, I will wear these trappings with a glad and thankful heart; for in sooth I would seek to do honour to His Majesty. As for my Lord in the Heavens, I trow that He doth look beneath such matters of gay adornment; yet even so, I would have His mission honoured in the sight of all men, and His messenger fitly arrayed."

So the Maid put on her spotless apparel, and looked more than ever like a youthful warrior, going forth with stainless shield, in the quest of chivalrous adventure. The whole Court was entranced by her beauty, her lofty dignity, her strange air of aloofness from the world, which made her move amongst them as a thing apart, and seemed to set a seal upon her every word and act.

When she spoke of the coming strife, and her plans for the relief of the beleaguered city, her eyes would shine, a ringing note of authority would be heard in her voice, she would fearlessly enter into debate with the King and his Ministers, and tell them that which she was resolved to do, whether they counselled it or no. At such moments she appeared gifted with a power impossible rightly to describe. Without setting herself up in haughtiness, she yet overbore all opposition by her serene composure and calm serenity in the result. Men of war said that she spoke like a soldier and a strategist; they listened to her in amaze, and wondered what the great La Hire would say when he should arrive, to find that a country maiden had been set over his head.

In other matters, too, the Maid knew her mind, and spoke it with calm decision. The Queen of Sicily had not been content with ordering the Maid's dress alone, she had also given orders to the first armourer in Tours to fashion her a suit of light armour for the coming strife. This armour was of white metal, and richly inlaid with silver, so that when the sun glinted upon it, it shone with a dazzling white radiance, almost blinding to behold. The King, also, resolved to do his share, had ordered for her a light sword, with a blade of Toledo steel; but though the Maid gratefully accepted the gift of the white armour, and appeared before all the Court attired therein, and with her headpiece, with its floating white plumes crowning it all, yet, as she made her reverence before the King, she gently put aside his gift of the sword.

"Gentle Dauphin," she said, "I thank you from my heart; but for me there is another sword which I must needs carry with me into battle; and I pray you give me leave to send and fetch it from where it lies unknown and forgotten."

"Why, Maiden, of what speak you?" he answered; "is not this jewelled weapon good enough? You will find its temper of the best. I know not where you will find a better!"

"No better a sword, Sire," she answered; "and yet the one which I must use; for so it hath been told me of my Lord. In the church of Fierbois, six leagues from hence, beneath the high altar, there lies a sword, and this sword must I use. Suffer me, I pray you, to send and fetch it thence. Then shall I be ready and equipped to sally forth against the foes of my country."

"But who has told you of this sword, my maiden?"

"My Lord did tell me of it, as I knelt before the altar, ere I came to Chinon. It is in the church of St. Catherine; and suffer only my good knight, Jean de Metz, to go and make search for it, and he will surely bring it hither to me."

Now I did well remember how, as we knelt in the church at Fierbois in the dimness of the early morn, the Maid had received some message, unheard by those beside her; and gladly did I set forth upon mine errand to seek and bring to her this sword.

When I reached Fierbois, which was in the forenoon of the day following, the good priests of the church knew nothing of any such sword; but the fame of the Maid having reached their ears, they were proud and glad that their church of St. Catherine should be honoured thus, and calling together some workmen, they made careful search, and sure enough, before we had dug deep, the spade struck and clinked against metal, and forth from beneath the altar we drew a sword, once a strong and well-tempered weapon, doubtless, but now covered with rust, so that the good priests looked askance at it, and begged to have it to cleanse and polish.

It was then too late for my return the same day, so I left it to them, and lodged me in the town, where all the people flocked to hear news of the Maid and of the coming campaign.

Then in the morning, with the first of the light, the sword was brought to me; and surely many persons in Fierbois must have sat up all the night, for every speck of rust had been cleansed away, and a velvet scabbard made or found for the weapon, which the priests begged of me to take with it to the Maid as their gift, and with their benediction upon it and her.

My return was awaited with some stir of interest, and before I had well dismounted I was hurried, all travel stained as I was, into the presence of the King. There was the Maid waiting also, calm and serene, and when she saw the thing which I carried in my hands, her face lighted; she took several steps forward, and bent her knee as she reverently took the sword, as though she received it from some Higher Power.

"It was even as she said?" questioned the King, quickly.

"Even so, Sire; the sword of which no man knew aught, was lying buried beneath the high altar of St. Catherine's Church, in Fierbois."

A murmur of surprise and gratification ran through the assembly. But there was no surprise upon the Maid's face.

"Did you doubt, Sire?" she asked, and he could not meet the glance of her clear eyes.

## VIII.

## HOW THE MAID MARCHED FOR ORLEANS.

Methinks the Maid loved that ancient sword better than all her shining armour of silver! Strange to say, the jewelled sheath of the King's Toledo blade fitted the weapon from Fierbois, and he supplemented the priests' gift of a scabbard by this second rich one. The Maid accepted it with graceful thanks; yet both the gorgeous cases were laid away, and a simple sheath of leather made; for the sword was to be carried at her side into battle, and neither white nor crimson velvet was suited to such a purpose.

Nor would the Maid let us have her sword sharpened for her. A curious look came upon her face as Bertrand pointed out that although now clean and shining, its edges were too blunt for real use. She looked round upon us as we stood before her, and passed her fingers lovingly down the edges of the weapon.

"I will keep it as it is," she answered; "for though I must needs carry it into battle with me, I pray my Lord that it may never be my duty to shed Christian blood. And if the English King will but listen to the words of counsel which I have sent to him, perchance it may even now be that bloodshed will be spared."

Evelyn Everett-Green

In sooth, I believe that she would far rather have seen the enemy disperse of their own accord, than win the honour and glory of the campaign, which she knew beforehand would bring to her renown, the like of which no woman in the world's history has ever win. She would have gone back gladly, I truly believe, to her home in Domremy, and uttered no plaint, even though men ceased after the event to give her the praise and glory; for herself she never desired such.

But we, who knew the temper of the English, were well aware that this would never be. Even though they might by this time have heard somewhat of the strange thing which had happened, and how the French were rallying round the standard of the Angelic Maid, yet would they not readily believe that their crushed and beaten foes would have power to stand against them. More ready would they be to scoff than to fear.

Now, at last, after all these many hindrances and delays, all was in readiness for the start. April had well nigh run its course, and nature was looking her gayest and loveliest when the day came that we marched forth out of the Castle of Chinon, a gallant little army, with the Maid in her shining white armour and her fluttering white pennon at our head, and took the road to Tours, where the great and redoubtable La Hire was to meet us, and where we were to find a great band of recruits and soldiers, all eager now to be led against the foe.

Much did we wonder how the Generals of the French army would receive the Maid, set, in a sense, over them as Commander-in-Chief of this expedition, with a mandate from the King that she was to be obeyed, and that her counsels and directions were to be followed. We heard conflicting rumours on this score. There were those who declared that so desperate was the condition of the city, and so disheartened the garrison and citizens that they welcomed with joy the thought of this deliverer, and believed already that she was sent of God for their succour and salvation. Others, on the contrary, averred that the officers of the army laughed to scorn the thought of being aided or led by a woman - a peasant - une peronelle de bas lieu, as they scornfully called her - and that they would never permit themselves to be led or guided by one who could have no knowledge of war, even though she might be able to read the secrets of the future.

In spite of what had been now ruled by the Church concerning her, there were always those, both in the French and English camps, who called her a witch; and we, who heard so many flying rumours, wondered greatly what view the redoubtable La Hire took of this matter, and Dunois, the Bastard of Orleans, as he was often called. For these two men, with Xaintrailles, were the ruling Generals in Orleans, and their voice would be paramount with the army there, and would carry much weight with those reinforcements for the relieving force which we were to find awaiting us at Tours and at Blois.

Now La Hire, as all men know, was a man of great renown, and of immense personal weight and influence. He was a giant in stature, with a voice like a trumpet, and thews of steel; a mighty man in battle, a daring leader, yet cautious and sagacious withal; a man feared and beloved by those whom he led in warfare; a gay roysterer at other times, with as many strange oaths upon his lips as there are saints in the calendar; what the English call a swashbuckler and daredevil; a man whom one would little look to be led or guided by a woman, for he was impatient of counsel, and headstrong alike in thought and action.

And this was the man who was to meet us at Tours, form his impression of the Maid, and throw the great weight of his personal influence either into one scale or the other. Truth to tell, I was something nervous of this ordeal, and there were many who shared my doubts and fears. But the Maid rode onward, serene and calm, the light of joy and hope in her eyes, untroubled by any doubts. At last she was on her way to the relief of the beleaguered city; there was no room for misgiving in her faithful heart.

We entered Tours amid the clashing of joy bells, the plaudits of the soldiers, and the laughter, the weeping, the blessings of an excited populace, who regarded the Maid as the saviour of the realm. They crowded to their windows and waved flags and kerchiefs. They thronged upon her in the streets to gaze at her fair face and greet her as a deliverer.

It was indeed a moving scene; but she rode through it, calm and tranquil, pausing in the press to speak a few words of thanks and greeting, but preserving always her gentle maidenly air of dignity and reserve. And so we came to the house which had been set apart for her use on her stay, and there we saw, standing at the foot of the steps which led from the courtyard into the house, a mighty, mailed figure, the headpiece alone lacking of his full armour, a carven warrior, as it seemed, with folded arms and bent brows, gazing upon us as we filed in under the archway, but making no move to approach us.

I did not need the whisper which ran through the ranks

of our escort to know that this man was the great and valiant La Hire.

As the Maid's charger paused at the foot of the steps, this man strode forward with his hand upraised as in a salute, and giving her his arm, he assisted her to alight, and for a few moments the two stood looking into each other's eyes with mutual recognition, taking, as it were, each the measure of the other.

The Maid was the first to speak, her eyes lighting with that deep down, indescribable smile, which she kept for her friends alone. When I saw that smile in her eyes, as they were upraised to La Hire's face, all my fears vanished in a moment.

"You are the Dauphin's brave General La Hire, from Orleans," she said; "I thank you, monsieur, for your courtesy in coming thus to meet me. For so can we take counsel together how best the enemies of our country may be overthrown."

"You are the Maid, sent of God and the King for the deliverance of the realm," answered La Hire, as he lifted her hand to his lips, "I bid you welcome in the name of Orleans, its soldiers, and its citizens. For we have been like men beneath a spell - a spell too strong for us to break. You come to snap the spell, to break the yoke, and therefore I bid you great welcome on the part of myself and the citizens and soldiers of Orleans. Without your counsels to His Majesty, and the aid you have persuaded him to send, the city must assuredly have fallen ere this. Only the knowledge that help was surely coming has kept us from surrender."

"I would the help had come sooner, my General,"

spoke the Maid; "but soon or late it is one with my Lord, who will give us the promised victory."

From that moment friendship, warm and true, was established betwixt the bronzed warrior and the gentle Maid, who took up, as by natural right, her position of equal - indeed, of superior - in command, not with any haughty assumption, not with any arrogant words or looks, but sweetly and simply, as though there were no question but that the place was hers; that to her belonged the ordering of the forces, the overlooking of all. Again and again, even we, who had come to believe so truly in her divine commission, were astonished at the insight she showed, the sagacity of her counsels, the wonderful authority she was able to exert over the soldiers brought together, a rude, untrained, insubordinate mass of men, collected from all ranks and classes of the people, some being little better than bands of marauders, living on prey and plunder, since of regular fighting there had been little of late; others, mercenaries hired by the nobles to swell their own retinues; many raw recruits, fired by ardour at the thought of the promised deliverance; a few regular trained bands, with their own officers in command, but forming altogether a heterogeneous company, by no means easy to drill into order, and swelled by another contingent at Blois, of very much the same material.

But the Maid assembled the army together, and thus addressed them. At least, this was the substance of her words; nothing can reproduce the wonderful earnestness and power of her voice and look, for her face kindled as she spoke, and the sunshine playing upon her as she sat her charger in the glory of her silver armour, seemed to encompass her with a pure white light, so that men's eyes were dazzled as they looked upon her, and they whispered one to the other:

"The Angelic Maid! The Angelic Maid! surely it is an Angel of God come straight down from Heaven to aid and lead us."

"My friends," she spoke, and her voice carried easily to every corner of the great square, packed with a human mass, motionless, hanging upon her words; "My friends, we are about to start forth upon a crusade as holy as it is possible for men to be concerned in, for it is as saviours and deliverers of your brethren and our country that we go; and the Lord of Hosts is with us. He has bidden us march, and He has promised to go with us, even as He was with the Israelites of old. And if we do not see His presence in pillar of cloud by day, and pillar of fire by night, we yet do know and feel Him near us; and He will give abundant proof that He fights upon our side!"

She lifted her face for a moment to the sky. She was bareheaded, and every head was bared in that vast crowd as she uttered the name of the Most High. It seemed as though a light from Heaven fell upon her as she spoke, and a deep murmur ran through the throng. It was as if they answered that they needed no other vision than that of the Maid herself.

"If then the Lord be with us, must we not show ourselves worthy of His holy presence in our midst? O my friends, since I have been with you these few days, my heart has been pained and grieved by that which I have heard and seen. Oaths and blasphemies fall from your lips, and you scarce know it yourselves. Drunkenness and vice prevail. O my friends, let this no

Evelyn Everett-Green

longer be amongst us! Let us cleanse ourselves from all impurities; let our conversation be yea, yea, nay, nay. Let none take the name of the Lord in vain, nor soil His holy cause by vice and uncleanness. O let us all, day by day, as the sun rises anew each morning, assemble to hear Mass, and to receive the Holy Sacrament. Let every man make his confession. Holy priests are with us to hear all, and to give absolution. Let us start forth upon the morrow purified and blessed of God, and let us day by day renew that holy cleansing and blessing, that the Lord may indeed be with us and rest amongst us, and that His heart be not grieved and burdened by that which He shall see and hear amongst those to whom He has promised His help and blessing!"

Thus she spoke; and a deep silence fell upon all, in the which it seemed to me the fall of a pin might have been heard. The Maid sat quite still for a moment, her own head bent as though in prayer. Then she lifted it, and a radiant smile passed over her face, a smile as of assurance and thankful joy. She raised her hand and waved it, almost as though she blessed, whilst she greeted her soldiers, and then she turned her horse, the crowd making way for her in deep reverential silence, and rode towards her own lodging, where she remained shut up in her own room for the rest of the day.

But upon the following morning a strange thing had happened. Every single camp follower - all the women and all the disorderly rabble that hangs upon the march of an army - had disappeared. They had slunk off in the night, and were utterly gone. The soldiers were gathered in the churches to hear Mass. All that could do so attended where it was known the Maid would be, and when she had received the Sacrament herself, hundreds crowded to do the like; and I suppose there were thousands in the city that day, who, having confessed and received absolution, received the pledge of the Lord's death, though perhaps some of them had not thought of such a duty for years and years.

And here I may say that this was not an act for once and all. Day by day in the camp Mass was celebrated, and the Holy Sacrament given to all who asked and came. The Maid ever sought to begin the day thus, and we of her personal household generally followed her example. Even La Hire would come and kneel beside her, a little behind, though it was some while before he desired to partake of the Sacrament himself. But to be near her in this act of devotion seemed to give him joy and confidence and for her sake, because he saw it pained her, he sought to break off his habit of profane swearing, and the use of those strange oaths before which men had been wont to quake.

And she, seeing how sorely tried he was to keep from his accustomed habit, did come to his aid with one of her frank and almost boy-like smiles, and told him that he might swear by his baton if he needs must use some expletive; but that no holy name must lightly pass his lips.

Strange indeed was it to see the friendship which had so quickly sprung up between that rough warrior and the Maid, whom he could almost have crushed to death between his mighty hands.

If all the Generals in the army were as noble minded as he, and as ready to receive her whom God had sent them, we should have little to fear; but there was Dunois yet to reckon with, who had promised to come forth and meet her outside the town (for the blockade, as I have before said, was not perfect; and on the south side men could still come and go with caution and care), and to lead her in triumph within its walls, if the English showed not too great resistance.

But even now we were to find how that they did not yet trust the Maid's authority as it should be trusted; and even La Hire was in fault here, as afterwards he freely owned. For the Maid had told them to lead her to the city on the north side, as her plan was to strike straight through the English lines, and scatter the besieging force ere ever she entered the town at all. But since the city lies to the north of the river, and the English had built around it twelve great bastilles, as they called them, and lay in all their strength on this side, it seemed too venturesome to attack in such a manner; and in this La Hire and Dunois were both agreed. But La Hire did not tell the Maid of any disagreements, but knowing the country to be strange to her, he led her and the army by a route which she believed the right one, till suddenly we beheld the towers of Orleans and the great surrounding fortifications rising up before our eyes; and, behold! the wide river with its bridge more than half destroyed, lay between us and our goal!

At this sight the eyes of the Maid flashed fire, and she turned them upon La Hire, but spoke never a word. His face flushed a dull crimson with a sudden, unexpected shame. To do him justice be it said, that (as we later heard) he had been against this deception after having seen the Maid; but there were now many notable generals and marshals and officers with the army, all of whom were resolved upon this course of action, which had been agreed upon beforehand with Dunois, and they had overborne his objections, which were something faint-hearted perhaps, for with his love and admiration for the Maid, he trembled, as he now explained to her, to lead her by so perilous a route, and declared that she could well be conducted into the city through the Burgundy gate, by water, without striking a blow, instead of having to fight her way in past the English bastions.

"I thank you for your care for me, my friend," she answered, "but it were better to have obeyed my voice. The English arrows could not have touched me. We should have entered unopposed. Now much precious time must needs be lost, for how can this great army be transported across yonder river? - and the bridge, even if we could dislodge the English from the tower of Les Tourelles, is broken down and useless."

Indeed it seemed plain to all that the Generals had made a great blunder; for though we marched on to Checy, where Dunois met us, and whence some of the provisions brought for the starving city could be dispatched in the boats assembled there, it was plain that there was no transport sufficient for the bulk of the army; and the Maid, as she and Dunois stood face to face, at last regarded him with a look of grave and searching scrutiny.

"Are you he whom men call the Bastard of Orleans?"

"Lady, I am; and I come to welcome you with gladness, for we are sore beset by our foes; yet all within the city are taking heart of grace, believing that a Deliverer from Heaven has been sent to them."

"They think well," answered the Maid, "and right glad

am I to come. But wherefore have I been led hither by this bank, instead of the one upon which Talbot and his English lie?"

"Lady, the wisest of our leaders held that this would be the safest way."

"The counsel of God and our Lord is more sure and more powerful than that of generals and soldiers," she answered gravely. "You have made an error in this. See to it that such error be not repeated. I will that in all things my Lord be obeyed."

The Generals stood dumb and discomfited before her; a thrill ran through the army when her words were repeated there; but, indeed, we all quickly saw the wisdom of her counsel and the folly of her adversaries; for the bulk of the army had perforce to march back to Blois to cross the river there, whilst only a thousand picked men with the chiefest of the Generals and the convoys of provisions prepared to enter the city by water and pass through the Burgundy Gate.

At the first it seemed as though even this would be a dangerous task, for the wind blew hard in a contrary direction, and the deeply-laden boats began to be in peril of foundering. But as we stood watching them from the bank, and saw their jeopardy, and some were for recalling them and waiting, the Maid's voice suddenly rang forth in command:

"Leave them alone, and hasten forward with the others. The wind will change, and a favouring breeze shall carry us all safe into the city. The English shall not fire a shot to hinder us, for the fear of the Maid has fallen upon them!"

We gazed at her in wonder as she stood a little apart, her face full of power and calm certainty. And indeed, it was but a very few minutes later that the wind dropped to a dead calm, and a light air sprang up from a contrary direction, and the laden boats gladly spreading sail, floated quietly onwards with their precious load towards the suffering city.

Then we embarked, somewhat silently, for the awe which fell upon those who had never seen the Maid before, extended even to us. Moreover, with those frowning towers of the English so close upon us, crowded with soldiers who seemed to know what was happening, and who were coming into Orleans, it was scarce possible not to look for resistance and hostile attack.

But curious as it may seem, not a shot was fired as we passed along. A silence strange and sinister seemed to hang over the lines of the enemy; but when we reached the city how all was changed!

It was about eight o'clock in the evening when at last we finished our journey by water and land, and entered the devoted town. There the chiefest citizens came hurrying to meet us, leading a white charger for their Deliverer to ride upon.

And when she was mounted, the people thronged about her weeping and shouting, blessing and hailing her as their champion and saviour. The streets were thronged with pale-faced men; women and children hung from the windows, showering flowers at our feet. Torches lit up the darkening scene, and shone from the breastplates and headpieces of the mailed men. But the Maid in her white armour seemed like a being from

Evelyn Everett-Green

another sphere; and the cry of "St. Michael! St. Michael himself!" resounded on all sides, and one did not wonder.

Nothing would serve the Maid but to go straight to the Cathedral first, and offer thanksgiving for her arrival here, and the people flocked with her, till the great building was filled to overflowing with her retinue of soldiers and her self-constituted followers. Some begged of her to address them from the steps at the conclusion of the brief service, but she shook her head.

"I have no words for them - only I love them all," she answered, with a little natural quiver of emotion in her voice. "Tell them so, and that I have come to save them. And then let me go home."

So La Hire stood forth and gave the Maid's message in his trumpet tones, and the Maid was escorted by the whole of the joyful and loving crowd to the house of the Treasurer Boucher, where were her quarters, and where she was received with acclamation and joy. And thus the Maid entered the beleaguered city of Orleans.

# IX.

## HOW THE MAID ASSUMED COMMAND AT ORLEANS.

The house of the Treasurer was a beautiful building in the Gothic style, and weary as was the Maid with the toils and excitements through which she had passed, I saw her eyes kindle with pleasure and admiration as she was ceremoniously led into the great banqueting hall, where the tables were spread with abundant good cheer (despite the reduced condition of the city), to do honour to her who came as its Deliverer.

There was something solemn and church-like in these surroundings which appealed at once to the Maid. She had a keen eye for beauty, whether of nature or in the handiwork of man, and her quick penetrating glances missed nothing of the stately grandeur of the house, the ceremonious and courtly welcome of the Treasurer, its master, or the earnest, wistful gaze of his little daughter Charlotte, who stood holding fast to her mother's hand in the background, but feasting her great dark eyes upon the wonderful shining figure of the Maid, from whose white armour the lights of the great hall flashed back in a hundred points of fire.

The greeting of the master of the house being over, the Maid threw off for a moment the grave dignity of her bearing throughout this trying day, and became a simple girl again. With a quick grace of movement she crossed the space which divided her from the little child, and kneeling suddenly down, took the wondering little one in her arms, and held her in a close embrace.

"Ma petite, ma mie, ma tres chere," those nearest heard her murmur. "Love me, darling, love me! I have a little sister at home who loves me, but I had to go away and leave her. Perhaps I may never see her again. Try to love me instead, and comfort my heart, for sometimes I am very, very weary, and hungry for the love that I have lost!"

Now, one might have thought that so young a child - for she was not more than eight years old, and small for her years - would have been affrighted at the sudden approach of the shining warrior, about whom so many stories had been told, and who looked more like the Archangel Michael, as many thought, than a creature of human flesh and blood. But instead of showing any fear, the child flung her arms about the neck of the Maid, and pressed kisses upon her face - her headpiece she had removed at her entrance - and when the mother would have loosened her hold, and sent the child away with her attendant, little Charlotte resisted, clinging to her new friend with all her baby strength, and the Maid looked pleadingly up into the kindly face of the lady, and said:

"Ah, madame, I pray you let her remain with me. It is so long since I felt the arms of a child about my neck!"

And so the little one stayed to the banquet, and was given the place of honour beside the Maid. But neither of these twain had any relish for the dainty meats and rich dishes served for us. As on the march, so now in the walls of the city, the Maid fared as simply as the rudest of her soldiers. She mixed water with her wine, took little save a slice or two of bread, and though to please her hosts she just touched one or two specially prepared dishes, it was without any real relish for them, and she was evidently glad when she was able to make excuse to leave the table and go to the room prepared for her.

But here again she showed her simple tastes, for when the great guest chamber was shown her she shrank a little at its size and luxury, and, still holding the child's hand in hers, she turned to the mother who was in attendance and said:

"I pray you, sweet lady, let me whilst I am your guest share the room of this little daughter of yours. I am but a simple country girl, all this grandeur weighs me down. If I might but sleep with this little one in my arms - as the little sister at home loved to lie - I should sleep so peacefully and have such happy dreams! Ah, madame! - let me have my will in this!"

And Madame Boucher, being a mother and a true woman, understood; and answered by taking the Maid in her arms and kissing her. And so, as long as the Maid remained in Orleans, she shared the little white bedroom of the child of the house, which opened from that of the mother, and the bond which grew up between the three was so close and tender a one, that I trow the good Treasurer and his wife would fain have regarded this wonderful Maid as their own daughter, and kept her ever with them, had duty and her voices not called her elsewhere when the first part of her task

Evelyn Everett-Green

was done.

Now Bertrand and I, together with Pierre, her brother, and the Chevalier d'Aulon and Sir Guy de Laval, were lodged in the same house, and entertained most hospitably by the Treasurer, who sat up with us far into the night after our arrival, listening with earnest attention to all we could tell him respecting the Maid, and telling us on his part of the feeling in Orleans anent her and her mission, and what we might expect to follow her arrival here.

"The townsfolk seem well-nigh wild for joy at sight of her," spoke De Laval, "and the more they see of her, the more they will love her and reverence her mission. I was one who did openly scoff, or at least had no faith in any miracle, until that I saw her with mine own eyes; and then some voice in my heart - I know not how to speak more plainly of it - or some wonderful power in her glance or in her voice, overcame me. And I knew that she had in very truth come from God, and I have never doubted of her divine commission from that day to this. It will be the same here in Orleans, if, indeed, there be any that doubt."

"Alas! there are - too many!" spoke the Treasurer, shaking his head, "I am rejoiced that our two greatest Generals, Dunois and La Hire, have become her adherents, for I myself believe that she has been sent of God for our deliverance, and so do the townsfolk almost to a man. But there are numbers of the lesser officers - bold men and true - who have fought valiantly throughout the siege, and who have great influence with the soldiers they lead, and these men are full of disgust at the thought of being led by a woman - a girl - and one of low degree. They would be willing for her to stand aloft and prophesy victory for their arms, but that she should arm herself and lead them in battle, and direct operations herself, fills them with disgust and contempt. There is like to be trouble, I fear, with some of these. There is bold De Gamache, for example, who declares he would sooner fold up his banner and serve as a simple soldier in the ranks, than hold a command subservient to that of a low-born woman!"

That name as applied to the Angelic Maid set our teeth on edge; yet was it wonderful that some should so regard her?

"Let them but see her - and they will change their tune!" spake Bertrand quickly. "A low-born woman! Would they speak thus of the Blessed Virgin? And yet according to the wisdom of the flesh it would be as true of one as of the other."

The Treasurer spoke with grave thoughtfulness:

"Truly do I think that any person honoured by the Lord with a direct mission from Himself becomes something different by virtue of that mission from what he or she was before. Yet we may not confound this mission of the Maid here in Orleans with that one which came to the Blessed Mary."

"Nor had I any thought," answered Bertrand, "of likening one to the other, save inasmuch as both have been maidens, born in lowly surroundings, yet chosen for purity of heart and life, and for childlike faith and obedience, for the honour of receiving a divine commission. There the parallel stops; for there can be no comparison regarding the work appointed to each.

Yet even as this Maid shall fulfil her appointed task in obedience to the injunctions received, she is worthy to be called the handmaid of the Lord."

"To that I have nought to say but yea," answered the Treasurer heartily, "and I pray our Lord and the Blessed Virgin to be with her and strengthen her, for I fear me she will have foes to contend with from within as well as from without the city; and as all men know, it is the distrust and contradiction of so-called friends which is harder to bear than the open enmity of the foe."

It was difficult for us, vowed heart and soul to the cause of the Maid, and honoured by her friendship and confidence, to believe that any could be so blind as not to recognise in her a God-sent messenger, whom they would delight to follow and to honour. Yet when I walked out upon the following morning - a sunny first of May - to have a good look round at the position of the fortifications, the ring of English bastilles to the north, the blockading towers upon the southern bank, I was quickly aware of a great deal of talk going on amongst the soldiers and the officers which was by no means favourable to the cause of the Maid.

Voices were hushed somewhat at my approach, for though none knew me, I was of course a stranger, and therefore likely to have entered the town in the train of the Maid, who had yesterday made her appearance there. But I heard enough to be sure that what the Treasurer had said last evening was likely to be true. The soldiers were disposed to scoff at being led by a woman, and the officers to grumble at having had to bear all the burden of the long siege, and then when the King did send an army for the relief, to send it under the command of this Maid, who would bear away the honour and glory which otherwise all might have shared.

From their point of view, perhaps, this discontent was not unreasonable; but as I looked upon the works around me, I marvelled how it had been possible for the English, unprotected as they must have originally been, to erect these great towers for their own shelter, and from which to batter the town with their cannon and great stone balls, when the French in great numbers and protected by strong walls, ought to have been able to sally forth continually and so to harass them that the construction of such buildings should have been impossible.

The great Dunois had shown considerable acumen. He had himself destroyed all the suburbs of the town which lay without the walls, so that the English might find no shelter there, and when they had effected a lodgment on the south side of the river, he had destroyed the greater part of the bridge, thus making it impossible for the enemy to cross and take possession of the town. But he had not stopped the erection of those threatening towers circling round the city to the north, nor the construction of those still stronger blockading fortresses on the south side, Les Tourelles guarding the fragment of the broken bridge, and Les Augustins not far away.

When I spoke to one grizzled old soldier about it, he shrugged his shoulders and made reply:

"What would you? Those English are helped of the devil himself. We have tried to stand against them, but it is all to no purpose. Some demon of fighting enters

Evelyn Everett-Green

into them, and they know that we shall fly - and fly we do. At last there were none who would face them. Our generals sought in vain to lead them. You should have heard La Hire swearing at them. O-he, O-he, he is a master of the art! Some of us would have followed him; but the rest - cne might as well have asked a flock of sheep to go against the wolf, telling them they were fifty to one! Not they! It was witchcraft, or something like it. They sat still on these ramparts and watched the English working like moles or like ants, and never lifted a finger. Pouf! When men get to that they are not fit to fight They had better go home and ply the distaff with the women."

"And let a woman come and lead their comrades to battle!" I said, laughing. "Have you seen the wonderful Maid of whom all the world is talking?"

"No; at least, I only caught a gleam of light upon her white armour last night; but as I said to the boys in the guardroom, I care not whether she be woman, witch, or angel; if she will bring back heart and courage, and make men again of all these chicken-hearted poltroons, I will follow her to the death wherever she may lead. I am sick with shame for the arms of France!"

"Bravely spoken, my friend!" I cried, giving him my hand; "and if that be the spirit of the army, I doubt not but that a few days will see such a turn in the tide of warfare as shall make the whole world stand aghast!"

"Then you believe in her?" quoth the old soldier, looking me shrewdly up and down.

"With my whole heart!" I answered, as I turned and took my way back to my quarters.

That same day the Maid held a council of war, at which all the officers of any importance were permitted to attend; and here it was that she received the first real check since she had received the King's commission and royal command.

"Let us attack the foe at once, and without delay, messires!" she said, sitting at the head of the council table, fully armed, save for her headpiece, and speaking in her clear, sweet, full tones, wherein power and confidence were blended; "the Lord of Hosts is on our side. Let us go forth in His strength, and the victory will be ours."

But they listened to her in silent consternation and amaze. Here was this inexperienced girl, blind with enthusiasm, drunk with success, her head completely turned by her reception last night, actually advising an assault upon the enemy before the arrival of the army of relief, which had been forced to return to Blois to cross the river, and which could not arrive for a few more days. What madness would she next propose? Well, at least La Hire and Dunois were there to curb her folly and impetuosity. A chit of a girl like that to sit and tell them all to go forth to certain death at her command! As though they would not want all their strength to aid the relieving army to enter when it should appear! As though they were going to weaken themselves beforehand by any mad scheme of hers!

Thus the storm arose. Even La Hire, Dunois, and the Treasurer himself, were against her. As for the lesser officers, when they began to speak, they scarce knew how to contain themselves, and restrain their anger and scorn from showing itself too markedly towards one who held the King's mandate of command.

Evelyn Everett-Green

And of late the Maid had always been listened to with such honour and respect! How would she bear this contradiction and veiled contempt, she who had come to assume the command of the city and its armies at the King's desire?

She sat very still and quiet at the table, as the storm hummed about her. Her clear gaze travelled from face to face as one or another of the officers rose and spoke. Sometimes a slight flush of red dyed her cheek for a moment; but never once did anger cloud her brow, or impatience or contempt mar the wonderful serenity of her beautiful eyes. Only once did she speak during the whole of the debate, after her opening words had been delivered, and that was after a very fiery oration on the part of a youthful officer, whose words contained more veiled scorn of her and her mission than any other had dared to show.

Instead of looking at him either in anger or in reproach, the Maid's own wonderful smile shone suddenly upon him as he concluded. Then she spoke:

"Captain de Gamache, you think yourself my foe now; but that will soon be changed, and I thank you beforehand for the brave, true service which you shall presently render me. But meantime, beware of rashness; for victory shall not come to the city without the Maid."

He gazed at her - we all gazed at her - in amaze, not knowing what her words portended. But she gave no explanation. She only rose to her feet and said:

"Then, gentlemen, since the attack is not to be yet - not till the arrival of the relieving force, let me make the tour of the battlements, and examine the defences of the city. I would that you had faith to let me lead you forth today; but the time will come when I shall not have to plead with you - you will follow gladly in my wake. For the rest, it would perchance be a sorrow to my brave men, who have marched so far with me, not to partake in the victory which the Lord is about to send us; wherefore I will the more readily consent to delay, though, let me tell you, you are in the wrong to withstand the wishes of the Commander of the King's armies, and the messenger of the King of Kings."

I verily believe that she shamed them by her gentle friendliness more than she would have done by any outburst of wrath. Had she urged them now, I am not sure but what they would have given her her way; but she did not. She put her white velvet cap, with its nodding plumes, upon her head, and taking with her the chiefest of the generals and her own immediate retinue, she made the tour of the walls and defences of the city, showing such a marvellous insight into the tactics of war that she astonished all by her remarks and by her injunctions.

Suddenly, as we were walking onwards, she paused and lifted her face with a wonderful rapt expression upon it. Then she turned to Dunois, and said with quiet authority:

"Mon General, I must ask of you to take a small body of picked men, and ride forth towards Blois, and see what bechances there. I trow there is trouble among the men. Traitors are at work to daunt their hearts. Go and say that the Maid bids them fear nothing, and that they shall enter Orleans in safety. The English shall not be suffered to touch them. Go at once!"

"In broad daylight, lady, and before the very eyes of the foe?"

"Yes, yes," she answered instantly; "I will stand here and watch you. No hurt shall be done to you or to your company."

So Dunois went at her command, and we saw him and his little band ride fearlessly through the English lines; and scarce could we believe our eyes when we noted that no weapon was raised against them; not even an arrow was shot off as they passed.

"She speaks the words of God. She is His messenger!" whispered the men who stood by; and her fame flew from mouth to mouth, till a strange awe fell upon all.

She was never idle during those days of waiting. She asked news of the letter she had sent to the English, and heard it had been delivered duly, though the herald had not returned. She gave commission to La Hire to demand his instant release, and this was accomplished speedily; for the bold captain, of his own initiative, vowed he would behead every prisoner they had in the city if the man were not given up at the command of the Maid. I am very sure no such act of summary vengeance would have been permitted, but the man was instantly released and came and told us how that the letter had been read with shouts of insulting laughter, and many derisive answers suggested; none of which, however, had been dispatched, as Talbot, the chief in command of the English armies, had finally decreed that it became not his dignity to hold any parley with a witch.

And yet she could scarce believe that they should none

of them understand how that she was indeed come from God, and that they must be lamentably overthrown if they would not hear her words. On the third day of her stay in the city she caused her great white banner to be carried forth before her, and riding a white horse, clad in her silver armour, and clasping her banneret in her hand she rode slowly out upon the broken fragment of the bridge opposite to the tower of Les Tourelles, and begged a parley from the English general in command.

It was not Lord Talbot who came forth and stood upon his own end of the bridge, gazing haughtily across the space which divided them; but it was a notable soldier, whom the French called Classidas, though I have been told that his real name was Sir William Glassdale To him the Maid addressed herself in her clear mellow voice, which could be heard across the flowing river:

"Retournez de la part Dieu a l'Angleterre!" was the burden of her charge, imploring him to have mercy upon himself and his soldiers, as else many hundreds of them, and himself also, must perish miserably, and perchance even without the offices of the Church.

But she was answered by roars of mocking laughter from the soldiers of the fort, and worse still, by gross insults from Classidas himself, hurled across at her from a biting tongue, which carried like the note of a trumpet.

Silently she stood and gazed at him; mournfully she turned and rode back to the town.

"May God have mercy upon their souls!" she prayed; and for the rest of the day she was sorrowful and sad.

"If it could have been done without bloodshed!" she murmured again and yet again.

Ah, and then the day when the news came that the relieving army was in sight! Was she sad or pensive then? No! She sprang to her feet; she set down the little Charlotte, who was playing in her arms; she seized her weapons, her page flew to bring her full armour. Her horse was already in waiting; she swung upon his back. She waved her hand and called to us to rally about her.

"The English are preparing to fight!" she cried (how did she know? none had told her), "but follow me, and they will strike no blow."

Already La Hire was at her side, seeking to dissuade her from leaving the shelter of the town. She smiled at him, and rode through the gate, her white banner floating in the wind.

"See yonder; that is the point of danger. We will station ourselves there, and watch our brave army march past. They shall not be hurt nor dismayed. All shall be well!"

So we rode, wondering and amazed, behind and around her, and at the appointed spot, in the very midst of the English lines, we halted, and made a great avenue for the army from Blois to pass through. All gazed in wonder at the Maid. All saluted deeply. The English in their towers gazed in amaze, but fired no shot. We all passed into the city in safety.

Great God, but how would it be with our Maid when the real battle and bloodshed should begin?

## X.

## HOW THE MAID LED US INTO BATTLE.

"It was well indeed that you sent me forth on that mission, my Chieftainess," spoke Dunois, as we sat at the long table in the Treasurer's house, refreshing ourselves after the fatigues of the march to and from the city, and the anxiety of awaiting an attack, which had not come. He bowed towards the Maid in speaking, calling her by a playful title in vogue amongst the officers and Generals who were her friends. "Though what prompted you to that act of sagacity is more than I know. I had no misgivings that there would be trouble with the army."

"My voices warned me," answered the Maid gently. "It was not much; yet a little leaven often leavens the whole lump. They needed just the leader's eye and voice to recall them to their duty."

"Truly that is just how the matter stood," spoke Sir Guy in low tones to us twain, Bertram and I, who sat on either side of him at the other end of the board.

He had been one to depart and return with Dunois, and we looked eagerly to him for explanation.

"There are ever timid spirits in all ranks, and traitors or

Evelyn Everett-Green

faint-hearted friends are never far away in such times as these. The army which would have followed the Maid to the death with joy, felt depression and disappointment at being parted from her. Had they been able to ford the river and march straight into the city, there would have been no trouble, no tremors or doubts; but the turning back was a discouragement, and alas! the French have had too much of this of late. There were whisperers at work seeking to undermine faith in the Maid and her mission. As she says, no great hurt was done; it was but the work of a few - and some of these priests, who should better have understood the counsels of God - but a little leaven will work mightily in the lump, as she herself did justly remark; and ere we reached Blois, we had heard rumours that the army was talking of disbanding itself and dispersing hither and thither. The truth was not so bad as that; but there was wavering and doubt in the ranks.

"Our appearance with the message from the Maid worked like a charm. The soldiers, when they knew that she had been told of their hesitation, were instantly horribly ashamed. They clamoured to be led back to her, to show the mettle of which they were made. I trow they will not waver again, now that she hath them beneath her eye."

"It is marvellous how she doth hold them by the power of her glance, by her gentleness and devotion. And, look you, what hath she done to the English? It was rumoured through the city that so soon as the relief army approached the English lines, there would be an attack in force, and our comrades would be driven back at the sword's point, and have to fight every inch of the way. Yet what has been the truth? The Maid led us to the spot which commanded the road - well in the heart of the English lines. Their fortresses were humming like hives of bees disturbed. The English knew what was being done, and watched it all; yet not a gun was fired, not an archer launched his shaft, not a man moved out to oppose the entrance of the relief force nor even the convoy of provisions for the garrison. They watched it all as men in a dream, not a dog moved his tongue against us."

"She told us it would be so," spoke I, leaning towards Sir Guy, "there will be fighting anon; but it was not to be then. Surely their arms were holden by a power they wot not of. If she herself had not gone forth to guard the way - standing like the flaming cherubim with the sword which turned every way - I misdoubt me but that a heavy action must have been fought, ere the army was suffered to enter the gates."

There was much talk all down the table of these matters; but the Maid took little part in this. Her eyes were heavy, and she looked weary and pale. I doubt not she had spent the night previous in vigil and prayer, as was so often her wont. When we rose from our repast, she retired into a small inner room reserved for her use, and the little Charlotte went with her. A curtain, partly drawn, shut off this room from the outer one in which we knights and some of her pages and gentlemen sat talking; and I was just able to see from where I sat that the Maid had laid herself down upon a couch, the little one nestled beside her, and I felt sure by her stillness and immobility that she was soon soundly asleep, taking the rest she sorely needed after the exertions and excitements of the early hours of the day.

Our conversation languished somewhat, for the

warmth of the May afternoon made us all drowsy. We, like the Maid herself, had laid aside our coats of mail, and were enjoying a spell of rest and leisure; and there was silence in both the rooms, when suddenly we - if indeed we slept - were awakened by the voice of the Maid speaking in the tones of one who dreams.

"I must up and against the English!" she cried, and at the first word I started broad awake and was on my feet at the door of communication, looking towards her.

She still lay upon the couch, but her eyes were wide open and fixed; her lips moved.

"I hear! I hear!" she went on, yet still as one who dreams, "I am ready - I will obey. Only tell me what I must do. Is it against the towers I must go, to assail them? Or is it that Fastolffe comes against us with yet another host?"

Little Charlotte here pulled the Maid by the hand, crying out:

"What are you saying? To whom do you speak? There is nobody here but you and me!"

The Maid sprang to her feet, wide awake now in an instant. She bent for one moment over the wondering child, and kissed her tenderly, as though to soothe the alarm in the baby eyes.

"Run to your mother, ma mie, for I must off and away on the instant," then wheeling round with her air of martial command, she called to me and said, "To arms at once! I must to the front! French blood is flowing.

They are seeking to act without me. O my poor soldiers, they are falling and dying! To horse! to horse! I come to save them!"

Was she dreaming? What did it mean? The town seemed as quiet as the still summer afternoon! Not a sound of tumult broke the silence of the streets. Yet the Maid was having us arm her with lightning speed, and Bertrand had rushed off at the first word for her horse and ours.

"I know not what they are doing," spoke the Maid, "but my voices tell me to fly to their succour! Ah! why could they not have told me before! Have I not ever been ready and longing to lead them against the foe?"

She was ready now. We were all ready, and the echoes of the quiet house awoke beneath our feet as we clattered down the staircase to the courtyard below, where already the horses were standing pawing the ground with impatience, seeming to scent the battle from afar. The Maid swung herself lightly to the saddle with scarce a touch from me.

"My banner! My banner!" she suddenly cried; and looking upwards we saw a pretty sight. The little Charlotte, her mother beside her, was hanging out of the window, the light staff of the Maid's white banneret clasped in her chubby hands; and she was leaning out of the window, holding it towards the white mailed figure, of whom (in armour) she always spoke, in hushed tone, as mon ange. The Maid looked upwards, kissed her gauntleted hand to the little one, seized the staff of her banner, and then, calling upon her followers in clear tones of command, dashed out through the gateway into the street beyond, and without an instant's hesitation turned towards that gate of the city nearest to the English bastille named St. Loup. And though we all spurred after her, so that the sparks flew from under our horses' feet, and the Chevalier d'Aulon brought up the rear bearing the great white standard, which was to lead the armies into battle, we none of us knew wherefore we had come forth nor whither we were going; and the city being yet still and quiet, the citizens rushed to doors and windows to watch us pass by, and shouted questions to us which we were not able to answer.

Now, the house of the Treasurer is hard by the Renart Gate, and we were making for the Burgundy Gate; so you who know Orleans will understand that we had the whole distance of the city to traverse ere we cleared the walls. And sure enough, as we approached the fortifications upon the eastern side, a change came over the spirit of the scene; signs of excitement and fear and wonder began to show themselves; the walls were alive with men at arms, gazing fixedly out eastward, shouting, gesticulating, wild with a tumult of emotion. Soldiers buckling on their arms, citizens with pale, yet resolute, faces, and swords or axes in their hands, were hurrying forth, and at sight of the Maid on her chestnut charger (for the Crusader was ever her favourite horse, and she had declared that he must carry her into her first battle whenever that should be) they shouted aloud with joy, and vowed themselves her servants and followers, wherever she should lead them.

A young blacksmith, armed with a great club, was hanging upon my stirrup, and bounding along beside my horse with a swiftness and strength which excited my admiration. From him I heard first of the thing which had taken place.

"It was De Gamache and some of the other lesser officers who designed it," he cried. "They declared that the power of the English was already broken; that they would not leave their walls or show fight today; that already they had grown faint hearted, and were ready to fly before the French.

"My Captain, I tell you the truth, these men are jealous of the Angelic Maid whom Heaven has sent us. They say that she will take from them all the honour and glory; that they will fight and risk their lives, but that she alone will have the praise. So they were full of bitterness and anger; and some, methinks, may have thought to shame her by showing that they could act without her aid, and do the work she has come to do, whilst she takes her rest and holds her councils. So, gathering a band of soldiers together, these officers have sallied forth to try and storm and take the fortress of St. Loup, which lies some two thousand English yards from the walls along the river banks. But the soldiers on the walls are shouting out that the English have swarmed forth like angry bees, and are beating back our soldiers and slaying them by the score."

"They should have known better than to go forth without the knowledge and command of the Maid," I said sternly, and the young man at my side nodded vehemently, his face alight.

"That is what we said - we others - we citizens, who have seen how powerless the soldiers are against the English. Have they not fought again and again, and what has come of it but loss and defeat? And now that the good God has sent a Deliverer, it is like flying in His face to seek and do without her. I said as much again and again. I knew no good would come of it. But when we saw the Maid herself flying to the rescue, then did I vow that I, too, would fight under her banner. For now I know that God will give us the victory!"

We were at the Burgundy Gate by this time and, dashing through, we saw a terrible sight. The whole open plain between the walls of the town and the fortress of St. Loup was covered with soldiers, strewn with dying and dead. A horrible sort of fight was going on, horrible to us, because the French were in full retreat before our foe, going down like sheep before the butcher's knife, rushing panic stricken hither and thither as men demented, whilst the English soldiers, as though ashamed of their recent inaction and paralysis, were fiercely pursuing, shouting "Kill! kill! kill!" as they went about their work of slaughter, driving back their enemies, and striking at them remorselessly.

Here and there a brave officer, with his band of chosen followers, would be presenting a bold face to the foe, making a stand and seeking to rally the flying ranks. I was certain that I saw De Gamache himself, hewing his way like a very Paladin through the ranks of the English, and dealing death and destruction wherever he went. But the valour of a few had no power to turn the fortunes of the field; and the rout had already begun, when the Maid and her attendants, closely followed by an enthusiastic band of soldiers and citizens, dashed forth from the Burgundy Gate, and mingled with the flying French hastening towards the city for safety.

"Courage, my children, courage!" cried the Maid, waving her white pennon. "Be not dismayed. The Lord has heard your cries. He has sent me to your aid. Take courage! Fear nothing, for the victory shall be ours!"

She did not even pause to note the effect of her words upon them, but sped onwards, fearless of danger, right into the very heart of the battle. We followed and closed up round her; but that shining white figure could not be hidden. The English saw it bearing down upon them, and instantly there was wavering in their ranks. Before our swords had had time to strike at them, something touched them as with an icy hand.

"The Maid! the Maid! The White Witch!" they cried, and they paused in their pursuit to gaze upon that dazzling figure, and methinks their hearts melted like wax within them.

From behind now arose a mighty tumult, and shouts and cries as of triumph thundered from the city walls. Dunois and La Hire, more tardily advised of what was happening, but prompt and decisive in action, were galloping out of the Gate at the head of the picked soldiers under their command. Rank behind rank we could see them flashing through the shadow into the sunshine, and dashing forward in compact order, their gaze fixed full upon the Maid in the centre of the plain, who stood with uplifted sword and fluttering pennon, a veritable angel of the battle.

But we saw other sights, too; for Lord Talbot was not idle on his side, but sent forth from other of the bastilles bodies of men to the aid of the defenders of St. Loup.

The whole plain was filled with surging masses of soldiers, rushing one upon the other in the fury of the fray.

Evelyn Everett-Green

How would the Maid bear it? She whose tender heart ached at the thought of human suffering, and whose soul was filled with yearning sorrow for men struck down in their sins. I pressed up towards her and saw her pitiful eyes fixed upon a convoy of wounded men, whom we had sent to rescue from their peril, lying as they did in the very heart of the plain. The eyes which had been flashing fire a moment before, were suffused with tears, as the melancholy procession passed her by.

She turned to her page and said, "Ride quickly into the city, and bid the priests come forth to hear the confessions and give absolution to the dying. Lose not a moment! Tell them that souls are every moment being hurried to their last account. Bid them make haste and come, and let them give equal care to friend and foe; for in death all men are equal in the sight of God, and I would not that any English soldier or prisoner should fall without the consolations of religion."

Then, having thus done all that she could for the wounded and the dying, the Maid was once again the resolute soldier. Her keen eyes swept the plain; she saw with lightning speed where the need was the greatest, where the peril to the French cause was direst, and sweeping into the midst of the press, her sword and her banner flashing in the sunshine, she ever brought succour and victory in her wake.

No foe could stand before her. Not that she struck blows with her own hand. There seemed no need for that, and when at the close of the day I relieved her of her arms, there was no spot of blood upon her shining blade, though her coat of silver mail had received stains from the fray. She was like the Angel of Victory, flashing through the ranks of the combatants. Wherever she appeared, the flying French turned back to face the foe, and the pursuing English wavered, paused, and finally broke rank and fled backwards to the shelter of their walls and forts. Our men fought gallantly - let me not deny them their due - soldiers and citizens alike, who had come forth with and after the Maid, all were inspired by confidence and courage. But it was her presence in the ranks which gave assurance of victory. Wherever French soldiers wavered it was when she was far away and her back towards them. Yet so soon as she turned in their direction - and some power seemed to whisper to her whenever her soldiers were dismayed - and galloped to their assistance, all was well again; and ere an hour had passed the English were driven back within their towers, and the victory was ours.

Dunois and La Hire rode up to the Maid and saluted. From the city in our rear we could already hear the pealing of the joy bells, the triumphant acclamation of the populace.

"Let us lead you back thither to receive the plaudits you have so well deserved," spoke Dunois, who was man enough to give all the credit of the victory to the Maid. "Right valiantly have you accomplished your task. Now let us take you to receive the gratitude of the town."

"Accomplished!" repeated the Maid with a glance of surprise. "Why, my friends, the task is scarcely yet begun!"

They gazed at her in amazement; but she calmly pointed towards the frowning walls and battlements

Evelyn Everett-Green

of St. Loup.

"We must take yonder tower," she said quietly, "that is what our brave, but rash young officers set themselves to do. They shall not be disappointed. It shall be ours ere night fall upon us. Call to me the bold De Gamache; I would have speech with him and his comrades."

The greater Generals looked at her and at one another, speaking no word. The walls and battlements of St. Loup were strong and well defended. The tower could spout fire and smoke like a living monster. Already the troops had marched far and fought hotly. Surely if assault were to be made it should wait for another day. Thus they communed together a stone's throw from the Maid; but she only looked upon them with her deep inward smile, and softly I heard her speak the words:

"No, it must be done today."

De Gamache rode up, and some half dozen other officers with him. His face was stained with blood and blackened by smoke. He had a scarf bound about his left arm; but his bearing was bold and resolute, and though his cheek flushed at the clear, direct gaze of the Maid's eyes, he neither faltered nor trembled as he stood before her.

"You did desire a good thing, my Captain," she said, "and had you told me of your brave wish, I would have put myself at your head and led you to victory forthwith. Yet this victory has not been forfeited, only delayed by your eager rashness. Say, if I lead you myself, this very hour, against yon frowning tower, will you follow me like brave soldiers of the Cross, and not turn back till my Lord has given us the victory? For He will deliver yon place into our hands, albeit not without bloodshed, not without stress or strife. Many must be slain ere we can call it ours, but will you follow and take it?"

The shout which arose from a thousand throats rang to the welkin, and methinks must have smote with dread import upon the English ears. The Maid's voice seemed to float through the air, and penetrate to the extreme limits of the crowd, or else her words were taken up and repeated by a score of eager tongues, and so ran through the mighty muster with thrilling import. The eyes were dazzled by the flashing blades as men swung them above their heads.

"Lead us, O Maid, lead us! We follow to death or victory! We fear nothing so that you are our leader and our guide!"

There was no withstanding a spirit like that! La Hire's voice was one of the foremost in the cry; his great blade the first to leap from its scabbard. Sage counsels of war, prompted by experience, had to give way before a power different from anything which the veterans had known before. With a dash, the elan of which was a marvellous sight to see, the soldiers poured themselves like a living stream against the walls of St. Loup. The English behind the fortifications rained upon them missiles of every description. The air was darkened by a cloud of arrows. The cannon from the walls belched forth smoke and flame, and great stone and iron balls came hurtling down into our midst, dealing death and destruction. The English soldiers with their characteristic daring sallied forth sword in hand to beat us back and yet we pressed on and ever on; driven backwards here and there by stress of fighting; but never giving great way, and always rallied by the sight of that gleaming white armour, and by the clear, sweet voice ringing out through all the tumult of arms.

"Courage, my children, courage. The fight is fierce; but my Lord gives you the victory. A little more courage, a little more patience, and the day is ours!"

She stood unscathed amid the hail of stones and arrows. Her clear glance never quailed; her sweet voice never faltered; she had thought for everyone but herself. Again and again with her own hands she snatched some follower from a danger unseen by him, but which a moment later would have been his death. She herself stood unmoved in the awful tumult. She even smiled when Dunois and La Hire would have drawn her from the hottest of the fighting.

"No, no, my friends, my place is here. Have no fear. I shall not suffer. I have guardians watching over me that you wot not of."

And so she stood unmoved at the foot of the tower, till the English, overcome with amaze, gave up the defence, and fled from a place they believed must surely be bewitched.

And as the last of the sunlight faded from the sky, the fortress of St. Loup was ours. The Maid had fought her first battle, and had triumphed.

## XI.

## HOW THE MAID BORE TRIUMPH
## AND TROUBLE.


The people of Orleans, and we her knights and followers, were well-nigh wild with joy. I do not think I had ever doubted how she would bear herself in battle; and yet my heart had sometimes trembled at the thought of it. For, after all, speaking humanly, she was but a girl, a gentle maid, loving and tender-hearted, to whom the sight of suffering was always a sorrow and a pain. And to picture a young girl, who had perhaps never seen blows struck in anger in her life - save perchance in some village brawl - suddenly set in the midst of a battle, arms clashing, blood flowing, all the hideous din of warfare around her, exposed to all its fearful risks and perils - was it strange we should ask ourselves how she would bear it? Was it wonderful that her confidence and calmness and steadfast courage under the trial should convince us, as never perhaps we had been convinced before, of the nearness of those supernatural beings who guarded her so closely, who warned her of danger, who inspired her with courage, and yet never robbed her for one moment of the grace and beauty and crown of her pure womanhood?

And so, whilst we were well-nigh mad with joy and triumph, whilst joy bells pealed from the city, and the

Evelyn Everett-Green

soldiers and citizens were ready to do her homage as a veritable saint from heaven, she was just her own quiet, thoughtful, retiring self. She put aside the plaudits of the Generals; she hushed the excited shouting of the soldiers. She exercised her authority to check and stop the carnage, to insist that quarter should be given to all who asked it, to see that the wounded upon both sides were carried into the city to receive attention and care, and in particular that the prisoners - amongst whom were several priests - should receive humane treatment, and escape any sort of insult or reprisal.

These matters occupied her time and thought to the exclusion of any personal pride or triumph. It was with difficulty that the Generals could persuade her to ride at their head into the city, to receive the applause and joyful gratitude of the people; and as soon as she could without discourtesy extricate herself from the crowd pressing round to kiss her hands or her feet, or even the horse upon which she rode, she slipped away to give orders that certain badly wounded English prisoners were to be carried to the Treasurer's house, and laid in the spacious guest chamber, which, having been prepared for her own reception, had been permitted to no one else. Here she begged of Madame Boucher permission to lodge them, that she might tend their hurts herself, and assure herself that all was well with them.

No one could deny the Maid those things she asked, knowing well that others in her place would have issued commands without stooping to petition. But with the Maid it was never so. Her gentle courtesy never deserted her. No association with men, no military dignity of command, which she could so well assume, ever tarnished the lustre of her sweet humility. A gentle maiden, full of tenderness and compassion, she showed herself now. Instead of resting after the sore strife of the battle, which had exhausted even strong men, nothing would serve her but that she must herself dress the wounds of these English prisoners; and so deft was her touch, and so soft and tender her methods with them, that not a groan passed the lips of any of them; they only watched her with wondering eyes of gratitude; and when she had left the room they looked at each other and asked:

"Who is it? Is it boy, or angel, or what? The voice is as the voice of a woman, and the touch is as soft; but the dress is the dress of a man. Who can it be?"

I understood them, for I knew something of the English tongue, and I saw that they were in great amazement; for all who had seen the Maid bore her image stamped upon their hearts; and yet it was impossible for these prisoners of war to believe that the triumphant, angelic Commander of the Forces could stoop to tend the hurts of wounded prisoners with her own hands.

"Gentlemen," I said, "that is the Angelic Maid herself - she who has been sent of Heaven for the deliverance of France. I trow that you soldiers and knights of England have called her witch, and threatened to burn her if you can lay hands upon her. Perchance now that you have seen her thus face to face, your thoughts towards her will somewhat change."

They gazed at me and at one another in amaze. They broke into questions, eager and full of curiosity. When I had answered them they were ready to tell me what was spoken of her in the English ranks; all averred that some strange power seemed to fall upon them with the advent of the Maid into the city - a power that withheld them from sallying forth to hinder her coming, or that of the relieving army.

"We had meant to fight her to the death," spoke one English knight. "I was in counsel with the Generals when it was so proposed; and yet more resolved were we to keep out the army from Blois, which we heard must needs pass straight through our lines - an easy prey, we said, to our gunners, archers and swordsmen. All was in readiness for the attack - and yet no word was ever given. No trumpet sounded, though the men were drawn up ready. We all stood to arms; but the sight of that dazzling white figure seemed to close the lips of our commanders, to numb the limbs of our soldiers. I can say no more. When the chance was gone - the hour passed - we gazed into each other's face as men awaking from a dream. We cursed ourselves. We cursed the witch who had bound us by her spells. We vowed to redeem and revenge ourselves another day. And when we saw the French issuing forward to the attack scarce two hours after the entry of the relieving army, and there was no white figure with them, then indeed did we tell ourselves that our time was come; and we thought to win a speedy victory over the men who had so often fled before us. Yet you know how the day did end. The Maid came - victory rode beside her! Nought we could do availed when she appeared. I had thought to be left to die upon the battlefield, but behold I am here, and she has dressed my wounds with her own hands! It is wonderful! Past belief! Tell me who and what is she? A creature of earth or of heaven?"

I had already told him all I knew; but they were never tired of hearing the story of the Maid; and as I, at her request, watched beside them during the night, ministering to their wants, and doing what I was able to relieve their pain, I found that nothing so helped them to forget the smart of their wounds as the narration of all the wonderful words and deeds of this Heavenly Deliverer of France.

They were frank enough on their side also, and told me much of the disposition of their forces, and how that they were expecting a strong army to join them quickly, headed by Sir John Fastolffe, a notable knight, whose name we well knew, and had trembled before ere this. They admitted that their ranks were somewhat thinned by disease and death, and that they had scarce sufficient force both to maintain all the bastilles erected on the north side of the river and also to hold the great forts of Les Tourelles and Les Augustins on the south; but that when the reinforcements should arrive all would be well, and but for the marvellous power of the Maid, they would have felt no doubt whatever as to the speedy reduction of the city either by assault or blockade.

With the first golden shafts of sunlight came the Maid once more, little Charlotte beside her, both bearing in their hands such cooling drinks and light sustenance as the condition of the wounded men required. The Maid wore the white, silver embroidered tunic and silken hose which Queen Yolande had provided for her indoor dress; she carried no arms, and her clustering curls framed her lovely face like a nimbus. All eyes were fixed upon her as upon a vision, and as she bent over each wounded man in turn, asking him of his welfare and holding a cup to his lips, I could see the amazement deepening in their eyes; and I am sure that they were well-nigh ready to worship the ground upon which she trod, so deep was the impression made upon them by her beauty and her gentle treatment.

When she left the room I followed her at her sign, and asked:

"Then you go not forth to battle today, General?"

"Nay," she replied, "for today the Church keeps the blessed Feast of the Ascension; which should be to all a day of peace and thanksgiving and holy joy. I am going forthwith to hear Mass and receive the Holy Sacrament; and I would have my faithful knights about me. Let us forget warfare and strife for this day."

Her own face was transfigured as she spoke. The light shone upon it all the time that she knelt before the high altar in the Cathedral, rapt in a mystery of thanksgiving and heavenly joy. O how real it all was to her - those things which were to us articles of faith, grounds of hope, yet matters which seemed too far above us to arouse that personal rapture which was shining from the eyes and irradiating the whole face of the Maid.

It was a beautiful beginning to the day; and all the early hours were spent by the Maid in meditation and prayer within the walls of the Cathedral, where the people flocked, as perhaps they had never done before, to give thanks for the mercies received with the advent of the Maid, and to gaze upon her, as she knelt in a trance of rapture and devotion in her appointed place not far from the altar. We, her knights, went to and fro, some of us always near to her, that the crowd might not too curiously press upon her when she went forth, or disturb her devotions by too close an approach.

I noted that none of the Generals appeared or took part in the acts of devotion that day. And as I issued forth into the sunny street at the close of the High Mass, Bertrand met me with a look of trouble and anger on his face.

"They are all sitting in council of war together," he said, "and they have not even told her of it, nor suffered her to join them! How can they treat her so - even Dunois and La Hire - when they have seen again and yet again how futile are all plans made by their skill without the sanction of her voice? It makes my gorge rise! Do they think her a mere beautiful image, to ride before them and carry a white banner to affright the foe? It is a shame, a shame, that they should treat her so, after all that they have seen and heard!"

I was as wroth as Bertrand, and as full of surprise. Even now, looking back after all these years, the blindness of these men of war astonishes and exasperates me. They had seen with their own eyes what the Maid could accomplish; again and again she had proved herself the abler in counsel as in fight; and yet they now deliberately desired to set her aside from their councils, and only inform her of their decisions when made, and permit her to take a share in the fighting they had planned.

Bertrand was furiously angry. He led me up into a lofty turret which commanded a bird's-eye view of the whole city and its environs, and he pointed out that which the Maid had declared she would straightway do, so soon as the Feast of the Ascension was over, and how the Generals were about to follow a quite

Evelyn Everett-Green

different course.

Orleans, as all men know, lies upon the right - the north - bank of the Loire, and the country to the north was then altogether in the power of the English; wherefore they had built their great bastilles around the city upon that side without molestation, and were able to receive supplies from their countrymen without let or hindrance.

But these bastilles were not the chiefest danger to the city, or rather I should say, it was not these which were the chiefest cause of peril, since no help could reach the garrison from that side. They looked to the country to the south to help them, and it was to stop supplies from reaching them by water or from the south that the English had long since crossed the river and had established themselves in certain forts along the south bank. Of these, St. Jean le Blanc was one; but by far the most important and dangerous to the city were the two great towers commanding the bridge, whose names I have given before. Let me explain how these great fortifications stood.

Les Augustins had once been a convent, and it stood on the south bank, very near to the end of the bridge, guarding it securely from attack, and commanding the waterway and the approach to the city. Les Tourelles was an even stronger tower, constructed upon the very bridge itself, and menacing the town in formidable fashion. Dunois had broken down the main portion of the bridge on the north side to prevent the advance into the city of the English from their tower; so it stood grimly isolated from either bank; for the permanent bridge at the south end had been destroyed to be replaced by a drawbridge which could rise or fall at will.

And it was these towers of Les Augustins and Les Tourelles which had reduced the city to such straits by hindering the entrance of food supplies. Moreover, from Les Tourelles great stone cannon balls had been hurled into the city in vast numbers, battering down walls and doing untold damage to buildings and their inhabitants.

Now it was evident to all that these fortresses must be taken if the city were to be relieved and the siege raised. But the Maid, with her far-seeing eyes, had decreed that first the bastilles upon the north bank should be attacked and destroyed; and it was easy to follow her reasoning; "For," she said, "when the English are fiercely attacked there, they will, without doubt, yield up these lesser fortresses without a great struggle, concentrating themselves in force upon the left bank, where they think to do us most hurt. We shall then destroy their bastilles, so that they will have no place of shelter to fly back to; and then we shall fall upon them hip and thigh on the south side, and drive them before us as chaff before the wind. They must needs then disperse themselves altogether, having no more cover to hide themselves in; so will the enemies of the Lord be dispersed, and the siege of Orleans be raised."

This was the plan she had confided to her own immediate attendants and staff the previous evening, and which Bertrand repeated to me, gazing over the ramparts, and pointing out each fortress and bastion as it was named. But now the Generals in Council, without reference to the Maid, had decreed something altogether different. What they desired to do was not to

Evelyn Everett-Green

make any real or vigorous attack upon any of the English forts, but to feign an assault upon the towers on the south bank, and whilst the attention of the foe was thus engaged, get great quantifies of stores - all lying in readiness at hand - into the city, enough to last for a long while, and then quietly sit down behind the strong walls, and tire out the English, forcing them thus to retreat of their own accord!

Think of it! After all that had been promised, all that had been performed! To be content to shut ourselves in a well-provisioned town, and just weary out the patience of the foe! And, moreover, of a foe who expected daily reinforcements from the north, and who would be quite capable of exercising as much patience, and perhaps more daring than ourselves.

Even now my blood boils at the thought, and I find it hard to conceive how such men as Dunois and La Hire let themselves be led from their allegiance and confidence in the Maid to listen to such counsel as this from her detractors, and those many lesser commanders who were sorely jealous of her success and influence. But so it was, not once nor twice, but again and again; though in action they were staunch to her, would follow her everywhere, rally round her standard, fly to her defence when danger threatened, and show themselves gallant soldiers and generous-hearted men, never denying her all her share of praise and honour. But when sitting in the council room, surrounded by officers and men of experience in war disposed to scorn the counsels of an unlettered girl, and scoff at her pretensions to military rule, they were invariably led away and overborne, agreeing to act without her sanction, or even contrary to her advice, notwithstanding their belief in her mission, and their trust in her power as a leader.

The shades of evening had fallen in the Treasurer's house before word was brought to the Maid of the decision of the Generals in Council. We were sitting around her after supper; and she had fallen into a very thoughtful mood. The Chevalier d'Aulon had been called away, and now returned with a troubled face. He stood just within the doorway, as though half afraid to advance. The Maid lifted her eyes to his and smiled.

"Do not fear to tell me your news, my kind friend. I know that your faithful heart is sore at the dishonour done to me; but let us not judge harshly. It is hard for men full of courage and fleshly power to understand how the Lord works with such humble instruments. Perchance, in their place, we should not be greatly different.

"So they have refused my plan, and made one of their own. We are to attack the foe upon the south? Is that agreed? And even so not with all our heart and strength?"

D'Aulon recoiled a step in amaze.

"Madame, that is indeed so - a feint upon the south bank has been decreed, whilst provisions are thrown into the city - "

"Yes, yes, I know. Well, so be it. We will attack on the south bank. It must have come sooner or later, and if we fight with a will, the Lord will be with us and uphold our cause. But, my friends, understand this, and let the men likewise understand it. There shall be no mockery of fighting. It shall be true and desperate warfare. Let the Generals decree what they will, the Maid will lead her soldiers to victory! Tomorrow Les Augustins shall be ours; upon the next day Les Tourelles shall fall - " she paused suddenly and turned towards Bertrand.

"What day will that be - the day after to-morrow?"

"The seventh day of May," he answered at once.

"Ah!" she said, "then it will be on that day - the day which shall see Orleans relieved - the power of the English broken."

She spoke dreamily, and only Madame Boucher, who sat in the shadows with her child upon her lap, ventured to ask of her:

"What will be on that day, gentle Jeanne?"

"That I shall be wounded," she answered quietly.

"Did I not tell you long since," turning to Bertrand and me, "that I should not come unscathed through the assault; but that on a certain day I should receive a wound?"

I pulled out my tablets, upon which I often recorded the sayings of the Maid, and sure enough there it was written down as she said. We felt a great burning revolt at the thought of any hurt befalling her, and somebody spoke vehemently, saying that the holy Saints would surely protect her from harm. But she lifted her hand with her gentle authority of gesture, and spoke:

"Nay, my kind friends, but thus it must needs be; nor

would I have it otherwise. Listen, and I will tell you all. I often had my days and hours of fear because this great work was put upon one so weak and ignorant as I, and it was long before I clearly understood that I was but the instrument in a mighty Hand, and that power for all would be given me. Then my fear left and great joy came; perhaps even some pride and haughtiness of spirit in that I had been chosen for such a task.

"And then it was that my voices asked of me: 'Jeanne, hast thou no fear?'

"And I answered without pause, 'I fear nothing now.'

"Then St. Catherine herself suddenly appeared to me in a great white light and said: 'Child, thou art highly favoured of heaven; but the flesh is easily puffed up. And for this cause, and because it may be well that thou thyself and all men shall know that thou art but human flesh and blood, thou shalt not escape unscathed in warfare; but thou too shalt feel the sting of fiery dart, and know the scald of flowing blood.'

"I bowed my head and made answer I would bear whatever my Lord thought fit to lay upon me; and I asked if I might know when this thing would happen. It was not told me then; but later it was revealed to me; and I know that upon the seventh day of May I shall be wounded - " and she touched her right shoulder as she spoke, just below the neck.

"But what matter will that be, when the siege of Orleans shall be raised?"

Her face was aglow; nothing could touch her joy, not the insults of the proud Generals, nor the knowledge of

Evelyn Everett-Green

coming pain for herself. Her thought was all of the mission entrusted to her; and so, though thwarted and set aside, she showed no petty anger, dreamed not of any paltry vengeance such as others might have dealt the soldiers, by refusing to march with them on the morrow. Oh, no; hurt she might be - indeed we knew she was - her pain being for the dishonour done her Lord in this disrespect of His messenger; but no thought of reprisal entered her head. She rose from her seat, and lifted the little Charlotte in her strong young arms.

"Gentlemen, let us early to rest," she said, holding her head proudly, "for tomorrow a great work shall be done, and we must all have our share in it."

## XII.

## HOW THE MAID RAISED THE SIEGE.

To tell the tale of how Les Augustins was taken is but to tell again the tale of St Loup.

I know not precisely what instructions the lesser officers received, nor what they told their men. But whether from preconcerted arrangement that the attack was only to be a feint, or whether from the dash and energy of the English, it appeared at first as though the tide of war was rolling back in its old track, and that the prowess of the English as destined to win the day.

For one thing the assault was commenced before the Maid had crossed the river and could put herself at the head of the men. A large body of troops had been transported to the south side in boats during the night, under cover of darkness; and this was all very well; but they should have waited hen daylight came for the Maid to march at their head, instead of which they sought to rush the fortress before ever she had appeared at all; and when we arrived at the river's bank, it was to see a furious battle raging round the base of Les Augustins, and ere we were half across the river, we saw only too plainly that the French were being badly beaten, were fleeing in all directions from the pursuing foe, and were making for the river bank once more as fast as their legs could carry them.

The Maid watched it all, with that strange, inscrutable look upon her face, and that battle light in her eyes which we were all learning to know. She was sitting upon her horse; for though a number of animals had been taken across in the night, no horse of hers had been so conducted, and we had led the creature with its rider into the great flat-bottomed boat; so that she was on a higher level than the rest of us, and could better see what was passing, though it was plain to all that our soldiers were getting badly beaten.

"O foolish children, silly sheep!" murmured the Maid as she watched, "and yet you are not to blame, but those who lead you. When will they understand? When will they believe?"

We reached the shore, and the Maid, without waiting for any of us to mount or form a bodyguard round her, leaped her horse to the bank, and charged up it, her pennon flying, her eyes alight with the greatness of her purpose.

But even as she climbed the slippery bank, a great rush of flying soldiers met her, and by their sheer weight forced back horse and rider almost to the river's brink before they were aware who or what it was.

Then her silver trumpet voice rang out. She called upon them to reform, to follow her. She cried that her Lord would give them the victory, and almost before we who had accompanied her had formed into rank for the charge, the flying, panic-stricken men from the front, ashamed and filled with fresh ardour, had turned themselves about, closed up their scattered ranks, and were ready to follow her whithersoever she might lead them.

Yet it was to no speedy victory she urged them. No angel with a flaming sword came forth to fight and overcome as by a miracle. But it was enough for that white-clad figure to stand revealed in the thickest of the carnage to animate the men to heroic effort. As I say, it was the story of St. Loup over again; but if anything the fighting was more severe. What the Generals had meant for a mere feint, the Maid turned into a desperate battle. The English were reinforced many times; it seemed as though we had a hopeless task before us. But confidence and assurance of victory were in our hearts as we saw our Deliverer stand in the thick of the fight and heard her clarion voice ringing over the field. Ere the shades of night fell, not only was Les Augustins ours, but its stores of food and ammunition had been safely transported into the city, and the place so destroyed and dismantled that never again could it be a source of peril to the town.

And now the Maid's eyes were fixed full upon the frowning bulk of Les Tourelles, rising grim and black against the darkening sky, with its little "tower of the Boulevard," on this side the drawbridge. Thither had the whole English force retired - all who were not lying dead or desperately wounded on the plain or round the gutted tower of Les Augustins - we saw their threatening faces looking down fiercely upon us, and heard the angry voices from the walls, heaping abuse and curses upon the "White Witch," who had wrought them this evil.

"Would that we could attack at once!" spoke the Maid. "Would that the sun would stay his course! Truly I do believe that we should carry all before us!"

The leaders came up to praise and glorify her prowess. They heard her words, but answered how that the men must needs have a night's rest ere they tried this second great feat of arms. But, they added, there should be no going back into the city, no delay on the morrow in crossing the river.

It was a warm summer-like night. Provisions were abundant, shelter could be obtained beneath the walls of the captured citadel. They, with the bulk of the army, would remain on the south bank for the nonce, and the Maid should return to the city with the convoys of wounded, to spend a quiet night there, returning with the dawn of the morrow to renew the attack and take Les Tourelles.

Thus they spoke, and spoke suavely and courteously. But I did note a strange look in the eyes of the Maid; and I wondered why it was that Dunois, the speaker, grew red and stumbled over his words, whilst that La Hire, who had done a giant's work in the fighting that day, ground his teeth and looked both ashamed and disturbed.

The Maid stood a brief while as though in doubt. But then she made quiet reply:

"Then, gentlemen, it shall be as you will. I will return to the city for the night. But with the dawn of day I will be here, and Les Tourelles shall be ours. The siege of Orleans shall be raised!"

They bowed low to her; every one of them made obeisance. Yet was there something ironical in the very humility of some? I could not tell; yet my heart burned within me as I followed our mistress; and never had I known her so silent as she was upon our journey back, or as we sat at supper, the rest of us telling of the day's doings, but the Maid speechless, save when she bent her head to answer some eager question of little Charlotte's, or to smile at her childish prattle.

Suddenly the door was flung open, and Sir Guy strode in with a face like a thundercloud. Behind him came a messenger sent by the Generals to the Maid, and this was the news he brought:

There had been a council held after dark, and it was then unanimously agreed that all now had been done that was necessary. The city was provisioned, the power of the English had been greatly weakened and broken. The army would now be content with the triumphs already won, and would quietly await further reinforcements before taking any fresh step.

The man who brought this message faltered as he delivered it. The Maid sat very still and quiet, her head lifted in a dignified but most expressive disdain.

"Monsieur," she replied, when the envoy ceased speaking, "go back to those who sent you. Tell them that they have had their council and I have had mine. I leave the city at dawn as I have said. I return not to it till the siege has been raised."

The man bowed and retired confusedly. The Maid lifted the little child in her arms, as was her wont, to carry her to bed. She turned to her chaplain as she did so:

Evelyn Everett-Green

"Come to me at dawn, my father, to hear my confession; and I pray you accompany me upon the morrow; for my blood will be shed. But do not weep or fear for me, my friends, nor spread any banquet for me ere I start forth upon the morrow; but keep all for my return in the evening, when I will come to you by the bridge."

She was gone as she spoke, and we gazed at her and each other in amaze; for how could she come back by a bridge which had been destroyed, and how did she brook such slights as were heaped upon her without showing anger and hurt pride?

"And there is worse yet to come!" cried Sir Guy in a fury of rage, "for I lingered behind to hear and see. If you will believe it, there are numbers and numbers of the lesser officers who would desire that the Maid should now be told that her work is done, and that she can retire to her home in Domremy; that the King will come himself with another reinforcing army to raise the siege, so that they may get rid of her, and take the glory to themselves whenever the place shall be truly relieved. Could you believe such folly, such treachery?"

We could not; we could scarce believe our ears, and right glad was I to hear how that La Hire had had no part in this shameful council; and I hope that Dunois had not either, though I fear me he was less staunch.

La Hire had returned to the city to seek to infuse into the citizens some of the spirit of the Maid. He was always for bold attack, and would be ready on the morrow, we did not doubt, for whatever might betide.

It was little after dawn when we rode forth, the Maid in her white armour at our head, carrying her small pennon, whilst D'Aulon bore the great white standard close behind. Her face was pale and rapt. None of us spoke to her, and Pasquerel, her good chaplain, rode behind telling his beads as he went.

We reached the Burgundy Gate; and behold it was fast shut. At the portal stood De Gaucourt, a notable warrior, with a grim look about his mouth. The Maid saluted him courteously, and quietly bid him open the gate. But he budged not an inch.

"Madam," he said, "I have my commands from the Generals of the army. The gate is to remain shut. No one is to be suffered to pass forth today."

We understood in a moment. This was a ruse to trap the Maid within the city walls. Our hands were upon the hilts of our swords. At a word from her, they would have flashed forth, and De Gaucourt would have been a dead man had he sought to hinder us in the opening of the gate. But the Maid read our purpose in our eyes and in our gestures, and she stayed us by her lifted hand.

"Not so, my friends," she answered gravely, "but the Chevalier de Gaucourt will himself order the opening of the gate. I have to ride through it and at once. My Lord bids it!"

Her eyes flashed full and suddenly upon him. We saw him quiver from head to foot. With his own hands he unlocked the gate, and it seemed to swing of its own accord wide open before us. The Maid bent her head in gracious acknowledgment, swept through and was off

Evelyn Everett-Green

to the river like a flash of white lightning.

The river lay golden in the glory of the morning. The boats which had transported us across last night bore us bravely over now. I know not how the Generals felt when they saw the Maid, a dazzling vision of brightness, her great white standard close behind, her phalanx of knights and gentlemen in attendance, gallop up to the scene of action, from which they thought they had successfully banished her. I only know that from the throats of the soldiers there arose a deafening shout of welcome. They at least believed in her. They looked to her as to none else. They would follow her unwaveringly, when no other commander could make them budge.

A yell that rent the very firmament went up at sight of her, and every man seized his arms and sprang to his post, as though inspired by the very genius of victory.

"Courage, my children, forward! The day shall be ours!" she cried, as she took her place at the head of the formidable charge against the walls which frowned and bristled with the pikes and arrows of the English. Her voice, like a silver clarion, rang clear through the din of the furious battle which followed:

"Bon coeur, bonne esperance, mes enfants, the hour of victory is at hand! De la part de Dieu! De la part de Dieu!"

That was her favourite battle cry! It was God who should give the victory.

But it was no easy victory we were to win that day. The English fought with the energy of despair. They knew as well as we that when Les Tourelles fell the siege would be raised. True they had their bastilles upon the north side of the river to fall back upon, since the Maid's counsel of destruction had not been followed. But once dislodged from the south bank, and Orleans would lie open to the support of her friends in the south, and the position of the English army would be one of dire peril. For now the French were no more cowed by craven fear of the power of their enemies. They had found them capable of defeat and overthrow; the spell was broken. And it was the Maid who had done it!

Oh, how we fought around her that day! She was on foot now, for the banks of the moat were slippery, and the press around the walls was too great to admit easily of the tactics of horsemen. I never saw her strike at any foe. It was her pennon rather than her sword in which she trusted. Here was the rallying point for the bravest and most desperate of the assailants, ever in the thickest of the strife, ever pointing the way to victory.

It was the tower of the Boulevard against which we were directing our attack. If that fell, Les Tourelles itself must needs follow, isolated as it would then be in the midst of the river. We did not know it then, but we were to learn later, that La Hire in the city with a great band of citizens and soldiers to help him, was already hard at work constructing a bridge which should carry him and his men across to Les Tourelles, to take the English in the rear, whilst their attention was concentrated upon our work on the other side.

No wonder that the clash and din was something deafening, that the boom of the great cannon ceased not; smoke and fire seemed to envelop the walls of the towers; the air was darkened by clouds of arrows; great stones came crashing into our midst. Men fell on every side; we had much ado to press on without treading under foot the dead and dying; but the white pennon fluttered before us, and foot by foot we crept up towards the base of the tower.

Victory! Victory! was the cry of our hearts. We were close to the walls now - the Maid had seized a ladder, and with her own hands was setting it in position, when - O woe! woe! - a great cloth-yard shaft from an English bow, tipped with iron and winged with an eagle's plume, struck upon that white armour with such crashing force that a rent was made in its shining surface, and the Maid was borne to the ground.

Oh, the terrible fear of that moment! The yell of triumph and joy which arose from the walls of the fortress seemed to turn my blood into liquid fire.

The English had seen the fall of our champion. They shouted like men drunk with victory! They knew well enough that were she dead, they would drive back the French as sheep are driven by wolves.

I had been close beside the Maid for hours; for I never forgot what she had spoken about being wounded that day; yet when she fell I had been parted from her a brief space, by one of those battle waves too strong for resistance. But now I fought my way to her side with irresistible fury, though there was such a struggling press all about her that I had much ado to force my way through it. But I was known as one of her especial personal attendants, and way was made for me somehow; yet it was not I who was the first to render her assistance.

When I arrived, De Gamache was holding her in his arms; someone had removed her headpiece, and though her face was as white as the snowy plumes, her eyes were open, and there was a faint brave smile upon her lips. De Gamache had his horse beside him, his arm slipped through the reins.

"My brave General," he said, as the Maid looked in his face, "let me lift you to my saddle and convey you to a place of safety. I have done you wrong before; but I pray you forgive me, and bear no malice; for I am yours till death. Never was woman so brave."

"I should be wrong indeed to bear malice against any, my good friend," spoke the Maid, in her gentle tones, "above all against one so courteous, so brave."

We lifted her upon the horse. We formed a bodyguard round her. We drew her out of the thick of the press, for once unresisting; and we laid her down in a little adjacent vineyard, where the good Pasquerel came instantly, and knelt beside her offering prayers for her recovery. But the great arrow had pierced right through her shoulder, and stood out a handbreadth upon the other side. We had sent for a surgeon; but we dreaded to think of the pain she must suffer; must be suffering even now. Her face was white; her brow was furrowed.

But suddenly, as we stood looking at her in dismay, she sat up, took firm hold of the cruel barb with her own hands, and drew it steadily from the wound.

Was ever courage like hers? As the blood came gushing forth, staining her white armour red, she uttered a little cry and her lips grew pale. Yet I think the cry was less from pain than to see the marring of

Evelyn Everett-Green

her shining breastplate; and the tears started to her eyes. Never before had this suffered hurt; the sight of the envious rent hurt her, I trow, as much as did the smart of her wound.

The surgeon came hurrying up, and dressed the wound with a pledget of linen steeped in oil; and the Maid lay very white and still, almost like one dying or dead, so that we all held our breath in fear. In sooth, the faintness was deathlike for awhile, and she did beckon to her priest to come close to her and receive her confession, whilst we formed round her in a circle, keeping off all idle gazers, and standing facing away from her, with bent, uncovered heads.

Was it possible that her Lord was about to take her from us, her task yet unfulfilled? It was hard to believe it, and yet we could not but fear; wherefore our hearts were heavy within us during that long hour which followed.

And the battle? It was raging still, but the heart of it seemed to be lacking. The English were crying out that the White Witch was dead, taunting their foes with being led by a woman, and asking them where she was gone to now.

Dunois came hurrying up for news of her. The Maid roused herself and beckoned to him to come to her where she lay, and asked him of the battle. Dunois told her that the courage of the men seemed failing, that he thought of sounding the retreat.

For a few moments she lay still; her eyes bent full upon the blinding blue of the sunny sky. Then she spoke:

"Sound no retreat, my General," she spoke, "but give the men a breathing space. Let them draw off for a brief moment. Let them eat and drink and refresh themselves. Tell them that I will come to them again; and when you and they see my standard floating against the wall, then know by that token that the place is yours."

Dunois went his way, and soon the sound of the struggle ceased. There came a strange hush in the heat of the noontide hours. The Maid lay still a while longer; then raising herself, asked that water should be brought to cleanse away all stains from her hands and face and her white armour.

That being done she called to D'Aulon and said to him:

"Take the great standard; plant it again upon the edge of the moat; and when the silken folds touch the tower wall, call and tell me; and you, my knights and gentlemen, be ready to follow me to victory!"

Did we doubt her ability, wounded as she was, to lead us? Not one whit. We looked to our arms; we stood silently beside her. We watched D'Aulon move quietly forward to the appointed place, and unfold the great white banner, which hung down limply in the sultry heat of the May afternoon. He stood there, and we stood beside the Maid a great while; she lay upon the heap of cloaks which had been spread to form a couch for her; her hands were clasped and her eyes closed as though in prayer.

Then a little puff of wind arose, followed by another, and yet another - soft, warm wind, but we saw the folds of the banner begin to unfurl. Little by little the breeze strengthened; breathlessly we watched the gradual lifting of the silken standard, till, with an indescribably proud motion - as though some spirit was infused into the lifeless silk - it launched itself like a living thing against the tower wall.

"It touches! It touches!" cried D'Aulon.

"It touches! It touches!" we shouted in response.

"It touches! It touches!" came an echoing wave sound from the soldiers watching from their resting places.

The Maid was on her feet in a moment. Where was the weakness, the feebleness, the faintness of the wounded girl? All gone - all swallowed up in the triumph of the victorious warrior.

"Onward! Onward, my children. Onward, de la part de Dieu! He has given you the victory! Onwards and take the tower! Nothing can resist you now!"

Her voice was heard all over the field. The white folds of the banner still fluttered against the wall, the white armour of the Maid shone dazzling in the sunshine as she dashed forward. The army to a man sprang forward in her wake with that rush, with that power of confidence against which nothing can stand.

The English shrieked in their astonishment and affright. The dead had come to life! The White Witch, struck down as they thought by mortal wound, was charging at the head of her armies. The French were swarming up the scaling ladders, pouring into their tower, carrying all before them.

Fighting was useless. Nothing remained but flight. Helter skelter, like rabbits or rats, they fled this way and that before us. Not an Englishman remained upon the south side of the river. The French flag waved from the top of the tower. The seven months' siege was raised by the Maid eight days after her entrance into the city.

## XIII.

## HOW THE MAID WON A NEW NAME.

"Entrez, entrez - de la part de Dieu - all is yours!"

Thus spoke the Maid, as we rushed the tower of the boulevard, the English flying this way and that before us. The Maid found herself face to face with the commander - that Sir William Glasdale, who had called her vile names a few days before, and had promised to burn her for a witch if once she fell into his hands.

But she had no ill words for him, as she saw him, sword in hand, seeking to make a last stand upon the drawbridge leading to Les Tourelles.

"Now yield you, Classidas," she said; "I bear you no ill will. I have great pity for your soul. Yield you, and all shall be well."

But he would not listen; his face was black like a thundercloud, and with his picked bodyguard of men, he retreated backwards, sword in hand, upon the bridge, seeking to gain the other tower, not knowing its desperate condition, and hoping there to make a last stand.

But he was not destined to achieve his end. Suddenly the bridge gave way beneath his feet, and he and his men were all precipitated into the water. It looked to us as though a miracle had been wrought before our eyes; as though the gaze of the Maid had done it. But the truth was afterwards told us, that a fire ship from the city had been sent across and had burned the bridge, cutting off the retreat of the English that way.

And now we heard the din of battle going on within Les Tourelles; for La Hire had crossed the repaired bridge with a gallant band of soldiers, and our men, hearing the shouts of their comrades, and the cries of the trapped English, flung themselves into boats, or swam over, sword in mouth, anything to get to the scene of the fray; whilst others set to work with planks, and whatever they could lay hands upon, to mend the broken drawbridge that they might swarm across into Les Tourelles and join in the final act of victory, that should free Orleans from the iron grip in which she had been held so long.

But the face of the Maid was troubled, as she looked into the dark water which had closed over the head of Glasdale and his men. She had seized upon a coil of rope; she stood ready to fling it towards them when they rose; but encased as they were in their heavy mail, there was no rising for them. Long did she gaze into the black, bloodstained water; but she gazed in vain; and when she raised her eyes, I saw that they were swimming in tears.

"I would we might have saved them," she spoke, with a little catch in her voice, "I have such great pity for their souls!"

These were the first words I heard the Maid speak after her wonderful victory had been won; and whilst others went hither and thither, mad or drunk with joy, she busied herself about the wounded, making no distinction betwixt friend or foe, sending urgent message into the city for priests to come forth and bring the last Sacraments with them, and so long as there were any dying to be confessed or consoled, or wounded to be cared for and transported into the city, she seemed to have no thought for aught beside. Thankful joy was indeed in her heart, but her tender woman's pity was so stirred by sights of suffering and death that for the moment she could think of nothing else.

Thus the daylight faded, and we began to think of return. How shall I describe the sight which greeted our eyes in the gathering dusk, as we looked towards the city? One might have thought that the English had fired it, so bright was the glare in which it was enveloped; but we knew better. Bonfires were blazing in every square, in every open place. Nay, more, from the very roofs of tower and church great pillars of flame were ascending to the heavens.

Joy bells had rung before this, but never with such a wild jubilation, such a clamour of palpitating triumph. The city had gone mad in its joy - and it was no marvel - and all were awaiting the return of the Maid, to whom this miraculous deliverance was due. Eight days - eight days of the Maid - and the seven-months' siege was raised! Was it wonderful they should hunger for her presence amongst them? Was it wonderful that every house should seek to hang out a white banner in honour of the Angelic Maid, and her pure whiteness of soul and body?

"I will come to you by the bridge," had been her own word; and now, behold, the bridge was there! Like Trojans had the men worked beneath the eagle eyes of La Hire. An army had already crossed from the city; now that their task was done, the Maid's white charger had been led across, and the cry was all for her, for her; that she should let the people see her alive and well, now that her task was accomplished and Orleans was free!

She let us mount her upon her horse, and D'Aulon marched in front with the great white standard. Weary and white and wan was she, with the stress of the fight, with the pain and loss of blood from her wound, above all, with her deep, unfailing pity for the sufferings she had been forced to witness, for the souls gone to their last account without the sacred offices of the Church.

All this weighed upon her young spirit, and gave a strange, ethereal loveliness to her pale face and shining eyes. Methought she seemed almost more like some angelic presence in our midst than a creature of human flesh and blood.

The Generals formed an advance guard before her. The soldiers followed, rank behind rank, in the rear. We of her household rode immediately in her wake, ready to protect her, if need be, from the too great pressure of the crowd. And so we crossed the hastily-repaired bridge, and entered by the Bride Gate - or St. Catherine's gate, as it was equally called; for a figure of St. Catherine stands carved in a niche above the porch, and I saw the Maid glance upwards at it as she passed through, a smile upon her lips.

Shall I ever forget the thunder of applause which fell

upon our ears as we passed into the city through the bridge? It was like the "sound of many waters" - deafening in volume and intensity. And was it wonder? Had not something very like a miracle been wrought? For had not rumours reached the city many times that day of the death of the Deliverer in the hour of victory? None well knew what to believe till they saw her in their midst, and then the cry which rent the heavens was such as methinks is heard but once in a lifetime.

I know not who first spoke the words; but once spoken, they were caught up by ten thousand lips, and the blazing heavens echoed them back in great waves of rolling sound:

"THE MAID OF ORLEANS! THE MAID OF ORLEANS! Welcome, honour, glory, praise to THE MAID OF ORLEANS!"

The people were well-nigh mad with joy; they rushed upon her to kiss her hands, her knees, the folds of her banner, the neck or the flanks of her horse. In the red glare of the hundred bonfires the whiteness of her armour seemed to take a new lustre. The rent upon the shoulder could be plainly seen, showing where the arrow had torn its way. Women sobbed aloud as they looked; men cursed the hand which had shot the bolt; all joined in frantic cheers of joy to see her riding alone, erect and smiling, though with a dreamy stillness of countenance which physical lassitude in part accounted for.

"I thank you, my friends, I thank you," she kept saying, as though no other words would come, save when now and again she would add, " But to God must you give your thanks and blessings. It is He who has delivered you."

It was not far to the house of the Treasurer, and there in the threshold stood the little Charlotte, a great wreath of bay and laurel in her tiny hands. She was lifted up in her father's strong arms, and ere the Maid was able to dismount from her horse the little one had placed the triumphal wreath upon her fair head.

O, what a shout arose! It was like the mighty burst of some great thunderstorm. The Maid, blushing now at the tumult of applause, stretched out her arms, took the little one into them, and held her in a close embrace whilst she bowed her last graceful thanks to the joy-maddened crowd. Then she slipped from her horse, and holding the little one fast by the hand, disappeared into the house, whilst the people reluctantly dispersed to hear the story all over again from the soldiers pouring in, each with some tale of his own to tell of the prowess of THE MAID OF ORLEANS.

Yes, that was the name by which she was henceforth to be known. The city was wild with joy and pride thus to christen her. And she, having crossed by the bridge, as she had said, sat down for a brief while to that festal board which had been spread for her. But fatigue soon over-mastering her, she retired to her room, only pausing to look at us all and say:

"Tomorrow is the Lord's own day of rest. Remember that, my friends. Let there be no fighting, no pursuit, no martial exercise, whatever the foe may threaten or do. Tomorrow must be a day of thanksgiving and praise. Look to it that my words are obeyed."

They said she slept like a child that night; yet with the

early light of day she was up, kneeling in the Cathedral with her household beside her, listening to the sound of chant and prayer, receiving the Holy Sacrament, the pledge of her Lord's love.

Not until we had returned from that first duty did she listen to what was told her anent the movements of the English. They were drawn up in battle array upon the north side of the river, spoke those who had gone to the battlements to look. Thinned as were their ranks, they were still a formidable host, and from the menace of their attitude it might be that they expected the arrival of reinforcements. Would it not be well, spoke La Hire, to go forth against them at once, whilst the soldiers' hearts were flushed with victory, whilst the memory of yesterday's triumphs was green within them?

But the Maid, hitherto all in favour of the most dashing and daring policy, answered now, with a shake of the head:

"It is Sunday, my Generals," she replied; "the day of my Lord. The day He has hallowed to His service."

She paused a moment, and added, quite gently, and without reproach, "Had you acted as I did counsel, the English would now have had no footing on the north side of the river; they must needs have fled altogether from the neighbourhood of the city. Nevertheless, my Lord is merciful. He helps, though men hinder His designs. Let no man stir forth with carnal weapons against the foe this day. We will use other means to vanquish them."

Then turning to me, she bid me go to the Bishop, and

ask him to give her audience; and shortly she was ushered into his presence, and we waited long for her to reappear.

How shall I tell of the wonderful scene which the sun looked down upon that bright May morning, when the purpose of the Maid became fully revealed to us? Even now it seems rather as a dream, than as an incident in a terrible war.

Out upon the level plain, in full sight of the city, in full view of the serried ranks of the English army, a great white altar was set up. The army from Orleans marched out and stood bareheaded beneath the walls, unarmed by order of the Maid, save for the small weapon every man habitually carried at his belt, citizen as well as soldier. The townspeople flocked to the walls, or out into the plain, as pleased them best; and from the Renart Gate there issued forth a grave and sumptuous procession; the Bishop in his vestments, accompanied by all the ecclesiastics within the city walls, each of them robed, attended by acolytes swinging censers, the incense cloud ascending through the sunny air, tapers swaying in the breeze, their light extinguished by the brilliance of the sunshine.

The Maid in her white tunic, with a white mantle over her shoulders, followed with bent head, leading the little Charlotte by the hand succeeded by her household.

And there, in the sight of the rival armies, High Mass was celebrated by the Bishop, both armies kneeling devoutly, and turning towards the Altar as one man. Never have I witnessed such a scene. Never shall I witness such another.

The Mass over, the procession filed back through the gate, both armies kneeling motionless till it had disappeared. Then the Maid rose, and we with her, and followed her in its wake, and the French army, in perfect order, re-entered the city by the appointed gates, as had been ordered.

One hour later and the Maid sent D'Aulon up to the battlements to look what the English army was doing. He returned to say that they were still drawn up in rank as before.

"Which way are their faces?" she asked.

"Their faces are turned away from the city," was the reply.

The countenance of the Maid brightened with a great light.

"Then let them go, a part de Dieu!" she answered. "My God, I thank Thee for this great grace!"

And so, without further battle or bloodshed, the English army marched away from Orleans; and upon the next morning not a man of the foe was left; and the citizens pouring out from the town, destroyed, with acclamations of joy, those great bastilles, which had so long sheltered the foe and threatened the safety of the city.

It was a day ever to be remembered. The bells pealed ceaselessly, the houses were decked with garlands, white banners or silken pennons floated everywhere, the townsfolk arrayed themselves in holiday garb, and poured out through the gates to wander at will over the plain, so lately held by the English. Gladness and the wonder of a great relief was stamped upon every face, and constantly songs of triumph arose or thunders of applause, of which the burden always was - THE MAID OF ORLEANS! THE MAID OF ORLEANS!

They would have kept her with them for ever, if it might so have been. They talked wildly, yet earnestly, of building her a palace, where she should live at ease all the rest of her days, the object of universal admiration and homage.

But the Maid listened to such words, when repeated to her, with a dreamy smile. Her wound required rest; and for two days she consented to remain quiet in the house of the Treasurer, lying for the most part upon a couch in a great cool chamber, with the little Charlotte for her companion and playfellow. She sometimes rose and showed herself at a window in answer to the tumultuous shoutings of the crowd without; and she received with pleasure some great baskets and bouquets of flowers which the wives and children of the citizens had culled for her. But she gently put aside all suggestions of rewards for herself, which some would fain have bestowed upon the Deliverer, and which men of all ranks were but too ready to claim and receive for service rendered.

"I have all that I want, myself - and more," she said; "if any would offer gifts, let them be thank offerings to the Lord. Let the poor receive alms, let Masses be sung for the souls of those killed in the war; but for me - I want nothing but the love of the people of France. I am come to do the will of my Lord. I ask only His approving smile."

And all the while she was eagerly desirous to return to the King, and urge upon him the need to repair instantly to Rheims, and there receive his crown. To her he was not truly King till he had been anointed as such. She knew that the blow to the English arms just struck must have a paralysing effect upon their forces, and that a rapid march with even a small army would be accomplished without resistance, if only it were quickly made.

I need not say that the city of Rheims lay in the very heart of territory owning the English sway. To reach that city we must perforce march right through a hostile country, garrisoned by the enemy. But of that the Maid made light.

"The hearts of the people will turn towards us," she said. "They have submitted to the English yoke; but they are Frenchmen still. Once let them see that the power of the enemy is broken, and they will rally to our standard. But precious time should not be lost. The Dauphin should place himself at the head of such an army as he can spare for the march, and journey forthwith to Rheims. There shall the crown be set upon his head - the pledge and earnest that one day he shall rule the whole realm of France, as his fathers did before him!"

And so, before a week had passed, we set forth with the Maid to go to the King, who had by this time moved his Court from Chinon to Loches, another fortress upon the Loire, where there was space for his train, and which could, if necessary, be fortified against a siege.

It was a strange journey - more like a triumphal

progress than anything we had yet met with. The fame of the Maid and her miraculous exploit in the matter of the siege of Orleans had gone before her, and from every town or village through which she passed the people flocked out to see her, bearing garlands and banners, crowding about her, asking her blessing, seeking to touch her, pouring out blessings and praises, so that the heart of anyone less filled with the humility which comes from above must needs have been altogether puffed up and filled with pride.

But it was never so with the Maid. Her gentle courtesy and devout humility never failed her. Lovingly and gratefully she received love and affection, but praise and honour she set aside, bidding all remember that to God alone belonged the issues from death, and that she was but an instrument in His mighty hands.

We wondered how she would be received at the Court, and whether La Tremouille and her other adversaries had been convinced of her divine mission, and would now remove all opposition. As we approached the fortress we saw that flags were floating from every tower; that the place wore a festive aspect, and that the town was pouring out to welcome us and gaze upon the Maid.

Then, with a great fanfare of trumpets, the gates of the fortress were flung wide open, and forth came a gay procession, in the midst of which, we could not doubt, rode the King himself.

Yes, there was no doubt of it. The crowd parted this way and that, and we saw how the young King himself was marching towards us, and at the sight of the Maid, not only did every courtier in the train uncover, but the

King himself bared his head, and bowed low to the MAID OF ORLEANS.

She was off her horse in a moment, kneeling at his feet; but he raised her instantly, held her hands in his, gave her thanks with true emotion in face and voice, and, turning to her brothers, who rode amongst us of her household, he cried to them in loud tones, saying how he had decreed that the family of the D'Arcs should henceforth have the right to quarter the hues of France on their arms! An empty honour, perhaps, to simple peasants; and yet an honour that the proudest families in the land might envy!

They carried her into the fortress. The two Queens and the ladies of the Court knew not how to make enough of her. They seemed to think that our coming must be regarded as the signal for an outburst of merrymaking and carousing, such as the King found so much to his liking.

It amazed us to find him still wrapped in idle luxury, joyful, it is true, over the relief of Orleans, over the discomfiture of the English; but as indisposed as ever to take the field himself, or to put himself at the head of an army and march to his coronation as the Maid instantly urged him.

"Gentle Dauphin, the Lord would have you King of your realm; He would set the crown upon your head. He has smitten your enemies and scattered them. Then wherefore not do His will and march to the appointed spot? All will be well if you but follow His counsels."

"But, Maiden, I have so few troops; and I have no money; and the way lies through a hostile land," the

King would urge, when day after day she pleaded with him. "All my counsellors advise delay. Is it not right that I should listen to them as well as to you? Wherefore such haste? Is it not wiser to act with deliberation and prudence?"

"It is right to follow the voice of the Lord," spoke the Maid with grave and forceful earnestness, "and to put your trust in Him rather than in any child of man."

But the King could not be persuaded; indolence and fear held him captive, whilst his traitorous advisers sought by every means to undermine the influence of the Maid. And although in this they were not successful, for he believed in her mission, admired her prowess, and looked to her for guidance and help, he must needs listen also to these others who were of contrary mind, and so the weary days dragged on, and nothing was done.

"Noble Dauphin," pleaded the Maid at last, "hold not such long or so many councils; or if, indeed, these be needful to you, let me, I pray you, go forth again with a small army and clear the way. And when all the country betwixt this place and Rheims has submitted to your power, then follow yourself, and take your kingdom!"

Ah me! - to think that he, a King, could consent again to let her go thus, whilst he remained in ease and indolence surrounded by his Court! But so it was. What she could not persuade him to do himself, she at last obtained leave to do for him, and with a joyful face she came to us with the news:

" Gentlemen and my good comrades, be ready for a

speedy march; we will go forward and clear the way; and afterwards the Dauphin shall follow and be made King!"

# XIV.

## HOW THE MAID CLEARED THE KING'S WAY.

We started forth from Selles, where the army which was to do this work had assembled. It was not so great a force as it would have been but for the hesitations of the King, and the delays imposed by his Council. For the men who had marched from Orleans, flushed with victory, eager to rush headlong upon the foe and drive them back to their own chores, had grown weary of the long waiting, and had been infected by the timidity or the treachery of those about the Court. They had melted away by little and little, carrying with them the booty they had found in the English bastilles round Orleans, glad to return to their homes and their families without further fighting, though had the Maid been permitted to place herself at their head at once, as she did desire, they would have followed her to the death.

Still, when all was said and done, it was a gallant troop that responded to her call and mustered at her summons. The magic of her name still thrilled all hearts, and throughout the march of events which followed, it was always the common soldiers who trusted implicitly in the Maid; they left doubts and disputings and unworthy jealousies to the officers and the statesmen.

Evelyn Everett-Green

The Maid went forth with a greater glory and honour than has, methinks, ever been bestowed upon woman before - certainly upon no humbly-born maiden of seventeen years. Some said that she was actually ennobled in her own person by the grant to quarter the lilies of France, and that her brothers ranked now amongst the knights and nobles. Others declared that she had refused all personal honours, and that she still remained a humble peasant, though so high in the favour of the King, and so great a personage in the realm.

As for me, I cared nothing for all this. To me she was always the Angelic Maid, heaven sent, miraculous, apart from the earth, though living amongst us and leading us on to victory.

To the army she was - and that was enough. She was the companion and friend of princes, nobles, and knights; but she was never as others were. An atmosphere of sanctity seemed ever to encompass her. All who approached her did her unconscious homage. None could be with her long without being conscious that she was visited by sounds unheard by them, that her eyes saw sights to which theirs were closed. We were to have added witness to this in the days which followed.

So here we were gathered at Selles upon that bright June morning, just one month after the relief of Orleans. The King had presented to the Maid a great black charger; a mighty creature of immense strength and spirit, but with something of a wicked look in his rolling eyes which made me anxious as he was led forward. The Maid in her white armour - its rent deftly mended, its silver brilliance fully restored - with her velvet white-plumed cap upon her head and a little axe in her hand, stood waiting to mount. But perhaps it was the gleaming whiteness of this slender figure that startled the horse, or else the cries and shouts of the populace at sight of the Maid excited him to the verge of terror; for he reared and plunged so madly as his rider approached that it was with difficulty he was held by two stalwart troopers, and we all begged of the Maid not to trust herself upon his back.

She looked at us with a smile, and made a little courteous gesture with her hand; then turning to the attendants she said:

"Lead him yonder to the cross at the entrance to the church; I will mount him there."

Snorting and struggling, casting foam flakes from his lips, and fighting every inch of the way, the great charger was led whither the Maid had said. But once arrived at the foot of the cross, he suddenly became perfectly quiet. He stood like a statue whilst the Maid approached, caressed him gently with the hand from which she had drawn her mailed gauntlet, and, after speaking kindly words to him, vaulted lightly on his back.

From that moment her conquest of the fierce creature was complete. He carried her throughout that wonderful week with a gentleness and docility, and an untiring strength which was beautiful to see. The brute creation owned her sway as well as did men of understanding, who could watch and weigh her acts and deeds.

So, amid the plaudits of the people, the fanfare of trumpets, the rolling of drums, the rhythmical tread of thousands of mailed feet, we rode forth from Selles, led by the Maid, beside whom rode the King's cousin, the Duc d'Alencon, now resolved to join us, despite his former hesitancy and the fears of his wife. He had marched with us to Orleans, but had then turned back, perhaps with the not unnatural fear of again falling into the hands of the English. This had happened to him at Agincourt, and only lately had he been released.

Perhaps his fears were pardonable, and those of his wife more so. She had sought earnestly to hold him hack from this new campaign; and, when she could not prevail with him, she had addressed herself to the Maid with tears in her eyes, telling her how long had been his captivity in England, and with how great a sum he had been rarsomed. Why must he adventure himself again into danger?

The Maid had listened to all with gentle sympathy. Though so fearless herself she was never harsh to those who feared, and the appeal of the Duchesse touched her.

"Fear nothing, Madame," she answered, "I will bring him back to you safe and sound. Only pray for him always - pray for us day and night. I will make his safety my special care. He shall return to you unharmed; but I pray you hinder him not from serving his country in this great hour of need."

So the Maid prevailed, and the Duc was entrusted with the command of the army, second only to the Maid herself, who was distinctly placed at the head of all - whose word was to be supreme; whilst the King's fiat went forth that no Council should be held without her, and that she was to be obeyed as the head in all things!

And men like Dunois, La Hire, and the Chevalier Gaucourt heard this without a murmur! Think of it! - a campaign conducted by a girl of seventeen, who, until a few weeks before, had never seen a shot fired in her life! Ah; but all men remembered Orleans, and were not surprised at the King's decree.

As we marched along in close array, we gathered many recruits by the way, notwithstanding that we were in the territory which had submitted to the English rule. Knights and gentlemen flocked forth from many a chateau to join themselves to the army of the miraculous Maid, whilst humble peasants, fired by patriotism and zeal, came nightly into our camp seeking to be enrolled amid those who followed and fought beneath her banner.

And so for three days we marched, our ranks swelling, our hearts full of zeal and confidence, till news was brought us that the Duke of Suffolk, one of the bravest and most chivalrous of English knights and soldiers, had thrown himself and his followers into Jargeau, and was hastily fortifying it for a siege.

This news reached us at Orleans itself, whither we had returned in the course of our march, to be received with wild acclamations by the people there. So loving were the citizens, that they were loth indeed to see the Maid set forth upon any mission which threatened danger to herself or her army; and their protestations and arguments so wrought upon many of the generals and officers, that they united to beg her to remain inactive awhile, and send to the King for fresh reinforcements before attempting any such arduous task.

Evelyn Everett-Green

The Maid listened with her grave eyes wide in amazement.

"You say this to me - here in Orleans! You who have seen what my Lord accomplished for us before! Shame upon you for your lack of faith - for your unworthy thoughts. We march for Jargeau at dawn tomorrow!"

Never before had we heard the Maid speak with quite such severity of tone and word. Her glorious eyes flashed with a strange lambent light. She looked every inch the ruler of men. All heads were bent before her. None dared speak a word to hinder her in her purpose.

The morrow saw us before Jargeau. Its walls were strong, it was well supplied with those great guns that belched forth fire and smoke, and scattered huge stone balls against any attacking force. But we had brought guns with us - great pieces of ordnance, to set against the city walls, and the Maid ordered these to be brought and placed in certain positions, never asking counsel, always acting on her own initiative, without hesitation and without haste, calm and serene; with that deep, farseeing gaze of hers turned from her own position to the city and back again, as though she saw in some miraculous vision what must be the end of all this toil.

"Mort de Dieu!" cried La Hire, forgetting in his wonder the loyally kept promise to swear only by his baton, "but the Maid has nothing to learn in the art of gunnery! Where hath she learnt such skill, such wisdom! We never had guns to place at Orleans! Where has the child seen warfare, that she places her artillery with the skill of a tried general of forces!"

Ah! - where had the Maid learned her skill in any kind of warfare? Had we not been asking this from the first? This was but another development of the same miracle. For my part I had ceased now to wonder at anything which she said or did.

At daybreak on the morrow the roar of battle began. The air was shaken by the crash and thunder of the guns from both sides. But it was plain to all eyes how that the cunning disposition of our pieces, set just where they could deal most effectively with a weak point in the fortifications, or a gateway less capable than others of defence, were doing far more hurt to the enemy than their fire did to us. For the most part their balls passed harmlessly over our heads, and the clouds of arrows were for us the greater danger, though our armour protected us from over-much damage.

But it was before Jargeau that the incident happened, which so many writers have told of the Maid and the Duc d'Alencon; how that she did suddenly call to him, nay more, drew him with her own hand out of the place where he had stood for some time near to her, saying in a voice of warning, "Have a care, my lord, there is death at hand!"

Another young knight boldly stepped into that very position from which she had snatched Alencon, and an instant afterwards his head was struck off by a cannon ball. The Maid saw and covered her eyes for a moment with her mailed hand.

"Lord have mercy on that brave soul!" she whispered, "but why did he not heed the warning?"

Well, the fighting round Jargeau was fierce and long;

but the Maid with her standard held stubbornly to the place beside the wall which she had taken up, and at sight of her, and at the sound of her clear, silvery voice, encouraging and commanding, the men came ever on and on, regardless of peril, till the scaling ladders were set, and through the breaches torn in the walls by the guns, our soldiers swarmed over into the town, shouting with the shout of those with whom is the victory.

Again the Maid triumphed. Again the hearts of the English melted within them at the sight of the White Witch, as they would tauntingly call her, even whilst they cowered and fled before her. The French were swarming into the city; the great gates were flung open with acclamations of triumph; and the Maid marched in to take possession, her white banner floating proudly before her, her eyes alight, her cheeks flushed.

One of the young gentlemen not long since added to her household, Guillame Regnault by name, from Auvergne, a very knightly youth, a favourite with us all, came striding up to the Maid, and saluting with deep reverence, begged speech with her. She was never too much occupied to receive those who came to her, and instantly he had her ear.

"My General," he said, "the Duke of Suffolk is close at hand. We pressed him hard, and it seemed as though he would die sword in hand, ere he would yield. But I did beg of him in his own tongues with which I am acquainted, not to throw away his noble life; whereupon he did look hard at me, pausing the while in thrust and parry, as all others did pause, for us to parley; and he said that he would give up his sword to THE MAID OF ORLEANS, and to none other.

Wherefore I did tell him that I would run and fetch her to receive his submission, or take him to her myself. But then his mind did change, and he said to me, 'Are you noble?' So I told him that my family was noble, but that I had not yet won my knighthood's spurs. Then forthwith did he uplift his sword, and I read his meaning in his eyes. I bent my knee, and there and then he dubbed me knight, and afterwards would have tendered me his sword, but I said, 'Not so, gentle Duke, but I hear by the sound of the silver trumpet that the Maid, our General, is close at hand. Suffer me to tell her of what has passed, and I trow that she will herself receive your sword at her hands.'"

"You did well, Sir Guillame," spoke the Maid, using the new title for the first time, whereat the youth's face kindled and glowed with pleasure. "Bring the Duke at once to me here. I will receive his surrender in person."

Truly it was a pretty sight to watch - the dignified approach of the stalwart soldier; tall, upright, a knightly figure in battered coat of mail; bleeding from several wounds, but undaunted and undauntable; and the slim, youthful white figure, with uncovered head, and a face regal in its dignity; and yet so full of sweet courtesy and honourable admiration for a beaten, yet noble foe. He gazed upon her with a great wonder in his eyes, and then, dropping upon one knee, tendered his sword to her, which the Maid took, held in her hands awhile, deep in thought, and then, with one of her wonderfully sweet smiles, held out to him again.

"Gentle Duke," she said, "it hath been told me that you are known in France as the English Roland; and if so, I would be loth to deprive so noble a foe of his knightly weapon. Keep it, then, and all I ask of you is that you use it no more against the soldiers of France. And now, if you will let my gentlemen lead you to my tent, your hurts shall be dressed, and you shall receive such tendance as your condition requires."

But I may not linger over every incident of that march, nor all the achievements of the Maid in the arts both of peace and of war. Towns and castles surrendered at her summons, or flung wide their gates at the news of her approach. Sometimes we fought, but more often the very sound of her name, or the sight of the white figure upon the great black horse was sufficient, and fortress after fortress upon the Loire fell before her, the English garrisons melting away or marching out, unable or unwilling to try conclusions with so notable a warrior, who came, as it were, in the power of the King of Heaven.

And not only did she achieve triumphs in war's domains; she was equally victorious as a promoter of peace. For when the news was brought to us that the Comte de Richemont, Constable of France, but hitherto inimical to the King, desired to join us with a body of men, the Duc d'Alencon would have sent him away with insult and refused his proffer of help; but the Maid, with her gentle authority and reasonable counsel, brought him to a different frame of mind, and the Constable was received with a fair show of graciousness. And although in the days which immediately followed his aid was not of great importance (for when France had the Maid to fight for her she wanted none beside), yet in the time to come, when she was no longer there to battle for the salvation of her country, De Richemont's loyal service to the King was of inestimable value, and had it not been for the Maid at this juncture, he might have been lost for ever to the French cause.

Her generosity shone out the more in that De Richemont was no friend to her; indeed, he had regarded her as little better than a witch before he came under the magic of her personality. His greeting to her was rough and blunt.

"Maiden," he said, "they tell me that you are against me, and that you are a witch. I know not whether you are from God or not. If you are from Him, I do not fear you. If you are from the devil, I fear you still less."

She looked him full in the face, gravely at first, but with a smile kindling deep down in her eyes. Then she held out her hand in token of amity.

"Brave Constable, this is well spoken. You have no cause to fear me. You are not here by my will, it is true; for I have enough men with me to do the will of my Lord; but since you have come for love of the Dauphin, who soon must be crowned King, you are welcome indeed; and I know that you will live to serve him faithfully, though in the present you have foes at Court who turn his heart from you."

So again she saw what lay beyond our ken, and which the future has brought to light. Alas, that she never saw the day when the King threw off his supine fear and idleness, and played the man in the conquest of his kingdom, and when De Richemont fought like a lion at his side! Yet who dare say that she did not see and did not rejoice even then? If the light came only in gleams and flashes, surely it came to her charged with an infinite joy!

　　　　Evelyn Everett-Green

And now I must tell of the last exploit of this wonderful eight days' triumphal march through a hostile country - that battle of Patay, where, for the first time, the Maid met the foe in the open, and directed operations not against stone walls, as in every case before, but against an army drawn up in a plain.

There had been marching and counter-marching which only a map could make clear. What matters it the route we pursued, so long only as our progress had been attended by victory, and the fortresses cleared of foes, so that the journey of the King could now be taken in safety? Yet there was one more peril to face; for the army so long expected, under Sir John Fastolffe, was now heard of somewhere close at hand. He had joined himself to Talbot, so it was rumoured, and now a great host was somewhere in our neighbourhood, ready to fall upon us if they could find us, and cut us to pieces, as they had done so often before - witness the fields of Crecy, Poictiers, and Agincourt!

For the first time there was uneasiness and fear in the ranks of the soldiers. They had infinite confidence in the Maid as a leader against stone walls, for had they not seen her take tower after tower, city after city? But she had never led them in the open field; and how could they expect to meet and triumph over the English, who had always vanquished them heretofore?

We knew not where the foe lay; all we knew was that it was somewhere close at hand; and so strong grew the fear in the hearts of Alencon and many others, that they begged the Maid to fall back upon the camp at Beaugency, and to wait there for further reinforce-ments. But she shook her head with decision.

"Let us find them first, and then ride boldly at them. Be not afraid; they will not stand. My Lord will give us the victory!"

And how did we come upon them at last? Verily, by a mere accident. We were marching in good order towards the great plain of Beauce, which at this time of the year was so thickly overgrown with vineyards and cornfields that we saw nothing of any lurking foe; and I trow that we were not seen of them, although a great host was lying at ease in the noontide heat, watching for our coming, I doubt not; but not yet drawn up in battle array.

A stag, frightened by our approach, broke from the thicket, and went thundering across the plain. All at once a shower of arrows let loose from English bows followed the creature's flight, together with eager shouts and laughter, betraying the presence of the unsuspecting foe.

With a lightning swiftness the Maid grasped the whole situation. Here was an army, waiting to fight, it is true, but for the moment off its guard. Here were we, in order of march. One word from her, and our whole force would charge straight upon the foe!

And was that word lacking? Was there an instant's hesitation? Need such a question be asked of the Maid? Clear and sweet rose her wonderful voice, thrilling through the hot summer air.

"Forward, my children, forward, and fear not. Fly boldly upon them, and the day shall be yours!"

She charged, herself, at the head of one column; but La

Evelyn Everett-Green

Hire, in the vanguard, was before her. With shouts of triumph and joy the old veteran and his followers thundered into the very midst of the startled English, and we followed in their wake.

The Duc d'Alencon rode beside the Maid. His face was pale with excitement - perhaps with a touch of fear. He remembered the fight at Agincourt, and the wound received there, the captivity and weary waiting for release.

"How will it end, my General, how will it end?" he said, and I heard his words and her reply, for I was riding close behind.

"Have you good spurs, M. de Duc?" she asked, with one flashing smile showing the gleam of white teeth.

"Ah Ciel!" he cried in dismay; "then shall we fly before them?"

"Not so," she answered; "but they will fly so fast before us that we shall need good spurs to keep up with them!"

And so, indeed, it was. Perhaps it was the sight of the elan of the French troops, perhaps the fear of the White Witch, perhaps because taken at unawares and in confusion, but the English for once made no stand. Fastolffe and his men, on the outer skirts of the force, rode off at once in some order, heading straight for Paris, but the braver and less prudent Talbot sought, again and again, to rally his men, and bring them to face the foe.

But it was useless. The rout was utter and complete.

They could not stand before the Maid; and when Talbot himself had fallen a prisoner into our hands, the army melted away and ran for its life, so that this engagement is called the "Chasse de Patay" to this day.

## XV.

## HOW THE MAID RODE WITH THE KING.

Thus the English were routed with great loss, their leading generals prisoners in the hands of the Maid, and the road for the King open, not to Rheims alone, but to the very walls of Paris, had he so chosen.

Indeed, there were those amongst us who would gladly and joyfully have marched under our great white banner right to the capital of the kingdom, and driven forth from it the English Regent and all the soldiers with him, whether Burgundians or those of his own nation. For Fastolffe was flying along the road which led him thither, and it would have been a joy to many of us to pursue and overtake, to rout him and his army, or put them to the sword, and to march up beneath the walls of Paris itself, and demand its surrender in the name of the Maid!

Those there were amongst us who even came and petitioned of her to lead us thither, and strike a death blow, once and for all, against the power of the alien foe who had ruled our fair realm too long; but though her eyes brightened as we spoke, and though all that was martial in her nature responded to the appeal thus made to her - for by this time she was a soldier through every fibre of her being, and albeit ever extraordinarily tender towards the wounded, the suffering, the dying - be they friends or foes - the soldier spirit within her burned ever higher and higher, and she knew in her clear head that humanly speaking, we could embark upon such a victorious march as perchance the world has never seen before - certainly not beneath such a leader.

And yet she shook her head, even whilst her cheek flushed and her eyes sparkled. Little as the King had done to merit the deep devotion of such a nature as hers, the Maid's loving loyalty towards, and faith in him never wavered. Although we all saw in him the idle, pleasure loving, indolent weakling, which in those days he was, she could, or would, find no fault with him. Often as he disappointed her, she never ceased to love and honour him. Perchance it was given to her to see something of that manlier nature which must have underlaid even then that which we saw and grieved over. For she would hear no word against him. He was the centre and sun of her purpose, and her answer to us was spoken without hesitation.

"Nay, my friends, we have other work to do ere we may stand before the walls of Paris. The Dauphin must be brought to Rheims, and the crown set upon his head; for thus hath my Lord decreed, and I may not act other than as my voices direct."

And when the Maid spoke thus, there was no contradicting or gainsaying her. We had such confidence in her by this, that whatever she did was right in our eyes The soldiers would have followed her eagerly to the very walls of Paris; but at her command they turned back and marched, with pennons flying and music sounding, to the Court of the King, where news of the Chasse of Patay had already preceded us, and where a joyous welcome awaited our return, though even now there were sour and jealous faces amongst the nearest advisers of the King.

If you would believe it, they still opposed the journey of the King to Rheims, working on his fears, his irresolution, his indolence, and seeking to undermine the influence of the Maid, when she went personally to see him, that she might speak with him face to face. He himself had many excuses to offer.

"Sweet Chevaliere," he would say, calling her by one of the names which circulated through the Court, "why such haste? Is it not time that you should rest and take your ease after your many and arduous toils? Think what you have accomplished in these few days! Flesh and blood cannot continue at such a strain. Let us now enjoy the fruits of these wonderful victories; let us feast and rejoice and enjoy a period of repose. Surely that is prudent counsel; for we must have care for our precious Maid, whom none can replace in our army, if she, by too arduous toil, should do herself an injury!"

But the Maid looked at him with her grave eyes full of earnest pleading and searching questioning.

"Gentle Dauphin, I beseech you speak not thus, nor reason after such carnal fashion. Think of what your Lord and my Lord has done for you! Think of what hath been accomplished by Him since first it was given to me to look upon your face. Think what He hath decreed and what He hath already wrought for the furtherance of His purpose towards your Majesty and this realm! And shall His will be set aside? Shall we, His children, hang back and thwart Him, just in the hour when He has put the victory in our hands? Ah, sweet Dauphin, that would be shame, indeed! That would be pain and grief to Him. Cast away all such unworthy thought! Press on to the goal, now in sight! When you stand, crowned and anointed, King of France, you shall know the power wherewith you have been upheld, and lifted from the very mire of humiliation and disgrace!"

And at these words the Duc d'Alencon, who was by this an ardent believer in the Maid, and devotedly attached to her service, prostrated himself before the King, and cried:

"Sire, this Maid speaks words of wisdom. I pray your Majesty to give full heed to what she says. Had you watched her as I have done, had you marched with her and seen her in battle as well as in scenes of peace, you would know well that the power of God is with her. Fear not to do her bidding! Go forth as she bids. Let us hail you King of your fair realm, and then let the Maid lead us on to other and greater victories!"

We all joined our entreaties to that of the Duke. We marvelled how the King could be so blind. But whilst others spoke and urged him, whilst we saw the light kindle in the monarch's eyes, and knew that her words had prevailed with him, she stood apart as one who dreams; and over her face there stole a strange, pale shadow, unlike anything I had seen there before. She saw nothing of the scene about her; heard no word of what passed. I think she did not even know what was meant by the great shout which suddenly went up when the King arose and declared, once and for all, that his mind was made up, that he would march with the Maid to Rheims; that he would not be daunted by

Evelyn Everett-Green

the fact that in Troyes and in Chalons English garrisons yet remained, which might give him trouble in passing. What the Maid had done before she could do again. All that hitherto she had promised had been fulfilled; the fear of her had fallen upon the English, and the terror of the English no longer weighed upon the spirits of the French. He would go, come what might. He would trust in the power of the Maid to finish that which she had begun.

The shouts and plaudits of the courtiers within the castle, and of the soldiers without, when this thing was known, was evidence enough of the confidence and enthusiasm which the exploits of the Maid had awakened. Not a soldier who had followed her heretofore but would follow her now, wherever she should lead them. Surely her heart must have swelled with joy and pride as she heard the clamour of frantic applause ringing through the place.

But when she was back in her own apartments, and I was able to approach her alone, I ventured to ask her something concerning her silence of a short time back.

I always think with a great pride and tender joy of the trust and friendship which the Maid reposed in me, thereby doing me a vast honour. I had often ridden beside her on our marches, especially in the earlier days, when she had not so many to claim her words and counsels. Methinks she had spoken to Bertrand, to me, and to Sir Guy de Laval with more freedom respecting her voices and her visions than to any others, save, perhaps, the King himself, of whom she had ever said she had revelations for his ear alone. She would talk to us of things which for the most part she kept locked away in her own breast; and now when I did ask her what it was that had robbed her cheek of its colour, and wrapped her in a strange trance of grave musing, she passed her hand across her eyes, and then looked at me full, with a strange intensity of gaze.

"If I only knew! If I only knew myself!" she murmured.

"Did your voices speak to you, mistress mine? I have seen you fall into such musing fits before this, when something has been revealed; but then your eyes have been bright with joy - this time they were clouded as with trouble."

"It was when the Duke spoke of other victories," she said, dreamily; "I seemed to see before me a great confusion as of men fighting and struggling. I saw my white banner fluttering, as it were, victoriously; and yet there was a darkness upon my spirit. I saw blackness - darkness - confusion; there was battle and strife - garments rolled in blood. My own white pennon was the centre of some furious struggle. I could not see what it was, waves of black vapour rose and obscured my view. Then, in the midst of the smoke and vapour, I saw a great pillar of fire, rising up as to the very sky itself, and out of the fire flew a white dove. Then a voice spoke - one of my own voices; but in tones different from any I have heard before - 'Have courage, even to death, Jeanne,' it said, 'for we will still be with you.' Then everything faded once more, and I heard only the shouting of the people, and knew that the King had made his decision, and that he had promised to receive his crown, which has waited for him so long."

As she spoke these last words, the cloud seemed to lift.

Her own wonderful smile shone forth again.

"If this be so; if, indeed, the Dauphin shall be made King, what matters that I be taken away? My work will end when the crown shall be set upon his head. Then, indeed, my soul shall say: 'Lord, now lettest Thou Thy servant depart in peace.'"

Her face was suddenly transfigured - radiant - with some great and glorious thought. I was glad at heart to see that the shadow had passed entirely away. Only for a moment could any presage of personal fear cloud the sweet serenity of the Maid's nature. And yet I went from her something troubled myself; for had I not reason to know what strange power she possessed of reading the future, and what did it mean, that confusion of battle, that intermingling of victory and defeat, that darkness of smoke and blaze of fire, and the white dove flying forth unscathed? I had heard too often the shouts of the infuriated English - "We will take you and burn you, you White Witch! You shall perish in the flames from whence the devil, your father, has sent you forth!" - not to hear with a shudder any vision of smoke and of fire. But again, had not the Maid ever prevailed in battle over her foes? Might she not laugh to scorn all such threats?

Ah me! It is well that we may not read the future, else how could we bear the burden of life?

Joyous and triumphant was the day upon which, after some inevitable delays, we started forth - a goodly company in sooth - an army at our back, swelling with pride and triumph - to take our young King to the appointed place, and see the crown of France there set upon his head. From all quarters news was pouring in of the hopeless disruption of the power of the English after the Chasse de Patay. Towns and villages which had submitted in sullen acquiescence before, now sent messages of loyalty and love to the King. Men flocked daily to join our standard as we marched. It was a sight to see the villagers come forth, clad in their holiday dress, eager to see and pay homage to the King, but yet more eager to look upon the white mailed figure at his side and shout aloud the name of THE MAID OF ORLEANS!

For the place of honour at the King's right hand was reserved for the Maid, and she rode beside him without fear, without protest, without shame. Gentle, humble, and simple as she always was, she knew herself the Messenger of a greater King than that of France, and the honour done to her she accepted as done to her Lord, and never faltered beneath it, as she was never puffed up or made haughty or arrogant thereby. Nor did she ever lose her tenderness of heart, nor her quick observation of trivial detail in the absorbing interests of her greatness.

She was the first to note signs of distress upon the part of the soldiers, during this march in the midsummer heat. It was she who would suggest a halt in the noontide, in some wooded spot, that "her children" might rest and refresh themselves, and it was she who, never tired herself, would go amongst them, asking them of their well being, and bringing with her own hands some luscious fruit or some cooling draught to any soldier who might be suffering from the effects of the sun.

She who rode beside a King, who was the greatest and most renowned of that great company, would minister

Evelyn Everett-Green

with her own hands to the humblest of her followers; and if ever King or Duke or courtier jested or remonstrated with her on the matter, her answer was always something like this:

"They are my own people. I am one of them. At home when any was sick in the village, I was always sent for. And wherefore not now? I am the same as I was then. Soon I shall be going back to them, my task accomplished. Wherefore should I not be their friend and sister still?"

Then all would laugh to think of the Maid of Orleans going back to take up the life of a peasant again at Domremy; but the Maid's face grew grave and earnest as she would make reply:

"Indeed, if my work for my King is accomplished, I would fain do so. I was so happy, so happy in my sweet home."

But now our triumphal march was suddenly brought to a halt; for we were approaching the town of Troyes - a place of ill omen to France, and to the young King in particular, for there the shameful treaty was signed which robbed him of his crown; and great was the dissension amongst the King's counsellors as to what should be done.

The place was strong, the English garrison there large. A summons to surrender sent on in advance had been ignored, and now came the question - should the army pass on its way to Rheims leaving this place in the rear unattacked and untaken, or should it run the risk of a long delay, and perhaps some peril and loss in attempting to reduce it?

La Hire and Dunois spoke out insistently. At all costs the town must be taken. It would be folly and madness to leave such a stronghold of the enemy in the rear. Other places had fallen before the victorious Maid, and why not this? The army would go anywhere with her. The soldiers only desired to be told what she counselled, and to a man they would support her. They had lost all fear of the foe, if only the Maid led them into battle, whether in the open or against massive walls.

But as usual the King's nearest counsellors were all for delay, for avoiding battle, for retreat rather than risk. The Archbishop of Rheims, instead of being eager to push on to the place which so far was only his in name, for he had never been aught but titular Archbishop as yet, was always one with La Tremouille in advising caution and a timid policy. Both were the enemies of the Maid, jealous of her gifts and of her influence with the King, and fearful lest her power over him should grow and increase. They even plotted that she should be excluded from the council now sitting anent this very matter, and it was only when the King and the Duc d'Alencon, growing restless and impatient at her absence, desired her presence instantly, that she was sent for.

There was a grave dignity about her as she entered, which sat impressively upon her young face, so fair and sweet and gentle. She knew that timid counsels were being held, and that she, the Commander-in-Chief of the army, was being set aside - the Messenger from the Lord was being ignored. Not for herself, but for Him was her spirit moved.

The Archbishop with much circumlocution told her of

Evelyn Everett-Green

the difficulty in which the King's Council was placed, and would have discoursed for long upon the situation, only that in his first pause the Maid spoke, addressing herself to the King:

"Shall I be believed if I speak my counsel?" she asked.

"You will be believed according as you speak," answered the King, thoroughly uneasy, as he ever was, when torn in twain by the multitude of counsellors with whom he must needs surround himself, though his heart ever inclined towards the Maid.

"I speak that which my Lord gives me to speak," she answered, her wonderful eyes full upon the King. "Shall I be believed?"

"If you speak that which is reasonable and profitable, I will certainly believe you," he answered, still uneasy beneath her look.

"Shall I be believed?" she questioned a third time, and there was a fire in her eyes which seemed to leap out and scathe the pusillanimous monarch as he sat quaking in his Council.

"Speak, Maiden," he cried out then, "I at least will believe!"

"Then, noble Dauphin," she cried, "order your army to assault this city of Troyes, where such despite has been done you, and hold no more councils; for my Lord has told me that within three days I shall lead you into the town, and false Burgundy and proud England shall there be overthrown!"

"Pouf!" cried the Chancellor, one of the Maid's worst foes, "if there was a chance of doing such a thing in six days we would willingly wait; but - "

He stopped suddenly - none knew why, save that the Maid's eyes were fixed full upon him, and in those eyes was that strange shining light which some of us knew so well. She did not speak to him, but when his voice suddenly wavered and broke, she addressed herself to the King, speaking as one who repeats a message.

"You shall be master of the city of Troyes, noble Dauphin, not in six days - but tomorrow."

And even as she spoke, without waiting for any response, she turned and went forth, walking with her head well up, and her eyes fixed straight before her, yet as one who walks in sleep, and pays no heed to what lies before him. She called for her horse; and leaping into the saddle, rode out bareheaded in the summer sun to the camp where the soldiers lay, in doubt and wonderment at this delay; and as they sprang up to a man at sight of her, and broke into the acclamations which always greeted her appearance amongst them, she lifted up her clear ringing voice and cried:

"Be ready, my children, against the morrow, confess your sins, make your peace with God and man. For tomorrow He will lead you victorious into yonder frowning city, and not a hair of your heads shall suffer!"

They crowded about her, filling the air with shouts of triumph; they clamoured to be led at once against the

Evelyn Everett-Green

grim frowning walls. I verily believe, had she put herself at their head then and there, that nothing could have withstood the elan of their attack; but the Maid received her orders from a source we knew not of, and fleshly pride never tempted her to swerve from the appointed path. She smiled at the enthusiasm of the men, but she shook her head gently and firmly.

"Do my bidding, my children, confess yourselves and pray till set of sun. Then I will come to you and set you your appointed tasks, and tomorrow I will lead you into the city!"

That night there was no sleep for the Maid or for her soldiers. At no time was it dark, for midsummer was over the land, and the moon hung in the sky like a silver lamp when the sun had set. The Maid came forth as she had said with the last of the daylight, and at her command a great mound was speedily raised, of earth, brushwood, faggots, stones - anything that the soldiers could lay hands upon; and when this hillock was of height sufficient to satisfy the young General, the great guns were brought and set upon it in such masterly fashion, and in such a commanding way, that La Hire, Dunois and Xantrailles, who came to see, marvelled at it, and we could note from the top of this earthwork that within the city great commotion reigned, and that it was as busy as a hive that has been disturbed.

As the first mystic glow of the summer's dawn kindled in the eastern sky, the Maid stood, a white luminous figure in full armour, poised lightly on the top of one of our pieces of ordnance, her drawn sword in her hand, pointing full in the direction of the city.

I have heard since from those within that the anxious

garrison and citizens saw this motionless figure, and cried aloud in terror and awe. To them it seemed as though St. Michael himself had come down to fight against them, and terror stricken they ran to the governors of the city and implored that surrender might be made, ere the heavens opened and rained lightnings down upon them.

And thus it came about that ere the dawn had fairly come, an embassy was sent to the King and terms of surrender offered. The King, from motives of policy or fear, the Maid, from pity and generosity, accepted the messengers graciously, and granted the garrison leave to depart with their horses and their arms, if the town were peacefully given up; and thus it came about that after the King had finished his night's slumber, and the Maid had done her gracious part in redeeming and releasing the French prisoners, which, but for her, would have been carried away by the retiring English and Burgundians, she rode beside the King, and at the head of the cheering and tumultuous army into the city of Troyes, which had surrendered to the magic of her name without striking a blow.

"O my Chevaliere," cried the happy and triumphant monarch, as he turned to look into her grave serene face. "What a wonderful Maid you are! Stay always with me, Jeanne, and be my friend and General to my life's end."

She looked at him long and earnestly as she made answer:

"Alas, Sire, it may not be! For a year - perhaps for a year. But I shall last no longer than that!"

# XVI.

## HOW THE MAID ACCOMPLISHED
## HER MISSION.

Shall I ever forget that evening? No, not if I live to be a hundred!

June had well-nigh passed ere we began our march from Gien - that triumphant march headed by the King and the Maid - and July had run half its course since we had been upon the road. For we had had a great tract of country to traverse, and a large army must needs have time in which to move itself.

And now upon a glorious golden evening in that month of sunshine and summertide, we saw before us - shining in a floating mist of reflected glory - the spires and towers, the walls and gates of the great city of Rheims - the goal of our journeyings - the promised land of the Maid's visions and voices!

Was it indeed a city of stone and wood which shone before us in the level rays of the sinking sun? I asked that question of myself; methinks that the Maid was asking it in her heart; for when I turned my eyes upon her, I caught my breath in amaze at her aspect, and I know now what it is to say that I have looked upon the face of an angel!

She had dropped her reins, and they hung loose upon her horse's neck; her hands were clasped together in a strange rapture of devotion. Her head was bare; for she often gave her headpiece to her page to carry for her, and in the evenings did not always replace it by any other covering. Her hair had grown a little longer during these months, and curled round her face in a loose halo, which in the strong and ruddy light of the setting sun, shone a glorious golden colour, as though a ray of heavenly light were enmeshed within it.

But it was the extraordinary brightness of those great luminous eyes, the rapt and intense expression of her face which arrested my attention, and seemed for a moment to stop the triumphant beating of my heart. It was not triumph which I read there, though there was joy and rapture and peace, beyond all power of understanding. It was the face of one who sees heaven open, and in the wonder and awe of the beatific vision forgets all else, and feels not the fetters of the flesh, heeds not those things which must needs intervene ere the spirit can finally be loosed to enter upon blessedness and rest, but soars upwards at once into heavenly regions.

The town of Rheims lay before us. The inhabitants were pouring forth to meet us. We saw them coming over the plain, as we watched the walls and buildings, glowing in the mystic radiance of the summer's evening, loom up larger and grander and sharper before us. It was no dream!

And yet who would have thought it possible three months ago? In mid-April the iron grip of the English lay all over the land north of the Loire, and the south lay supine and helpless, stricken with the terror of the

Evelyn Everett-Green

victorious conqueror. Orleans was at its last gasp, and with its fall the last bulwark would be swept away; all France must own the sway of the conqueror. The King was powerless, indolent, ready to fly at the first approach of peril, with no hope and no desire for rule, doubtful even if he had the right to take upon himself the title of King, careless in his despair and his difficulties. The army was almost non-existent; the soldiers could scarce be brought to face the foe. One Englishman could chase ten of ours. The horror as of a great darkness seemed to have fallen upon the land.

And yet in three months' time what had not been accomplished!

The King was riding into the ancient city of Rheims, to be crowned King of France; Orleans was relieved; a score of fortresses had been snatched from the hands of the English. These were fleeing from us in all directions back to Paris; where they hoped to make a stand against us, but were in mortal fear of attack; and now it was our soldiers who clamoured to be led against the English - the English who fled helter-skelter before the rush and the dash of the men whom heretofore they had despised.

And all this was the work of yonder marvellous Maid - a girl of seventeen summers, who, clad in white armour, shining like an angelic vision, was riding at the King's side towards the city.

He turned and looked at her at the moment my gaze was thus arrested, and I saw his face change. He put out his hand and touched hers gently; but he had to touch her twice and to speak twice ere she heard or knew.

"Jeanne - fairest maiden - what do you see?"

She turned her gaze upon him - radiant, misty, marvellous.

"I see the Land of Promise," she answered, speaking very low, yet so clearly that I heard every word. "The chosen of the Lord will go forward to victory. He will drive out the enemy before the face of him upon whom He shall set the crown of pure gold. France shall prosper - her enemies shall be confounded. What matter whose the work, or whose the triumph? What matter who shall fall ere the task be accomplished - so that it be done according to the mind of the Lord?"

"And by the power of the Maid - the Deliverer!" spoke the King, a gush of gratitude filling his heart, as he looked first at the slight figure and inspired face of the Maid, and then at the city towards which we were riding, the faint clash of joy bells borne softly to our ears. "For to you, O my General, I owe it all; and may the Lord judge betwixt us twain if I share not every honour that I may yet win with her who has accomplished this miracle!"

But her gaze was full of an inexplicable mystery.

"Nay, gentle Dauphin, but that will not be," she said; "One shall increase, another shall decrease - hath it not ever been so? My task is accomplished. My work is done. Let another take my place after tomorrow, for my mission will be accomplished."

"Never!" cried the King firmly and earnestly, and when I heard him thus speak my heart rejoiced; for I, no more than others, believed that success could attend the King's further efforts without her who was the inspiration of the army, and the worker of these great miracles which had been wrought. How often have I wondered since - but that is no part of my story. Let me tell those things which did happen to us.

How can I tell of our entry into Rheims? Have I not spoken in other places of other such scenes, often in the early dusk of evening, when whole cities flocked out to meet the Maid, to gaze in awe and wonder upon her, to kiss her hands, her feet, her knees, the neck and flanks of the horse she rode, and even his very footprints in the road, as he moved along with his precious burden?

As it was there, so was it here - the same joy, the same wonder, the same enthusiasm. The King was greeted with shouts and acclamations, it is true; but the greater admiration and wonder was reserved for the Maid, and he knew it, and smiled, well pleased that it should be so; for at that time his heart was full of a great gratitude and affection, and never did he seek to belittle that which she had wrought on his behalf.

Thankfulness, peace, and happiness shone in the eyes of the Maid as she rode; but there was a nearer and more personal joy in store for her; for as we passed through the town, with many pauses on account of the greatness of the throng, pouring in and out of the churches (for it was the vigil of the Madelaine), or crowding about the King and the Maid, she chanced to lift her eyes to the windows of an inn in the place, and behold her face kindled with a look different from any I had seen there before, and she looked around for me, and beckoning with her hand, she pointed upwards, and cried in tones of strange delight and exultation:

"My father, fair knight, my father! I saw his face!"

Now, I knew that Jacques d'Arc had been greatly set against his daughter's mission, and it had been declared that he had disowned her, and would have withheld her from going forth, had such a thing been within his power. She had never received any message of love or forgiveness from him all these weeks, though her two younger brothers had joined the army, and were always included in her household. So that I was not surprised at the kindling of her glance, nor at the next words she spoke.

"Go to him, my friend; tell him that I must needs have speech with him. Ah, say that I would fain return home with him when my task is done, if it be permitted me. Go, find him speedily, ere he can betake himself away. My father! My father! I had scarce hoped to look upon his face again!"

So whilst the King and the Maid and their train rode on to the huge old palace of the Archeveche, hard by the Cathedral, I slipped out of my place in the ranks, and passed beneath the archway into the courtyard of the old inn, where the Maid declared that she had seen the face of her father looking forth.

I had not much trouble in finding him; for already a whisper had gone forth that certain friends and relatives of the wonderful Maid had journeyed from Domremy to witness her triumphant entry into Rheims. Indeed, some of these had followed us from Chalons, all unknown to her, who would so gladly have welcomed them. Chalons, though a fortified town, and with a hostile garrison, had opened its gates to us without resistance , feeling how hopeless it was to

Evelyn Everett-Green

strive against the power of the Maid.

The wonder and awe inspired by her presence, and by her marvellous achievements, had sunk deeply into the spirits of these simple country folk, who had only heretofore known Jeanne d'Arc as a gentle village maiden, beloved of all, but seeming not in any way separated from her companions and friends. Now they had seen her, white and glistening, in martial array, riding beside a King, an army at her back, acclaimed of the multitude, the idol of the hour, a victor in a three months' campaign, the like of which never was before, and methinks can never be again.

So now, when I stood face to face with the rugged prud'homme, the father of this wonderful Maid, and told him of her desire to speak with him upon the morrow, when the King should have received his crown, I saw that many emotions were struggling together in his breast; for his soul revolted yet, in some measure, at the thought of his girl a leader of men, the head of an army, the friend of kings and courtiers, whilst it was impossible but that some measure of pride and joy should be his at the thought of her achievements, and in the assurance that at last the King, whom loyal little Domremy had ever served and loved, was to receive his crown, and be the anointed sovereign of the land.

"She desires speech with me? She, whom I have seen riding beside the King? What have I to do with the friends of royalty? How can she consort with princes and with peasants?"

"Let her show you that herself, my friend," I answered. "We, who have companied with her through these wonderful weeks, know well how that she is no less a loving daughter, a friend of the people, for being the friend of a King and the idol of an army. Give me some message for her. She longs for a kind word from you. Let me only take her word that you will see her and receive her as a father should receive his child, and I trow that it will give her almost the same joy as the knowledge that by her miraculous call she has saved her country and crowned her King."

I scarce know what answer Jacques d'Arc would have made, for he was a proud, unbending man, and his face was sternly set whilst I pleaded with him. But there were others from Domremy, entirely filled with admiration of the Maid, and with desire to see her again; and their voices prevailed, so that he gave the answer for which I waited. He would remain at the inn over the morrow of the great function of the coronation, and would receive his daughter there, and have speech with her.

"Tell her that I will take her home with me, if she will come," he spoke; "for she herself did say that her work would be accomplished when the crown was placed upon the King's head. Let her be true to her word; let her return home, and become a modest maiden again beneath her mother's care, and all shall be well betwixt us. But if pride and haughtiness possess her soul, and she prefers the company of courtiers and soldiers to that of her own people, and the life of camps to the life of home, then I wash my hands of her. Let her go her own way. She shall no longer be daughter of mine!"

I did not tell those words to the Maid. My lips refused to speak them. But I told her that her father would remain in the place till she had leisure to have speech with him; and her eyes kindled with joy at hearing such news, for it seemed to her as though this would be the pledge of his forgiveness, the forgiveness for which she had longed, and for the lack of which none of her triumphs could altogether compensate.

There was no sleep for the city of Rheims upon that hot summer's night. Although the coming of the King had been rumoured for some time, it had never been fully believed possible till news had been brought of the fall of Troyes, and the instant submission of Chalons. Then, and only then, did citizens and prelates truly realise that the talked-of ceremony could become an accomplished fact, and almost before they had recovered from their amazement at the rapidity of the march of events, courtiers brought in word that the King and his army were approaching.

So all night long the people were hard at work decorating their city, their churches, above all their Cathedral; and the priests and prelates were in close conference debating what vestments, what vessels, what rites and ceremonies should be employed, and how the lack of certain necessary articles, far away at St. Denis, could be supplied out of the rich treasuries of the Cathedral.

As the dawn of the morning brightened in the east, the sun rose upon a scene of such splendour and magnificence as perhaps has seldom been witnessed at such short notice. The whole city seemed one blaze of triumphal arches, of summer flowers, of costly stuffs and rich decoration. Every citizen had donned his best and brightest suit; the girls and children had clothed themselves in white, and crowned themselves with flowers. Even the war-worn soldiers had polished their arms, furbished up their clothes, and borrowed or bought from the townsfolk such things as were most lacking; and now, drawn up in array in the great square, with tossing banners, and all the gay panoply of martial glory, they looked like some great victorious band - as, indeed, they were - celebrating the last act of a great and wonderful triumph.

As for the knights, nobles, and courtiers, one need not speak of the outward glory of their aspect - the shining armour, the gay dresses, the magnificent trappings of the sleek horses - that can well be pictured by those who have ever witnessed a like brilliant scene.

But for the first part of the day, with its many and varied ceremonies, there was lacking the shining figure of the Maid; nor did the King himself appear. But forth from the Palace of the Archeveche rode four of the greatest and most notable peers of the realm, attended by a gorgeous retinue; and with banners waving, and trumpets blowing great martial blasts, they paced proudly through the streets, between the closely-packed ranks of soldiers and citizens, till they reached the ancient Abbey of Sainte Remy, where the monks of Sainte Ampoule guard within their shrine the holy oil of consecration, in that most precious vial which, they said, was sent down from heaven itself for the consecration of King Clovis and his successors.

Upon bended knees and with bared heads these great peers of France then took their solemn oath that the sacred vial should never leave their sight or care, night or day, till it was restored to the keeping of the shrine from which the Abbot was about to take it. Then, and only then, would the Abbot, clothed in his most sumptuous vestments, and attended by his robed monks, take from its place that holy vessel, and place it in the hands of the messengers - Knights Hostages, as they were termed for the nonce - and as they carried it slowly and reverently forth, and retraced their steps to the Cathedral, accompanied now by the Abbot and monks, every knee was bent and every head bowed.

But all the while that this ceremony was taking place, the Maid was shut up in her room in the Palace, dictating a letter of appeal to the Duke of Burgundy, and praying him in gentle, yet authoritative terms, to be reconciled to his King, join hands with him against the English foe, and then, if need there were to fight, to turn his arms against the Saracens, instead of warring with his brethren and kinsmen. I trow that this thing was urged upon her at this time, in that she believed her mission so nearly accomplished, and that soon she would have no longer right to style herself "Jeanne the Maid," and to speak with authority to princes and nobles.

As yet she was the appointed messenger of Heaven. Her words and acts all partook of that almost miraculous character which they had borne from the first. I will not quote the letter here; but it is writ in the page of history; and I ask of all scholars who peruse its words, whether any village maiden of but seventeen years, unlettered, and ignorant of statecraft, could of herself compose so lofty and dignified an appeal, or speak with such serene authority to one who ranked as well-nigh the equal of kings. It was her last act ere she donned her white armour, and passed forth from her chamber to take part in the ceremony of the coronation. In some sort it was the last of her acts performed whilst she was yet the deliverer of her people.

When I looked upon those words, long after they had been penned, I felt the tears rising in mine eyes. I could have wept tears of blood to think of the fate which had befallen one whose thoughts were ever of peace and mercy, even in the hour of her supremest triumph.

How can my poor pen describe the wonders of the great scene, of which I was a spectator upon that day? Nay, rather will I only seek to speak of the Maid, and how she bore herself upon that great occasion. She would have been content with a very humble place in the vast Cathedral today; she had no desire to bear a part in the pageant which had filled the city and packed the great edifice from end to end.

But the King and the people willed it otherwise. The thing which was about to be done was the work of the Maid, and she must be there to see all, and the people should see her, too - see her close to the King himself, who owed to her dauntless courage and devotion the crown he was about to assume, the realm he had begun to conquer.

So she stood near at hand to him all through that long, impressive ceremony - a still, almost solemn figure in her silver armour, a long white velvet mantle, embroidered in silver, flowing from her shoulders, her hand grasping the staff of her great white banner, which had been borne into the Cathedral by D'Aulon, and beside which she stood, her hand upon the staff.

She was bareheaded, and the many-coloured lights streamed in upon her slim, motionless figure, and the face which she lifted in adoration and thanksgiving. I trow that none in that vast assembly, who could see her as she thus stood, doubted but that she stood there the accredited messenger of the Most High. The light from Heaven itself was shining on her upturned face, the reflection of an unearthly glory beamed in her eyes. From time to time her lips moved, as though words of thanksgiving broke silently forth; but save for that she scarcely moved all through the long and solemn ceremony. Methinks that she saw it rather in the spirit than in the flesh; and the knights and nobles who had poured in from the surrounding country to witness this great function, and had not companied with the Maid before, but had only heard of her fame from afar, these regarded her with looks of wonder and of awe, and whispering together, asked of each other whether in truth she were a creature of flesh and blood, or whether it were not some angelic presence, sent down direct from Heaven.

And so at last the King was anointed and crowned! The blare of the thousand trumpets, the acclamations of a vast multitude proclaimed the thing done! Charles the Seventh stood before his people, their King, in fact as well as in name.

The work of the Maid was indeed accomplished!

# XVII.

## HOW THE MAID WAS PERSUADED.

The ceremony was over. The Dauphin stood in our midst a crowned and anointed King. We were back in the great hall of the Archeveche, and the thunders of triumphant applause which had been restrained within the precincts of the sacred edifice now broke forth again, and yet again, in long bursts of cheering, which were echoed from without by the multitudes in the street and great square Place, and came rolling through the open windows in waves of sound like the beating of the surf upon the shore.

The King stood upon a raised dais; his chiefest nobles and peers around him. He was magnificently robed, as became so great an occasion, and for the first time that I had ever seen, he looked an imposing and a dignified figure. Something there was of true kingliness in his aspect. It seemed as though the scene through which he had passed had not been without effect upon his nature, and that something regal had been conveyed to him through the solemnities which had just taken place.

The Maid was present also; but she had sought to efface herself in the crowd, and stood thoughtfully apart in an embrasure of the wall, half concealed by the arras, till the sound of her name, proclaimed aloud in a hundred different tones, warned her that something was required of her, and she stepped forward with a questioning look in her startled eyes, as though just roused from some dream.

She had been one of the first to prostrate herself at the new-made King's feet when the coronation ceremony was over; and the tears streaming down her face had been eloquent testimony of her deep emotion. But she had only breathed a few broken words of devotion and of joy, and had added something in a choked whisper which none but he had been able to hear.

"The King calls for the Maid! The King desires speech with the Maid!" such was the word ringing through the hall; and she came quietly forth from her nook, the crowd parting this way and that before her, till she was walking up through a living avenue to the place where the King was now seated upon a throne-like chair on the dais at the far end of the hall.

As she came towards him the King extended his hand, as though he would meet her still rather as friend than as subject; but she kneeled down at his feet, and pressing her lips to the extended hand, she spoke in a voice full of emotion:

"Gentle King, now is the pleasure of God fulfilled towards you. Now is the will of my Lord accomplished. To Him alone be the praise and glory! It was His will that I should be sent before you to raise the siege of Orleans, to lead you to this city of Rheims, there to receive your consecration. Now has He shown to all the world that you are the true King - that it is His will you should reign over this fair realm, that this kingdom of France belongs to you and you alone. My task is now accomplished. His will in me is fulfilled. Go forward, then, noble King - strong in the power of your kingly might and right, doubting not that He will aid you still; though He will work with other instruments, with other means, for my task in this is now accomplished!"

There was a little stir and thrill throughout the hall as these words were spoken. Dismay fell upon many, wonder upon all, triumph gleamed from the eyes of a few; but most men looked one at the other in consternation. What did she mean by these words? - this Heaven-sent Maid to whom we owed so much? Surely she did not think to leave us just in the hour of her supreme triumph? How could we hope to lead on the armies to fresh victories, if the soldiers were told that the Maid would no longer march with them? Who would direct us with heavenly counsel, or with that marvellous clearness of vision which is given only to a few in this sinful world, and to those only whose hearts are consecrated by a great devotion, and a great love? She could not mean that! She loved France with an overwhelming fervour. She was devoted to the service of the King, in whom she had never been able or willing to see wrong. She knew her power with the army; she loved the rough soldiers who followed her unshrinkingly in the teeth of the very fiercest perils, and who would answer to her least command, when they would obey none other general.

O no, she could not think of deserting France in this her hour of need! Much had been done; but much yet remained to do. If she were to quit her post, there could be no telling what might not follow. The English, cowed and bewildered now, might well pluck up heart of grace, and sweep back through the country once owning their sway, driving all foes before them as in the days of old. The victories won in these last weeks might soon be swallowed up in fresh defeat and disaster. How could we expect it to be otherwise if the presence of the Maid were withdrawn?

These and a hundred other questions and conjectures were buzzing through the great hall. Wonder and amaze was on every face. The King himself looked grave for a moment; but then his smile shone out carelessly gay and confident. He looked down at the Maid, and there was tender friendliness in his glance. He spoke nothing to her at the first as to what she had said; he merely asked of her a question.

"My Chevaliere, my guardian angel, tell me this, I pray. You have done all these great things for me; what am I to do in return for you?"

She raised her eyes towards him, and the light sprang into them - that beautiful, fearless light which shone there when she led her soldiers into battle.

"Go forward fearlessly, noble King. Go forward in the power of your anointing; and fear nothing. That is all I ask of you. Do that, and you will give to me my heart's desire."

"We will talk of that later, Jeanne," he answered, "I have many things to speak upon that matter yet. But today I would ask you of something different. You have done great things for me; it is not fitting that you should refuse to receive something at my hands. This day I sit a King upon my father's throne. Ask of me some gift and grace for yourself - I your King and your friend demand it of you!"

It was spoken in a right kingly and gracious fashion, and we all held our breath to listen for the answer the Maid should give. We had known her so long and so well, and we had learned how little she desired for herself, how hard it was to induce her to express any wish for her own gratification. She was gentle and gracious in her acceptance of the gifts received from friends who had furnished her from the beginning with such things as were needful for her altered life; but she had ever retained her simplicity of thought and habit; and though often living in the midst of luxury and extravagance, she was never touched by those vices herself. And now she was bidden to ask a boon; and she must needs do it, or the displeasure of the King would light upon her.

He had raised her to her feet by this time, and she stood before him, a slim boy-like figure in her white point-device dress, her cheeks a little flushed, her slender fingers tightly entwined, the breath coming and going through her parted lips.

"Gentle King," she answered, and her low full voice thrilled through the hall to its farthermost end in the deep hush which had fallen upon it, "there is one grace and gift that I would right gladly ask of you. Here in this city of Rheims are assembled a few of mine own people from Domremy; my father, my uncle, and with them some others whom I have known and loved from childhood. I would ask this thing of you, noble King. Give me at your royal pleasure a deed, duly signed and sealed by your royal hand, exempting the village of Domremy, where I was born, from all taxes such as are levied elsewhere throughout the realm. Let me have this deed to give to those who have come to see me here, and thus when I return with them to my beloved childhood's home, I shall be witness to the joy and gladness which such a kingly boon will convey. Grant me this - only this, gentle King, and you will grant me all my heart desires!"

The King spoke aside a few words to one of those who stood about him, and this person silently bowed and quitted the hail; then he turned once more to the Maid, standing before him still with a happy and almost childlike smile playing over her lips.

"The thing shall be done, Jeanne," he said; "and it shall be done right soon. The first deed to which I set my hand as King shall be the one which shall for ever exempt Domremy from all taxation. You shall give it to your father this very day, to take home with him when he goes. But as for those other words of yours - what did you mean by them? How can you witness the joy of a distant village, when you will be leading forward the armies of France to fresh victories?"

He gazed searchingly into her face as he spoke; and she looked back at him with a sudden shrinking in her beautiful eyes.

"Sire," she faltered - and anything like uncertainty in that voice was something new to us - "of what victories do you speak? I have done my part. I have accomplished that which my Lord has set me to do. My task ends here. My mission has been fulfilled. I have no command from Him to go forward. I pray you let me return home to my mother and my friends."

"Nay, Jeanne, your friends are here," spoke the King

gravely, "and your country is your mother. Would you neglect to hear her cry to you in the hour of her need? Her voice it was that called you forth from your obscurity; she calls you yet. Will you cease to hear and to obey?"

The trouble and perplexity deepened in the eyes of the Maid.

"My voices have not bidden me to go forward," she faltered.

"Have they bidden you to go back - to do no more for France?"

"No," she answered, throwing back her head, her eyes kindling once again with ardour; "they have not bidden me return, or I would have done it without wavering. They tell me nothing, save to be of a good heart and courage. They promise to be with me - my saints, whom I love. But they give me no commands. I see not the path before me, as I have seen it hitherto. That is why I say, let me go home. My work is done; I have no mission more. Shall I take upon me that which my Lord puts not upon me - whether it be honour or toil or pain?"

"Yes, Jeanne, you shall take that upon you which your country calls upon you to take, which your King puts upon you, which even your saints demand of you, though perchance with no such insistence as before, since that is no longer needed. Can you think that the mind of the Lord has changed towards me and towards France? Yet you must know as well as I and my Generals do, that without you to lead them against the foe, the soldiers will waver and tremble, and perchance turn their backs upon our enemies once more. You they will follow to a man; but will they follow others when they know that you have deserted them? You tell me to go forward and be of good courage. How can I do this if you turn back, and take with you the hearts of my men?"

"Sire, I know not that such would be the case," spoke the Maid gravely. "You stand amongst them now as their crowned and anointed King. What need have they of other leader? They have followed me heretofore, waiting for you; but now - "

"Now they will want you more than ever, since you have ever led them to victory!" cried the King; and raising his voice and looking about him, especially to those generals and officers of his staff who had seen so much of the recent events of the campaign, he cried out:

"What say you, gentlemen? What is our chance to drive away the English and become masters of this realm if the MAID OF ORLEANS take herself away from us, and the soldiers no longer see her standard floating before them, or hear her voice cheering them to the battle?"

Some of those present looked sullenly on the ground, unwilling to own that the Maid was a power greater than any other which could be brought into the field; but there were numbers of other and greater men, who had never denied her her meed of praise, though they had thwarted her at times in the council room; and these with one accord declared that should the Maid betake herself back to Domremy, leaving the army to its fate, they would not answer for the effect which this desertion would have, but would, in fact, almost expect the melting away of the great body of the trained soldiers and recruits who had fought with her, and had come to regard her presence with them as the essential to a perfect victory.

But we were destined to have a greater testimony than this, for a whisper of what was passing within the great hall had now filtered forth into the streets, and all in a moment we were aware of a mighty tumult and hubbub without, a clamour of voices louder and more insistent than those which had hailed the King a short time before, and the words which seemed to form themselves out of the clamour and gradually grow into the burden of the people's cry was the repeated and vehement shout, "THE MAID OF ORLEANS! THE MAID OF ORLEANS! We will fight if the Maid goes with us - without her we be all dead men!"

They came and told us what the crowd of soldiers in the street was shouting; they begged that the Maid would show herself at some window, and promise that she would remain with the army. Indeed, there was almost a danger of riot and disaster if something were not done to quell the excitement of the soldiery and the populace; and at this news the Maid suddenly drew her slender, drooping figure to its full height, and looked long and steadfastly at the King.

"Sire," she said, "I give myself to you and to France. My Lord knows that I seek in this to do His will, though differently from heretofore. You will be disappointed. Many will misjudge me. There will be sorrow and anguish of heart as well as triumph and joy. But if my country calls, I go forth gladly to meet her cry - even though I go to my death!"

I do not know how many heard her last words; for they were drowned in the roar of joyful applause which followed her declaration. The King gave her his hand, and led her forth upon a balcony, where the great concourse in the street below could see them; and by signs he made them understand that she would continue with him as one of his Commanders-in-Chief; and in hearing this the city well nigh went mad with joy; bonfires blazed and bells pealed madly; and the cry heard in the streets was less "Long live the King!" than that other frantic shout, "THE MAID OF ORLEANS! THE MAID OF ORLEANS!"

But the Maid returned to her apartments with a strange look upon her face, and she held out her hand to me as one who would fain ask help and sympathy of a trusted comrade, as I am proud to think I was regarded at that time by her.

"The King's word has prevailed, O my friend," she said, "but I would that I were sure it will be for the best!"

"How can it be otherwise than for the best?" I answered as I held her hand in mine, and looked searchingly into her fair, grave face. "Will not your Lord help you yet? Do not all men trust in you? Will not the soldiers fight for and with you? And are you not sure in your heart that the cause of the French King will yet triumph?"

Her eyes were misty with unshed tears as she made reply:

"I know that my Lord will not desert me; and I trust I may serve Him yet, and the King whom I love. I know that all will be well - at the last - for this fair realm of France. But I have no commission direct from my Lord as I have had hitherto. My voices yet speak gentle and kindly words. I trow that my saints will watch over me, and that they will give me strength to strive and to overcome. For myself I fear not - I am ready to die for my King and my country if that be the will of God. Only the shadow lies athwart my path, where until today all was brightness and sunshine. It would have been so sweet to go home to my mother, to see the Fairy Tree, and the old familiar faces, and listen once more to the Angelus bell! I had thought that I should by this have earned my rest. I had not thought that with so many to serve him, the King would have had further use for me."

"Yet how could it be otherwise, my General, when the soldiers will follow you alone? - when all look to you as their champion and their friend?"

"Nay, but I have enemies too," she answered sadly, "and I know that they will work me ill - greater ill in the future than they have had power to do heretofore, when I was watched over and guarded for the task that was set me. That task is now accomplished. Can I look to receive the same protection as before? The Lord may have other instruments prepared to carry on His work of deliverance. I doubt not that He will use me yet, and that I shall never be forsaken; but my time will not be long. I shall only last a year. Let the King use me for all that I am worth!-after that he must look for others to aid him!"

I could not bear to hear her speak so. I would have broken in with protestations and denials; but something in the look upon her face silenced me. My heart sank strangely within me, for had I not learned to know how truly the Maid did read that which the future hid from our eyes? I could only seek to believe that in this she might be mistaken, since she herself did say how that things were something different with her now.

She seemed to read the thoughts that crowded my brain; for she looked into my face with her tender, far-seeing smile.

"You are sad, my kind friend, my faithful knight, and sometimes mine own heart is sad also. But yet why should we fear? I know that I have enemies, and I know that they will have more power to hurt me in the times that are coming, than has been permitted hitherto, yet - "

With an uncontrollable impulse I flung myself at her feet.

"O my General - O my dear lady - speak not such things - it breaks my heart. Or if, indeed, the peril be so great, then let all else go, and bid your father to take you back to Domremy with him. There, at least, you will be safe and happy!"

Her eyes were deep with the intensity of her emotion.

"It may not be," she said with grave gentleness and decision. "I had hoped it for myself, but it may not be. My word is pledged. My King has commanded. I, too, must learn, in my measure, the lesson of obedience, even unto death!"

Her hands were clasped; her eyes were lifted heaven-wards. A shaft of light from the sinking sun struck in through the coloured window behind her, and fell across her face with an indescribable glory. I was still upon my knees and I could not rise, for it seemed to me as though at that moment another Presence than that of the Maid was with us in the room. My limbs shook. My heart seemed to melt within me; and yet it was not fear which possessed me, but a mysterious rapture the like of which I can in no wise fathom.

How long it lasted I know not. The light had faded when I rose to my feet and met her wonderful gaze. She spoke just a few words.

"Now you know what help is given us in our hours of need. My faithful knight need never mourn or weep for me; for that help and comfort will never be withheld. Of this I have the promise clear and steadfast!"

I was with her when she went to see her father. It was dark, and the old man sat with his brother-in-law, Durand Laxart - he who had helped her to her first interview with De Baudricourt - in one of the best rooms of the inn. Since it had been known that these men were the kinsfolk of the Maid, everything of the best had been put at their disposal by the desire of the citizens, and horses had been provided for them for their return to Domremy. For the city of Rheims was filled with joy at that which had been accomplished, and the Maid was the hero of the hour.

But I could see that there was a cloud upon the old man's face - the father's; and he did not rise as his daughter entered - she before whom nobles had learnt to bend, and who sat at the Council of the King. His sombre eyes dwelt upon her with a strange expression in their depths. His rugged face was hard; his knotted hands were closely locked together.

The Maid gazed at him for a moment, a world of tender emotions in her eyes; and then she quickly crossed the room and threw herself at his feet.

"My father! My father! My father!"

The cry seemed to come from her heart, and I saw the old man's face quiver and twitch; but he did not touch or embrace her.

"It is the dress he cannot bear," whispered Laxart distressfully to me, "it is as gall and wormwood to him to see his daughter go about in the garb of a man."

The Maid's face was raised in tender entreaty; she had hold of her father's hands by now. She was covering them with kisses.

"O my father, have you no word for me? Have you not yet forgiven your little Jeanne? I have but obeyed our Blessed Lord and His holy Saints. And see how they have helped and blessed and guided me! O my father, can you doubt that I was sent of them for this work? How then could I refuse to do it?"

Then the stern face seemed to melt with a repressed tenderness, and the father bent and touched the girl's brow with his lips. She uttered a little cry of joy, and would have flung herself into his arms; but he held her a little off, his hands upon her shoulders, and he looked into her face searchingly.

"That may have been well done, my daughter; I will not say, I will not judge. But your task is now accomplished - your own lips have said it; and yet you still are to march with the King's army, I am told. You love better the clash of arms, the glory of victory, the companionship of soldiers and courtiers to the simple duties which await you at home, and the protection of your mother's love. That is not well. That is what no modest maiden should choose. I had hoped and believed that I should take my daughter home with me. But she has chosen otherwise. Do I not well to be angry?"

The Maid's face was buried in her hands. She would have buried it in her father's breast, but he would not have it so.

I could have wept tears myself at the sight of her sorrow. I saw how utterly impossible it would be to make this sturdy peasant understand the difficulty of the Maid's position, and the claims upon her great abilities, her mysterious influence upon the soldiers. The worthy prud'homme would look upon this as rather a dishonour and disgrace than a gift from Heaven.

The words I longed to speak died away upon my tongue. I felt that to speak them would be a waste of breath. Moreover, I was here as a spectator, not as a partaker in this scene. I held the document, signed and sealed by the King, which I was prepared to read to the visitors from Domremy. That was to be my share in this interview - not to interpose betwixt father and child.

For a few moments there was deep silence in the room; then the Maid took her hands from her face, and she was calm and tranquil once again. She possessed herself of one of her father's reluctant hands.

"My father, I know that this thing is hard for you to understand. It may be that my brothers could explain it better than I, had you patience to hear them. But this I say, that I long with an unspeakable desire to return home with you, for I know that the path I must tread will darken about me, and that the end will be sad and bitter. And yet I may not choose for myself. My King commands. My country calls. I must needs listen to those voices. Oh, forgive me that I may not follow yours, nor the yearnings of mine own heart!"

The old man dropped her hand and turned away. He spoke no word; I think perchance his heart was touched by the tone of the Maid's voice, by the appealing look in her beautiful eyes. But he would not betray any sign of weakness. He turned away and leant his brow upon the hand with which he had grasped the high-carved ledge of the panelled shelf beside him. The Maid glanced at him, her lips quivering; and she spoke again in a brighter tone.

"And yet, my father, though you may not take me back with you, you shall not go away empty-handed. I have that to send home with you which shall, I trust, rejoice the hearts of all Domremy; and if you find it hard to forgive that which your child has been called upon to do, yet methinks there will be others to bless her name and pray for her, when they learn that which she has been able to accomplish."

Then she made a little sign to me, and I stepped forward with the parchment, signed and sealed, and held it towards the Maid's father. He turned to look at me, and his eyes widened in wonder and some uneasiness; for the sight of so great a deed filled him and his kinsman with a vague alarm.

"What is it?" he asked, turning full round, and I made answer:

"A deed signed by the King, exempting Domremy from all taxation, henceforward and for ever, by right of the great and notable services rendered to the realm by one born and brought up there - Jeanne d'Arc, now better known as THE MAID OF ORLEANS."

The two men exchanged wondering glances, and over Laxart's face there dawned a smile of intense joy and wonder.

"Nay, but this is a wonderful thing - a miracle - the like of which was never heard or known before! I pray you, noble knight, let me call hither those of our kinsfolk and acquaintance from Domremy as have accompanied us hither, that they may hear and understand this marvellous grace which hath been done us!"

I was glad enough that all should come and hear that which I read to them from the great document, explaining every phrase that was hard of comprehension. It was good to see how all faces glowed and kindled, and how the people crowded about the Maid with words of gratitude and blessing.

Only the father stood a little apart, sorrowful and stern. And yet I am sure that his heart, though grieved, was not altogether hardened against his child; for when at the last, with tears in her eyes (all other farewells being said), she knelt at his feet begging his blessing and forgiveness , he laid his hand upon her head for a moment, and let her embrace his knees with her arms.

"Go your way, my girl, if needs must be. Your mother will ever pray for you, and I trust the Lord whom you serve will not leave you, though His ways are too hard of understanding for me."

That was all she could win from him; but her heart was comforted, I think; for as she reached her lodging and turned at the door of her room to thank me in the gracious way she never forgot, for such poor services as I had rendered, she said in a soft and happy voice:

"I think that in his heart my father hath forgiven me!"

# XVIII.

## HOW I LAST SAW THE MAID.

I had thought, when I started, to tell the whole tale of the Angelic Maid and all the things which she accomplished, and all that we who companied with her did and saw, both of success and of failure. But now my brain and my pen alike refuse the task. I must needs shorten it. I think my heart would well nigh break a second time, if I were to seek to tell all that terrible tale which the world knows so well by now.

Ah me! Ah me! - what a world is this wherein we live, in which such things can be! I wake sometimes even yet in the night, a cold sweat upon my limbs, my heart beating to suffocation, a terror as of great darkness enfolding my spirit.

And is it wonderful that it should be so? Can any man pass through such experiences as mine, and not receive a wound which time can never wholly heal? And though great things have of late been done, and the Pope and his Court have swept away all such stain and taint as men sought to fasten upon the pure nature of the wonderful and miraculous Maid, we who lived through those awful days, and heard and saw the things which happened at that time, can never forget them, and (God pardon me if I sin in this) never forgive.

Evelyn Everett-Green

There are men, some living still, and some passed to their last account, whom I would doom to the nethermost hell for their deeds in the days of which I must now write - though my words will be so few. And (with horror and shame be it spoken) many of these men were consecrated servants of the Holy Church, whose very office made the evil of their deeds to stand out in blacker hues.

It is easy for us to seek to fasten the blame of all upon the English, who in the end accomplished the hideous task; but at least the English were the foes against whom she had fought, and they had the right to hold her as an adversary whose death was necessary for their success; and had the English had their way she would have met her end quickly, and without all that long-drawn-out agony and mockery of a trial, every step and process of which was an outrage upon the laws of God and of man. No, it was Frenchmen who doomed her to this - Frenchmen and priests. The University of Paris, the officers of the Inquisition, the Bishops of the realm. These it was who formed that hideous Court, whose judgments have now been set aside with contumely and loathing. These it was who after endless formalities, against which even some of themselves were forced in honour to protest, played so base and infamous a part - culminating in that so-called "Abjuration," as false as those who plotted for it - capped by their own infamous trick to render even that "Abjuration" null and void, that she might be given up into the hands of those who were thirsting for her life!

Oh, how can I write of it? How can I think of it? There be times yet when Bertrand, and Guy de Laval, and I, talking together of those days, feel our hearts swell, and the blood course wildly in our veins, and truly I do marvel sometimes how it was that we and others were held back from committing some desperate crime to revenge those horrid deeds, wrought by men who in blasphemous mockery called themselves the servants and consecrated priests of God.

But hold! I must not let my pen run away too fast with me! I am leaping to the end, before the end has come. But, as I say, I have no heart to write of all those weary months of wearing inactivity, wherein the spirit of the Maid chafed like that of a caged eagle, whilst the counsellors of the King - her bitter foes - had his ear, and held him back from following the course which her spirit and her knowledge alike advocated.

And yet we made none so bad a start.

"We must march upon Paris next," spoke the Maid at the first Council of War held in Rheims after the coronation of the King; and La Hire and the soldiers applauded the bold resolve, whilst La Tremouille and other timid and treacherous spirits sought ever to hold him back.

I often thought of the words spoken by the Maid to those friends of hers from Domremy, when she bid them farewell on the evening of which I have just written.

"Are you not afraid, Jeanne," they asked, "of going into battle, of living so strange a life, of being the companion of the great men of the earth?"

And she, looking at them with those big grave eyes of hers, had made answer thus:

Evelyn Everett-Green

"I fear nothing but treachery."

I wondered when she spoke what treachery she was to meet with; but soon it became all too apparent. The King's ministers were treacherously negotiating with false Burgundy, some say with the Regent Bedford himself. They cared not to save France. They cared only to keep out of harm's way - to avoid all peril and danger, and to thwart the Maid, whose patriotism and lofty courage was such a foil to their pusillanimity and cowardice.

So that though she led us to the very walls of Paris, and would have taken the whole city without a doubt, had she been permitted, though the Duc d'Alencon, now her devoted adherent, went down upon his very knees to beg of the King to fear nothing, but trust all to her genius, her judgment; he could not prevail, and orders were sent forth to break down the bridge that she had built for the storming party to pass over, and that the army should fall back with their task undone!

Oh, the folly, the ingratitude, the baseness of it all! How well do I remember the face of the Maid, as she said:

"The King's word must be obeyed; but truly it will take him seven years - ah, and twenty years now - to accomplish that which I would do for him in less than twenty days!"

Think of it - you who have seen what followed. Was Paris in the King's hands in less than seven years? Were the English driven from France in less than twenty?

She was wounded, too; and had been forcibly carried away from the field of battle; but it was against her own will. She would have fought through thick and thin, had the King's commands not prevailed; and even then she begged to be left with a band of soldiers at St. Denis.

"My voices tell me to remain here," she said; but alas! her voices were regarded no longer by the King, whose foolish head and cowardly heart were under other influences than that of the Maid, to whom he had promised so much such a short while since.

And so his word prevailed, and we were perforce obliged to retreat from those walls we had so confidently desired to storm. And there in the church of St. Denis, where she had knelt so many hours in prayer and supplication, the Maid left her beautiful silver armour, which had so often flashed its radiant message of triumph to her soldiers, and with it that broken sword - broken outside the walls of Paris, and which no skill had sufficed to mend - which had been taken from St Catherine's Church in Fierbois.

It was not altogether an unwonted act for knights to deposit their arms in churches, though the custom is dying away, with so many other relics of chivalry; but there was something very strange and solemn in this act of the Maid. It was to us a significant sign of that which she saw before her. We dared not ask her wherefore she did it. Something in her sad, gentle face forbade us. But I felt the tears rising to my eyes as I watched her kneel long in prayer when the deed was done, and I heard stifled sobs arising from that end of the building where some women and children knelt. For the Maid was ever the friend of all such, and never

Evelyn Everett-Green

a woman or child whom she approached, whether she were clad in peasant's homespun or in shining coat of mail, but gave her love and trust and friendship at sight.

Henceforth the Maid went clothed in a light suit of mail, such as any youthful knight might wear. She never spoke again of her fair white armour, or of the sword which had shivered in her hand, none save herself knew how or when.

Alas! for the days of glory which had gone before! Why did we keep her with the King's armies, when the monarch's ear was engrossed by adverse counsel, and his heart turned away from her who had been his Deliverer in the hour of his greatest need?

Methinks she would even now have returned home, but for the devotion of the soldiers and the persuasions of the Duc d'Alencon, and of some of the other generals, amongst whom the foremost were Dunois and La Hire. These chafed equally with the Maid at the supine attitude of the King; and the Duke, his kinsman, spoke out boldly and fearlessly, warning him of the peril he was doing to his kingdom, and the wrong to the Maid who had served him so faithfully and well, and to whom he had made such fair promises.

But for the present all such entreaties or warnings fell upon deaf ears. The time for the King's awakening had not yet come.

Nevertheless, we had our days of glory still, under the banner of the Maid, when, after many months of idleness, the springtide again awoke the world, and she sallied forth strong in the assurance of victory, whilst fortress after fortress fell before her, as in the days of yore. Oh, how joyous were our hearts! Now did we believe truly that the tide had turned, and that we were marching on to victory.

But upon the Maid's face a shadow might often be seen to rest; and once or twice when I would ask her of it, she replied in a low, sorrowful voice:

"My year is well-nigh ended. Something looms before me. My voices have told me to be ready for what is coming. I fear me it will be my fate to fall into the hands of the foe!"

I would not believe it! Almost I was resolved to plunge mine own dagger into her heart sooner than she should fall into the hand of the pitiless English. But woe is me! I was not at her side that dreadful evening at Compiegne, when this terrible mishap befell. I had been stricken down in that horrid death trap, when, hemmed in between the ranks of the Burgundians and English, we found our retreat into the city cut off.

Was it treachery? Was it incapacity upon the part of the leaders of the garrison, or what was the reason that no rush from the city behind took the English in the rear, and effected the rescue of the Maid?

I know not - I have never known - all to me is black mystery. I was one of those to see the peril first, and with Bertrand and Guy de Laval beside me, to charge furiously upon the advancing foe, crying aloud to others to close round the Maid and bear her away into safety, whilst we engaged the enemy and gave them time.

Evelyn Everett-Green

That is all I know. All the rest vanishes in the mists. When these mists cleared away, Bertrand and I were in the home of Sir Guy, tended by his mother and grandmother - both of whom had seen and loved well the wonderful Maid - and she was in a terrible prison, some said an iron cage, guarded by brutal English soldiers, and declared a witch or a sorceress, not fit to live, nor to die a soldier's death, but only to perish at the stake as an outcast from God and man.

Months had passed since the battle of Compiegne. Fever had had me fast in its grip all that while, and the news I heard on recovery brought it all back again. Bertrand and Guy were in little better case. We were like pale ghosts of our former selves during those winter months, when, hemmed in by snow, we could learn so little news from without, and could only eat out our hearts in rage and grief.

With the spring came the news of the trial at Rouen - the bitter hatred of Bishop Cauchon - the awful consummation he had vowed to bring about.

I know not whether it were folly to hope such a thing, but we three knights made instantly for the coast and crossed to England, to seek the ear of the young King there, and plead the cause of the Maid before him. I need not say how our mission failed. I care not to recall those sickening days of anxiety and hope deferred, and utter defeat at the last.

Heartbroken and desperate we returned; and made our way to Rouen. The whole city was in confusion. Need I say more? That very day, within an hour, the Maid, the Messenger from God, the Deliverer of the King, the Saviour of France, was to die by fire, to perish as a heretic. And the King whom she had saved had not lifted a hand to save her; the country she had delivered from a crushing disgrace, stood idly by to watch her perish thus!

Oh, the shame! - the treachery! - the horror! Let me not try to write of it. The King has striven now to make amends; but I wonder how he feels sometimes when he sees the May sunshine streaming over the fair earth - over that realm which he now rules from sea to sea, when he thinks of the Maid who was led forth in that blaze of glory to meet her fiery doom.

O God of Heaven look down and judge! How shall I tell of the sight I beheld?

Suddenly I came upon it - mad with my grief, desperate with horror and despair. I saw the face of the Maid again! I saw her upraised eyes, and her hands clasped to her breast, holding thereto a rough wooden cross, whilst someone from below held high in the air a crucifix taken from some church and fastened upon a long wand.

The pile on which she stood was so high - so high; they said it was done in mercy, that the rising clouds of smoke might choke her ere the flame touched her. She was clad in a long white garment from head to foot; her hair had grown and fell about and back from her face in a soft cloud gilded by the sun's rays. Her face was rapt - smiling - yes, I will swear it - smiling, as a child smiles up into the face of its father.

There was an awful hush throughout the wide place. Everything reeled and swam before me; but I saw that face - that serene and smiling face, wan and pale, but

Evelyn Everett-Green

tranquil and glad and triumphant.

Then came the rush of smoke, and the glare of ruddy fire. A stifled cry, like one immense groan rose from below - above in the reek and blaze all was silent. But from out that fire I saw - yes, and another saw it too (an English soldier, rushing to add a faggot to the pyre, a token of his hate to the Maid), and it so wrought upon him that he dropped his burden, fell upon his knees and was like to die of the fear - I saw a white dove rise from the smoke wreaths of that ghastly pile, hover a moment, just touched by the glare of the fire, and then dart heavenwards as upon eagle's wings.

Yes, I saw it. To the day of my death will I swear it. I saw what she had seen in vision long ago; and upon my heart there fell a strange sense of peace and calm. It had not hurt her - it had been as she once said. Her saints had been with her to the end. She had triumphed. All was well. Called of her Country, she had answered nobly to the call. Her Country had awarded her a fiery death; but in that fiery chariot she had ascended to the Lord, in whom she trusted, hereafter to receive the crown of glory that fadeth not away.

# Choose from Thousands of 1stWorldLibrary Classics By

Adolphus William Ward
Aesop
Agatha Christie
Alexander Aaronsohn
Alexander Kielland
Alexandre Dumas
Alfred Gatty
Alfred Ollivant
Alice Duer Miller
Alice Turner Curtis
Alice Dunbar
Ambrose Bierce
Amelia E. Barr
Andrew Lang
Andrew McFarland Davis
Anna Sewell
Annie Besant
Annie Hamilton Donnell
Annie Payson Call
Anton Chekhov
Arnold Bennett
Arthur Conan Doyle
Arthur Ransome
Atticus
B. M. Bower
Basil King
Bayard Taylor
Ben Macomber
Booth Tarkington
Bram Stoker
C. Collodi
C. E. Orr
C. M. Ingleby
Carolyn Wells
Catherine Parr Traill
Charles A. Eastman
Charles Dickens
Charles Dudley Warner
Charles Farrar Browne
Charles Ives
Charles Kingsley
Charles Lathrop Pack
Charles Whibley
Charles Willing Beale
Charlotte M. Braeme
Charlotte M.Yonge
Clair W. Hayes
Clarence Day Jr.
Clarence E. Mulford

Clemence Housman
Confucius
Cornelis DeWitt Wilcox
Cyril Burleigh
D. H. Lawrence
Daniel Defoe
David Garnett
Don Carlos Janes
Donald Keyhole
Dorothy Kilner
Dougan Clark
E. Nesbit
E.P.Roe
E. Phillips Oppenheim
Edgar Allan Poe
Edgar Rice Burroughs
Edith Wharton
Edward J. O'Biren
John Cournos
Edwin L. Arnold
Eleanor Atkins
Elizabeth Cleghorn
Gaskell
Elizabeth Von Arnim
Ellem Key
Emily Dickinson
Erasmus W. Jones
Ernie Howard Pie
Ethel Turner
Ethel Watts Mumford
Eugenie Foa
Eugene Wood
Evelyn Everett-Green
Everard Cotes
F. J. Cross
Federick Austin Ogg
Ferdinand Ossendowski
Francis Bacon
Francis Darwin
Frances Hodgson Burnett
Frank Gee Patchin
Frank Harris
Frank Jewett Mather
Frank L. Packard
Frederick Trevor Hill
Frederick Winslow Taylor
Friedrich Kerst
Friedrich Nietzsche
Fyodor Dostoyevsky

Gabrielle E. Jackson
Garrett P. Serviss
Gaston Leroux
George Ade
Geroge Bernard Shaw
George Ebers
George Eliot
George MacDonald
George Orwell
George Tucker
George W. Cable
George Wharton James
Gertrude Atherton
Grace E. King
Grant Allen
Guillermo A. Sherwell
Gulielma Zollinger
Gustav Flaubert
H. A. Cody
H. B. Irving
H. G. Wells
H. H. Munro
H. Irving Hancock
H. Rider Haggard
H. W. C. Davis
Hamilton Wright Mabie
Hans Christian Andersen
Harold Avery
Harold McGrath
Harriet Beecher Stowe
Harry Houidini
Helent Hunt Jackson
Helen Nicolay
Hendy David Thoreau
Henrik Ibsen
Henry Adams
Henry Ford
Henry Frost
Henry James
Henry Jones Ford
Henry Seton Merriman
Henry Wadsworth
Longfellow
Henry W Longfellow
Herbert A. Giles
Herbert N. Casson
Herman Hesse
Homer
Honore De Balzac

Horace Walpole
Horatio Alger, Jr.
Howard Pyle
Howard R. Garis
Hugh Lofting
Hugh Walpole
Humphry Ward
Ian Maclaren
Israel Abrahams
J.G.Austin
J. Henri Fabre
J. M. Barrie
J. Macdonald Oxley
J. S. Knowles
J. Storer Clouston
Jack London
Jacob Abbott
James Allen
James Lane Allen
James Andrews
James Baldwin
James DeMille
James Joyce
James Oliver Curwood
James Oppenheim
James Otis
Jane Austen
Jens Peter Jacobsen
Jerome K. Jerome
John Burroughs
John F. Kennedy
John Gay
John Glasworthy
John Habberton
John Joy Bell
John Milton
John Philip Sousa
Jonathan Swift
Joseph Carey
Joseph Conrad
Joseph Jacobs
Julian Hawthrone
Julies Vernes
Justin Huntly McCarthy
Kakuzo Okakura
Kenneth Grahame
Kate Langley Bosher
L. A. Abbot
L. T. Meade
L. Frank Baum
Laura Lee Hope

Laurence Housman
Leo Tolstoy
Leonid Andreyev
Lewis Carroll
Lilian Bell
Lloyd Osbourne
Louis Tracy
Louisa May Alcott
Lucy Fitch Perkins
Lucy Maud Montgomery
Lydia Miller Middleton
Lyndon Orr
M. H. Adams
Margaret E. Sangster
Margaret Vandercook
Maria Edgeworth
Maria Thompson Daviess
Mariano Azuela
Marion Polk Angellotti
Mark Overton
Mark Twain
Mary Austin
Mary Cole
Mary Rowlandson
Mary Wollstonecraft
Shelley
Max Beerbohm
Myra Kelly
Nathaniel Hawthrone
O. F. Walton
Oscar Wilde
Owen Johnson
P.G.Wodehouse
Paul and Mable Thorn
Paul G. Tomlinson
Paul Severing
Peter B. Kyne
Plato
R. Derby Holmes
R. L. Stevenson
Rabindranath Tagore
Rahul Alvares
Ralph Waldo Emmerson
Rene Descartes
Rex E. Beach
Richard Harding Davis
Richard Jefferies
Robert Barr
Robert Frost
Robert Gordon Anderson
Robert L. Drake

Robert Lansing
Robert Michael Ballantyne
Robert W. Chambers
Rosa Nouchette Carey
Ross Kay
Rudyard Kipling
Samuel B. Allison
Samuel Hopkins Adams
Sarah Bernhardt
Selma Lagerlof
Sherwood Anderson
Sigmund Freud
Standish O'Grady
Stanley Weyman
Stella Benson
Stephen Crane
Stewart Edward White
Stijn Streuvels
Swami Abhedananda
Swami Parmananda
T. S. Ackland
The Princess Der Ling
Thomas A. Janvier
Thomas A Kempis
Thomas Anderton
Thomas Bailey Aldrich
Thomas Bulfinch
Thomas De Quincey
Thomas H. Huxley
Thomas Hardy
Thomas More
Thornton W. Burgess
U. S. Grant
Valentine Williams
Victor Appleton
Virginia Woolf
Walter Scott
Washington Irving
Wilbur Lawton
Wilkie Collins
Willa Cather
Willard F. Baker
William Makepeace
Thackeray
William W. Walter
Winston Churchill
Yei Theodora Ozaki
Young E. Allison
Zane Grey